ANIMAL VOICES, UNICORN WHISPERS

MARY E. LOWD

CONTENTS

1. Stranger than a Swan — 1
2. Gerty and the Doesn't-Smell-Like-a-Melon — 5
3. Sheeperfly's Lullaby — 14
4. One Night in Nocturnia — 20
5. The Otter's Mermaid — 36
6. The Canoe Race — 73
   written with Daniel Lowd
7. Fox in the Hen House — 87
8. Frankenstein's Gryphon — 96
9. The Freedom of the Queen — 130
10. Hide the Honey — 133
11. Jellyfish for Dinner — 140
12. One Sheep — 164
13. Sarah Flowermane and the Unicorn — 167
14. An Otter's Soul — 186
15. Frond Farewell — 196
16. The Best Puppy Ever — 209
17. Excerpt from Purride and Purrejudice — 213
18. Treegadoon — 215
19. The Muddy Unicorn — 294

About the Author — 305
Also by Mary E. Lowd — 307

"Stranger than a Swan" (c) 2022 by Mary E. Lowd

First published in *All Worlds Wayfarer, Issue XII*

"Gerty and the Doesn't-Smell-Like-a-Melon" (c) 2010 by Mary E. Lowd

First published in *Golden Visions Magazine*

"Sheeperfly's Lullaby" (c) 2016 by Mary E. Lowd

First published in *A Glimpse of Anthropomorphic Literature, Issue 2*

"One Night in Nocturnia" (c) 2012 by Mary E. Lowd

First published in *Tails of a Clockwork World: A Rainfurrest Anthology*

"The Otter's Mermaid" (c) 2018 by Mary E. Lowd

First published in *Furry Trash*

"The Canoe Race" (c) 2011 by Daniel Lowd & Mary E. Lowd

First published in *Stories of Camp RainFurrest*

"Fox in the Hen House" (c) 2013 by Mary E. Lowd

First published in *Dancing in the Moonlight: Rainfurrest 2013 Charity Anthology*

"Frankenstein's Gryphon" (c) 2015 by Mary E. Lowd

First published in *Ember: A Journal of Luminous Things*

"The Freedom of the Queen" (c) 2022 by Mary E. Lowd

First published in *Oxfurred Comma Flash Fiction Contest*

"Hide the Honey" (c) 2023 by Mary E. Lowd

First published in *Deep Sky Anchor*

"Jellyfish for Dinner" (c) 2024 by Mary E. Lowd

First published in *Animal Voices, Unicorn Whispers*

"One Sheep" (c) 2012 by Mary E. Lowd

First published in *Allasso, Volume 2: Saudade*

"Sarah Flowermane and the Unicorn" (c) 2022 by Mary E. Lowd

First published in *Deep Sky Anchor*

"An Otter's Soul" (c) 2022 by Mary E. Lowd

First published in *The Lorelei Signal*

"Frond Farewell" (c) 2024 by Mary E. Lowd

First published in *Animal Voices, Unicorn Whispers*

"The Best Puppy Ever" (c) 2014 by Mary E. Lowd

First published in *AE: The Canadian Science Fiction Review*

"Excerpt from Purride and Purrejudice" (c) 2020 by Mary E. Lowd

First published in *Deep Sky Anchor*

"Treegadoon" (c) 2024 by Mary E. Lowd

First published in *Animal Voices, Unicorn Whispers*

"The Muddy Unicorn" (c) 2024 by Mary E. Lowd

First published in *Deep Sky Anchor*

For my ever-changing constellation of pets. You are the stars who guide my way. You may not understand me—or this dedication—but trying to understand you brings so much joy and meaning to my life.

1
STRANGER THAN A SWAN

EGGSHELL CRACKED, and the dome of the world broke away, showing a whole other world, infinitely larger and more complicated, beyond the confines of the duckling's natal home. It was time to lift her head—breaking the eggshell further, widening the crack in it—and then spread her wings, shaking out the scraggly, wet feathers plastered to her dimpled skin, letting them begin to dry into soft, yellow down.

The duckling sat in the bottom half of her shattered egg, rump cupped by the curve of shell. She stared out at the chaos of colors and confusion of shapes, all so much more than she'd ever expected while curled into a fetal pretzel of duckling limbs inside a perfect oblong spheroid. Her own heartbeat had been everything. Now it was merely a pinpoint, and the world was so huge, it could swallow her up and never notice her at all.

Blue stretched across the horizon, blotted with sways

and spikes of green around the edges, mirroring even more blue up above. More green and dark brown stretched and reached towards the higher blue. Other colors—stars of yellow and sworls of pink—dotted the various greens. It would have been peaceful, perhaps, if it were familiar. For the duckling, it was entirely new, and entirely overwhelming.

Then her bright, dark, confused, and troubled eyes landed on a shape that instantly triggered a sensation of warmth and comfort deep in her tiny, flickering breast. Her heart stuttered; her breathing slowed. And she knew this was her mother:

Purple tentacles writhed around her mother's face, ringing her glowing, red eyes. Darker purple, almost black, feathers and spines prickled from her hunched back, and her limbs were even more tentacles, pale lavender and puckered with perfectly round sucker disks. She was beautiful. She was glorious. And she made her duckling daughter feel safe.

The duckling flapped her wings and opened her flat beak to cheep her love. Her voice came out high and strong, and the tentacled mother creature looked down, noticing the duckling for the first time.

The two beings stared at each other, bright brown eyes and glowing red eyes, sizing each other up. The duckling had literally nothing to compare this mother to. The tentacled creature had become, in an instant, the measure by which she would judge the rest of the world, for the rest of her life.

The tentacled creature, though, had visited many worlds in her flying saucer. She had lived for relativistic centuries, trading any semblance of a permanent life on a planet, surrounded by loved ones, for the temporary skipping of a stone across the lake of the sky. She dipped down to visit planets, see their wonders, and then move on.

Today, she had come to Earth.

Today, she looked at a brand new, just hatched duckling, and her tentacular mouthparts twisted and curled into her species' semblance of a smile. The duckling was adorable. A funny little thing with wet black feathers already drying into downy yellow fluff. Its round head wobbled at the end of a long neck, and its eyes stared at her so steadily.

She felt, perhaps, like a human feels when a butterfly deigns to land on your hand, delicate, breakable, and yet, even if for just a moment, trusting.

The elder creature reached one of her lavender limbs down and stroked the duckling's soft yellow neck with her puckering sucker discs. The duckling closed her eyes, shutting out the visual chaos of the world, so she could focus better on this tender expression of her mother's love.

But the moment was a moment. Only a moment.

And then the tentacled creature moved on. Her lavender limbs pulled her across the grassy ground, back over the hill beside the lake, to where she'd parked her gleaming, silver, flying saucer. Pictures of it flying through the sky would flood social media and show up on human news shows later that day, snapped with camera apps on personal cell phones. Everyone would say they were a hoax.

And of everyone in the world, only one duckling, wordless and confused, would know who had been inside.

Two grown ducks—one brown and speckled; the other with a handsome, gleaming, green head—waddled down to the bank, followed by a gaggle of fluffy yellow ducklings, just like the one still sitting in her half egg.

The ducks flapped their wings joyously at the sight of their lost egg, now a hatchling. The other ducklings mimicked their parents, flapping their stubby little wings too.

But the duckling in her half egg shell stared at the family of ducks, confused. Her mother was gone. The moment of imprinting had passed. She didn't know who these ducks were, or why they weren't a glorious range of purples, from sunrise lavender tentacles to royal dusk spines. They looked like her, and they would care for her. But they were not like the image of herself that she would carry in her head for the rest of her days.

An image mirroring the mother who had never been her mother.

An image that no one else would ever understand.

2

GERTY AND THE DOESN'T-SMELL-LIKE-A-MELON

GERTY HAD BEEN snuffle-snorting about the melon patches all morning. She was looking for Little People to play with, but all the bugs and mice seemed to be hiding today. Dormancy was in the air.

She tried asking a bird to play with her, but it was so high in the branches of the karillow tree that she had to shout at it. And the master scolded her for barking. The bird flew away anyway. They always did.

So, Gerty gave up her search and scratched out a comfortable spot under the karillow tree. She napped and dozed, keeping her ears tuned for the voice of the master. When he spoke, she woke.

"Damned converter!" he shouted, and Gerty knew he was working on the vehicle parked beside the house. She was proud; her master was handy.

"Does the sky know what I know?" he sang, and Gerty knew he had moved inside, his voice carrying through an open window as he washed the dishes. She was proud; her master's voice was beautiful. She drowsed to sleep again.

"Lainey!" he cried, and Gerty woke again. She knew he was calling to his eight-year-old daughter; he was such a good family-man. Gerty was proud and began to close her eyes to go back to sleep.

"Lainey!" he cried again, "...Lainey?" and Gerty reopened her eyes. She picked her head up off the comfortable, dusty ground to listen better.

"Lainey??" There was strain in the master's voice. Gerty stood up and woofed, a soft woof her master wouldn't hear. She started sniffing the air, her nose working overtime in search of the scent of Lainey. But, before Gerty could get too worried, a high, piping voice answered, "Here, Papa!"

Lainey came skipping along the road completely unaware of the great concern she'd caused Gerty.

"Come with me," the master said, "we'll check the melon patches."

Gerty circled around the little girl several times, wagging her tail eagerly. She was glad the master's daughter was all right, but to be sure—to be on the safe side—Gerty decided to accompany master and daughter on their excursion.

Besides, it was a lazy day.

"Clomp, clomp, clomp," Lainey announced with each enthusiastic, stomping, footstep. Though, despite her *clomp*ing,' Lainey was actually stepping carefully, placing each foot delicately between the tender green melon vines. Whenever they came to a hub where the vines thickened around a round lump of melon, Lainey squatted down to get a look at it. Gerty, being a quadruped and shorter, already had the melons at nose height.

The two girls, biped and quadruped, sniffed at the melon while Master laid his hands on it, gently rocking the bulbous green-striped sphere, just enough to judge its ripeness—not too much, for that might rip its life-giving vines.

The master didn't stop at every melon. Sampling a few here and there, as the troupe continued progressing around the curve of the lake, was enough to ensure the overall health of their melon patch.

Gerty, however, was a diligent servant, and she made it her job to sniff all the melons the master didn't rock in his hands. Her nose was a more sensitive tool than the master's hands anyway.

As they walked, the master told his daughter about ancient times, many, many years before, when the master was a mere boy. Neither Lainey nor Gerty could picture it.

Gerty had to miss parts of the story as she strayed farther and closer to the lake than the master, checking every melon. But, she tried to listen and catch what she could.

"My dad bought this farm when I was about your age, Lainey. It was already a melon farm, but a little run down. So, Dad had to renovate it."

The melons all smelled so good. Gerty's mouth watered as she checked them.

"We checked the vines, like we're doing now. And we cleared the forest over there of vermin that came to eat our melons. Little rodents that would burrow into them, making homes as well of meals of the melons."

Gerty wrinkled her nose. She didn't smell vermin in any of *these* melons, but she could sure imagine them. The imagined smell made the fur on her neck bristle.

"There were bigger animals in the forest too. Gryphons used to nest in the trees. They slept in their nests, but during the day they'd run around the ground, hunting vermin like dogs."

"They didn't fly?" Lainey asked.

"Not much. I think the wings were mostly vestigial. They used them to glide down from their nests, but they climbed the trees to get back up."

Lainey held her arms out and jumped up and down, pretending she was a gryphon. Gerty watched affectionately, before turning back to her important business. Checking melons. *All* the melons.

"It took a few years for Dad to clear all the vermin. I think they were pretty much gone by the time I was ten. I tried to keep a small one as a pet." The master looked his daughter up and down. "I was about your age when I got that idea in my head. Mom was furious."

"A gryphon would be a better pet," Lainey said.

"Harder to catch," the master said. "And harder to hide under my bed."

They continued on for a while, neither father nor daughter speaking. They were to the far side of the lake when Lainey said, "I've never seen a gryphon in the forest." She was looking over her shoulder at the thick green of the woods. Gerty looked over at the woods too. She sniffed the air.

There was no gryphon scent. As far as Gerty knew, there never had been.

"Of course not," the master said, crouched down, still mostly paying attention to the melon cupped in his hands. The melon must have checked out okay, because he set it back and stood up. "What do you think they'd eat with the vermin gone?"

Lainey shrugged. "Melons?"

The master laughed. "Right," he said and tousled Lainey's hair. "Vegetarian gryphons. Good idea."

Master and daughter continued on. Lainey kept asking about what the gryphons had been like, and the master told her what he remembered about them. Gerty, however, couldn't keep listening. She was too worried by her latest find.

It was oblong-round and green with paler green stripes: it looked like a melon. But... She sniffed all around it. And, then, she sniffed all around it again. It did not *smell* like a melon.

There was no full, gonging sweetness. It lacked the tang of fresh green vine. Instead, it was musty with the slight sour of twigs soaking in the lake's edge. There was something very wrong with this melon. Gerty wasn't even sure it *was* a melon. It was... It was... Well, it was a *doesn't-smell-like-a-melon*. And it was right here at the edge of the lake in the melon patch. With the other melons. The *real* melons.

Gerty ran back to the master and circled around his feet looking up at him, concern about the doesn't-smell-like-a-melon deep in her eyes. The master offered her no reassurance. He merely stepped around Gerty and kept telling Lainey about water dragons. Apparently, gryphons had been essential to their life cycle.

Gerty had more pressing concerns. She ran back to the wolf in melon's clothing. She took another sniff; then a hacking sneeze to get the sour smell out of her nostrils. A few plaintive whines leaked from her jowls. A quick look over her shoulder showed Gerty that the master still wasn't paying attention. His words floated across the melon patch toward her, "Well, the last owners said there was one... But I never swam to the bottom of the lake to find out. And you're not going to either." After a pause, "Water dragons may not bother humans when they're left alone, but I wouldn't want to find out what a cranky one does if you wake it up at the bottom of its lair."

Gerty huffed her frustration. She was having to shoulder this burden all on her own. She pawed at the doesn't-smell-like-a-melon, and it rocked in its place among the watery vines. It wasn't attached to the vines, she realized.

She afforded the master a few more hopeful whines, followed by one or two more urgent *woofs*. No response.

Lainey was crouched at the edge of the lake further along, trying to peer deep enough into the water to see a dragon curled up underneath. The master was telling her about how they only laid eggs every hundred years.

Gerty huffed. She'd have to deal with the doesn't-smell-like-a-melon on her own. She pawed it again, scratching its surface with her claws. Its texture was harder than a melon's. After another snuffle, she pawed the offending object, digging her claws in until she'd rolled it entirely out of its place, splashing a little in the shallow water.

Having rolled it over, Gerty could now see the doesn't-smell-like-a-melon's other side: a crack ran perpendicular to the pale green stripes. The fur on Gerty's neck hackles started prickling, and she could feel her lip twitching into a snarl. Her snarl found full release and quickly turned into all out howling when the crack widened, growing and branching at either end.

The master came running. Lainey was right behind.

"What's wrong girl?" the master asked.

Gerty had backed away from the doesn't-smell-like-a-melon and was still bristling at it. The master looked down at the cracked, almost-melon-like object and said, "Well, I'll be." He squatted down and peered more closely. "Just look at what the lake's washed up. I didn't think I'd ever see one of these."

The master's presence emboldened Gerty and she edged her way closer to the cracking sphere again. She sniffed and huffed and quietly, nervously woofed. But she got her nose right up to it, and she could smell something inside. The smell was warm and pungent. Also, strangely pleasant and appealing. Gerty heard movement inside, and then she saw a blackened horn chipping away at the crack. Widening it.

"Can you tell what it is?" the master asked Lainey. She nodded, voraciously, her teeth biting her lower lip in anticipation. "I halfway thought I was telling you myths," the master said.

Gerty was becoming ever more fascinated as she watched the crack grow. The creature inside was getting closer to breaking out of its camouflaged egg. Already, the crack was large enough for Gerty to stick her nose in and get a real smell.

"Who'll take care of it?" Lainey asked. She watched Gerty nose the tiny, sinewy creature with its bewhiskered, leonine head and golden scales. "If the gryphons always raised the baby..." She trailed off, not quite able to bring herself to say the word 'dragon' in the actual face of it.

Master and daughter watched their dog snuffle the tiny dragon, checking every length of its body. The two animals couldn't have been shaped more differently—the one a straightforward quadruped with that most familiar of all animal shapes; the other bizarrely twisty, with little feet all along its curving body and tiny, angular wings sprouting from its back here and there.

Yet, it was also like watching a bereaved mother dog find an abandoned stray puppy. The dragon-baby was clearly already imprinted on Gerty, and Gerty would be facing fewer lazy days of fruitlessly asking bugs and birds to be her playmates.

"I wouldn't worry about that," the master said. "Shall we look and see if we can find any more of them?"

The rest of the circuit around the lake revealed six more eggs, all close to the edge of the water where they'd surfaced after floating up from the depths. Two of the eggs never hatched, but the other four produced wriggling, writhing, puppy-sized dragons just like the first. All of them imprinted on Gerty and followed her wherever she went.

In the days that came, Lainey and the master looked at the lake a little differently, knowing what was obscured beneath it. Lainey said, it made her feel like she lived at the end of a rainbow. "They're like living gold! Just *imagine* what their mother must be like." The master wasn't sure he wanted to... Despite his assurances to Lainey that water dragons were perfectly safe, he couldn't help but wonder. Gerty, however, was too absorbed in her new role, caring for and cavorting with the brood of five dragonlings, to worry about the giant they had come from. Or the giants they would one day become.

3

SHEEPERFLY'S LULLABY

SHEEP TELL many tales as they graze. There's little to do in a grassy field but count the clouds, search for four-leafed clovers, and tell tall tales. Yet, some of the sheep's tales are true, and when Soft-as-Snow stares at the clouds with her liquid brown eyes, she isn't counting them. She's searching, seeking, and hoping against hope—waiting for White Wings to return to her.

Soft-as-Snow is an old sheep now, and she spends her days watching the sky and waiting. But she isn't sad. She knows that White Wings will return and fill the sky with the fluffy span of her cirrostratus wings.

When Soft-as-Snow was a young sheep, she watched and waited too—she watched the other ewes birth and raise lambs every spring; she waited through every winter, wondering why her body didn't grow thick like the other ewes. She frolicked with the rams as much as any of them; she was healthy and ate well; but she bore no lambs. Other ewes swore she was blessed. Yet her heart filled with sadness.

One spring, Soft-as-Snow could stand watching the other ewes with their new lambs, hassled but happy, no longer. She waited until Sharp Eyes, the barker who guarded the sheep herd, was distracted by a lamb gamboling too close to the creek. Then she sneaked away from the meadow, and disappeared into the shadows of the alder tree woods.

Soft-as-Snow wandered among the ferns and foxgloves, peaceful but still sad. She sang the song that she had always longed to sing to a lamb of her own, bleating the words with such sorrow and longing that a tiny presence was moved by her emotion.

"Do not cry, Mother Sheep," chimed a tiny voice.

"I am not a mother sheep," said Soft-as-Snow peering into the fluttering shadows of the alder trees, searching for the source of the bell-like voice. "My name is Soft-as-Snow; who are you?"

Gold light dappled the undergrowth between the shadows. A gust of air rustled the leaves far above, and all the shadows moved. One of the gold dapples—at the tip of a fern frond—tilted, folded, and then flapped from the fiddlehead to the tip of Soft-as-Snow's black, wet nose.

"A butterfly!" Soft-as-Snow exclaimed.

"A fairy," the butterfly answered, preening his curled antenna with his foremost legs. "With a fairy's magic. I can help you."

With his gold wings and delicate legs, the butterfly

perched between Soft-as-Snow's eyes was the most beautiful thing she'd ever seen.

"For a price," the butterfly added in his tinkling voice.

"Name your price." She would have given this handsome stranger anything, but all he asked was, "Some of your wool. It looks so soft and light; I could make a nest from it and stay warm when the cool night breezes come."

"Done." Soft-as-Snow ripped a hank of her wool out with her own teeth, and the butterfly grasped it with his six legs. He flew the ball of wool up into the trees, promising to return with everything Soft-as-Snow would need to bear a lamb of her own.

The butterfly took so long that Soft-as-Snow began to wonder if she had dreamed it all—dazzled, hypnotized by the dancing, dappled light of the wood. Then a spot of gold in the sky flapped toward her and the butterfly returned. He held a tiny, minuscule globe in one clawed hand—gold as his wings, luminescent, and small as a poppy seed.

The butterfly landed behind Soft-as-Snow's ear and planted the tiny globe deep in her thick, white wool.

"Sing to it every night," the butterfly said. "If your song is as heartfelt as the one I heard today, you'll have a lamb of your own in no time."

So Soft-as-Snow returned to the meadow with a secret. Sharp Eyes barked at her but was clearly relieved that he was no longer missing a sheep.

That night, Soft-as-Snow whisper-sang her lullaby to the tiny globe nestled in the wool behind her ear. As the days passed, Soft-as-Snow began to feel foolish; her body was not growing thick; had she given the butterfly a piece of her wool for nothing? It was a small price to pay, even for nothing... But she felt her heart would break permanently if she didn't bear a lamb of her own this time.

Yet while she worried, a bump grew behind her ear as if her wool were developing a terrible mat. The bump grew to a lump the size of an acorn; then a chestnut; then one morning, when the meadow was fresh with dew and Soft-as-Snow had stayed up all night whisper-singing, she felt a pulling sensation in the lump of wool behind her ear. She roused herself and rambled over to the stream where she could see herself in the water's reflection.

Tiny black hooves—as small as the butterfly's claws—broke through the matted wool behind her ear. Two hooves, then two more, then a third pair. Soft-as-Snow's lamb was no larger than a butterfly; its body was woolly but segmented; curling antenna sprouted from its head; and snow white wings unfurled from its back. It wasn't quite sheep, nor quite butterfly. "I'll call you White Wings," Soft-as-Snow cooed to her newborn sheeperfly, and she was profoundly happy.

Through the summer, Soft-as-Snow and her miniature lamb grazed the meadow together. White Wings fluttered from one blade of grass to the next, always staying safely hidden in the shadow cast by her wooly white mother. Soft-as-Snow sang to her lambkin and told her all the tales that sheep tell. All except this one, for she didn't know it yet. She and White Wings weren't done living it.

When autumn came, the air grew chill, and White Wings shivered. Soft-as-Snow pulled out hanks of her own wool to give the tiny lamb, much as she had given to the lamb's fairy father. White Wings wrapped herself in the wool like a coat, growing fatter and fuzzier, until one day she could no longer fly by her mother's side.

Butterflies don't live as long as sheep, and Soft-as-Snow feared her tiny daughter would die. So she sang White Wings lullabies filled with sadness and fear, hope and protection, woven through and through with love. Yet the ball of wool encasing her daughter grew cold, and Soft-as-Snow nearly gave up hope.

Then gold dappled the sky. It was White Wings' fairy father, summoned by the pain in Soft-as-Snow's voice yet again. "I cannot bear to hear you sing this way," he chimed to her.

Soft-as-Snow's brown eyes filled with tears. "Our daughter is dying."

The golden butterfly landed on Soft-as-Snow's nose once again, just as he had on the day they'd met. "No," he chimed. "This is but a cocoon. My kind change shapes. It is our way. Our daughter cannot stay with you in this form, but she will emerge again when the first snow falls."

Soft-as-Snow guarded her daughter's cocoon through the rest of the autumn, and true to the golden butterfly's word, when the first flake of snow landed on her nose that winter, White Wings' cocoon began to tremble. The second flake landed on the wooly cocoon like a frozen kiss, and the ball of wool grew light. It puffed and swirled and stretched and expanded around Soft-as-Snow like a fog or an embrace. Like a memory. Like a hope. Like her daughter—everything that White Wings was to her, deep inside Soft-as-Snow's heart.

The fog lifted, drifting upward, condensing, dancing with the falling snowflakes, until White Wings was the most beautiful butterfly-shaped cloud in the sky. Her body was a puff of cumulonimbus; her wings stretched out cirrostratus. She snowed down kisses in the form of snowflakes to her beloved mother and promised that, though she would wander and graze the sky, she would come back to bathe her mother in loving raindrops every summer when the days were at their hottest.

Soft-as-Snow watched her daughter float away into the winter sky, safe in her shadow and complete in her love.

When other ewes bear new lambs, spring after spring, Soft-as-Snow tells them the tale of her darling sheeperfly. The lambs laugh and call her crazy, but every summer—when the days are at their hottest—the whole herd comes to stand beside Soft-as-Snow in the cooling kiss-like raindrops that fall from the sky.

4

ONE NIGHT IN NOCTURNIA

Mice tell a myth of fearsome creatures with scaly talons, massively muscled bodies, and sharp, hooked beaks. Death from the sky, instant death, for any mouse foolish enough to be above ground when these creatures come hunting.

The name of the myth is owl, and few mice see one and live to tell the tale. Owls are creatures of shadow—both the shadows of trees in a darkening forest and the shadows of misremembered tales retold by forgetful minds.

My name is Randal, and I am a mouse who has seen an owl up close and lived. My story is not second-hand, nor is it misremembered. For every moment of that night is burned into my brain with the mortal terror that coursed through my body every second that I was in *Nocturnia*.

How did I survive? I did not go to Nocturnia as a mouse.

I am an inventor, and before my voyage to Nocturnia I built many small conveniences for the mice of my village. Doors that hinge and lock; a pulley-drawn elevator that carries mice up to the bountiful branches of our village's oak trees; a powerful vice that crushes acorns into a tasty mash. Yes, the mice of my village were happy with me. Then I began work on my machine.

I scavenged the supplies from a brown dumpster across the concrete lot that all the other mice in my village avoided. There was never any food in this particular dumpster; however, I'd found many useful materials there for my inventions. Then, one day, among the scraps of wire and broken slats of gray plastic, I found some old green boards, dotted with colored knobs and traced with lines of silver. I was enthralled. There was energy in those boards that made my paws tingle as soon as I touched them. I knew they were magic, and I needed to harness that magic.

Much to the consternation of my fellow villagers, I stopped answering their requests to construct minor doodads—toys for their children, more efficient cooking tools, and the like—and devoted myself full-time to building a machine that could uncover and test the powers of the magical green boards I'd found.

My experiments were exhausting and produced strange results. One board reversed my sense of taste and sight when I hooked myself up to it with a wired-up skullcap I'd built from a thimble. That was a strange experience. Undaunted, I began wiring the boards together, adjusting the locations of the colored knobs, and, all the while, keeping detailed, *ever so detailed* notes.

One by one, the mice who used to call on me stopped visiting my laboratory. I suppose that rumors must have spread, flying wild as rumors are wont to do. I did not care. My studies were far too fascinating to concern myself with the uneducated fears of my fellow villagers. What did they know of the wondrous twin powers of magic and science?

Eventually, I could reliably swap my consciousness with that of an ant who lived in my lab and cooperated with my experiments in return for bits of sugar and candy. Like me, Brielle was a social recluse, an outcast from her anthill, disavowed by her queen for heretical thinking. Unlike me, she could not return to her society. I suppose I *could* have thrown my work away... Given up my anti-social tendencies, scorned the dark sciences that were making the other mice frightened of me, and rejoined the happy society of rodents living between the hawthorn tree and two oaks.

I did not. And the discoveries I have made since have opened my eyes to an indescribable *vastness* of experience. I can no longer go back.

When I found the owl feather in the concrete lot, fate's dark hand moved my paw. It was small and downy to the touch. Slips of silk, sewn together into one thin spine, drawn down to the sharp point of the quill. Trace of my enemy. The signature of *death*. Yet, I grabbed the feather and clutched it to my heart, scurrying all the way back to my lab.

I had been possessed by an idea, body and soul. A dangerous idea. My paws moved without me to wire the feather into the machine of green boards. My mouth moved against my will, describing my plan to Brielle.

As she listened, she bowed her head, compulsively cleaning her antennae with her forelegs, denoting her clear nervousness. But I pressed hard, for my plan would not work without her assistance. And, heaven help me, Brielle gave in.

The cage I constructed for myself was built from a cheese grater. I firmly wired extra panels to the top and bottom. The panel on the top was spring-loaded, but the latch only worked from outside.

Working the latch: that was all Brielle had to do, wait out the night and open the latch for me. She left my lab after that night. I wonder where she went. Where does an outcast ant go?

I'm getting ahead of myself.

I fed wires through one of the holes in the cheese grater, connecting my thimble skull-cap and a portable power switch to the machine. When the time came, I crouched inside the dark, claustrophobic cheese grater. The only light there streamed in through the tiny holes. Brielle watched me, her antennae stenciling tiny circles in the air, as I put on the skull-cap. I held the power switch in my paws. My ant and I stared at each other through the hole. She held my gaze as I steeled my nerves.

I threw the switch, and my paws were gone.

I was falling! *Flapping...*

I had wings. My god, it had worked.

Dizziness and elation filled me as my new broad, strong, *feathery* arms swept back and forth in rhythmic strokes. My talons curled, tucked tight beneath me. *Beneath me!* Alack! It was as if the entire universe had turned upside down, and the endless night sky stretched nauseatingly away... *beneath me.*

I faltered. Realizing the power I'd assumed in a moment by stealing a *flying* body, I lost the power, broke the rhythm, and, thrashing, truly fell.

The next part is hard to remember. In retrospect, I find my mind rests more where it is used to... In this old mouse's body. The visceral feel of flying, forgetting how to fly, and re-finding it again mid-fall eludes me. It is a sensation shaped wrong for this mouse brain.

Instead, I wonder how the owl, in those first moments of being robbed of his usual self, railed against the cheese-grater cage. Did he scream? Did he claw? Did he try to tear out his own, foreign limbs? *My limbs.*

How must it have been for Brielle to watch me... but not me... gripped by an insane rage? Did I threaten her? I know it was bad, because she wouldn't speak of it. But, I must admit, while I lived in that owl's body for one night, I was far too lost in my own experience to spare a single thought for the body I'd left behind or the friend I'd left guarding it.

Looking back, I find my expectations, my *plans*, for

that night hard to believe. I was so misguided. Naive. In my ignorance, I reveled in visions of taking that dragon-beast body and flying it back to its nest, the den of inequity and horror that must be the owls' city. There, I would wreck what damage and savage recompense I could for the lives of friends I'd seen lost to owl hunger over my years. I thought I knew those hateful beasts. I thought when I got to their city, I knew what I would find...

I did fly to the owls' city. Following my new winged brethren, I found my way deeper into that forest than my mouse legs could have carried me in many days.

I circled the sky, hearing the shrieks of other owls. "Nocturnia!" their voices rang. My head rang too. Even clothed in my wolf-body, the idea of infiltrating owl society terrified my little sheep-self to the bone.

"Join me," the voice of death chittered near my ear. My heart leapt in terror, but my wings stayed steady.

The voice belonged to a she-owl, and my sight of her was the first clear sight I ever had of an owl. For, though I inhabited one's body, I could not see myself, and the other owls I'd seen were the same feathered bolts of death in the distance that I'd glimpsed as a mouse. Only now, I shared the sky with them, instead of peering up at them above.

My beak and voice felt strange to me, but I managed to hoot a hoarse, "Yes." She angled her wings and swooped ahead. I followed her, and she led my way, wending between the trees, to a building nestled in a giant oak's upper branches.

The building was a splash of clashing colors in the dark of the forest night. The roof was constructed from overlapping umbrellas in red, yellow, blue—all settled in the natural architecture of the trees. The walls were more muted tones but even more riotous in pattern—patchwork quilts with all their little triangles and squares, draped down from the umbrellas' edges.

The she-owl and I lit on a branch and side-stepped our way between a gap in two quilts. The space inside was complex, riddled with the umbrellas' hanging handles and the tree's snaking branches. Stolen road signs—red octagons and green rectangles—were arranged as tables, and many owls perched around them, hooting and cooing conversationally.

"A bite to eat?" my she-owl companion asked, settling comfortably on the curve of an umbrella handle. I perched on a branch beside her still in too much shock to answer her. "They have voles here," she said. "I'll buy."

"No!" I squawked, abusing my borrowed vocal cords horribly. Coughing and hemming in the awkward silence that followed while all the nearby owls stare at me, I got slightly better control of my voice. "I mean," I hazarded, "I'm... fasting tonight."

Broad gold eyes blinked around me, but most of the other owls turned away. My companion shifted her talons and puffed the feathers on her chest, "I didn't mean to offend. Do you mind..."

I thought she was going ask if I minded whether she

ate in front of me, but she must have picked up my unconscious body language.

"Why are you fasting?" she asked instead.

"Out of respect for voles. And mice," I said. There was a hint of challenge in my voice, and I expected her to laugh at me. That would have been an experience to carry with me all my days... Death laughing in my face.

Instead, she stared at me with eyes round as the moon and gold as the sun. For a moment, I forgot myself and thought I was a tiny mouse before her. About to be eaten. In that frozen terror, I couldn't help but notice how beautiful the face of death was... Brown flecked feathers ringed her eyes in ever darkening circles, meeting at a V that extended from her hooked beak upward into ear-like tufts. She was a horrible vision, but beautiful nonetheless.

"They do poetry here," she said. "We could stay for that."

Speechless, I remembered myself again. I was an owl. Apparently a handsome one, as this goddess of death was *courting* me. Not preparing to assault me.

"If you prefer," she offered, "we could fly into the city."

"This isn't the city?"

She bobbed her round face, swaying her thickly feathered neck. "You've never been to the city?"

"Barn owl," I answered, wondering how much more damage I could do to owl society in their *city* than I could here.

"Let's go," she said, stepping off of her perch on the umbrella handle. "A country owl that's this close to

Nocturnia without having seen it..." She tut-tutted. "We can come back for the poetry."

So we soared together, through the deepening night. I marveled at the mental and physical acuity that I continued to feel as I followed her. The brain and body I inhabited felt well-rested and strong. I knew when I returned to my mouse body at the end of the night, it would be exhausted and the rising of the sun would drag me unwillingly into sleep. But, what if I had thought to drug my own body before making the switch? Then I could return to a second well-rested body, even after a full night's activity.

How much more could I achieve with my life if I began to live it dually? I could rotate my normal sleep schedule. Mouse by day; owl by night. Always awake, myself, while locking one of these devil-creatures into an eternal sleep, getting my rest during the night for me.

Except... I'd have to eat, in my owl form. That thought gave me pause. However, I quickly reasoned that I could switch from one owl to another, always fasting at night and leaving each owl whose life I borrowed a little weaker for the wear. I'd steal their time and leave them all slowly wasting away!

Giddy from the strength of my pumping wings and the speed of my buzzing mind, it seemed a nearly perfect plan. Diabolical. Much more effective than merely attacking their city once. Tonight, I would scout the city and lay plans for a much larger scale assault, carried out— subtly—over the rest of my life. A life that was suddenly to be filled with twice as many days—half mouse days, and half owl nights.

And in this frame of mind, I first laid eyes on Nocturnia. Through the dark of the night, my powerful owl's eyes saw the forest branches grow together, twined in ways that must have taken years to train. This was not the tacky scavenger's architecture I'd seen at the bar. This was the work of generations of dedicated arborists and craftsmen working closely with the living trees to bend trunks and branches out of their natural form and interweave them into the walls, floors, and arches of living buildings. The ancient wooden structures yet breathed with the rustle of new green leaves!

I was impressed. But, my heart stayed cold and determined. *I must find a way to tear down this work of art and nature*, I thought. *For the good of all mice.*

My tour began with a litany of the places that held sentimental value for my tour guide: the hollow knothole where she hatched; the branch in the ceiling of that great atrium where she perched to rest after her first hunt; that sort of thing. I hardly listened, but she didn't notice. The tour grew more interesting when we moved on to the sites of cultural significance.

We visited an art gallery filled with exquisitely delicate paintings and carved stone statues. The paintings ranged from simple portraits of owls to abstract swirls that seemed to me to relate to wind patterns somehow. The most troubling paintings, however, depicted mice, chipmunks, voles... Creatures that the owls should see as food and that I see as friends. These paintings gave me an eerie feeling, as if owls must always be watching us from the sky, observing us closely, and apparently painting our likenesses before the inevitable attack.

The exhibit of statues was more confusing, and I asked the owl curating the exhibit about them. He informed me that they were on loan from a nearby colony of bats and that many of the gallery's other visitors found them confusing as well. Apparently, they made more sense to creatures with sonar. In trade for the statues, Nocturnia's artist community had loaned the bats an exhibit of bonsai trees and other miniature topiary. The curator told me that the topiary was proving quite popular there.

Next my she-owl companion flew with me past the center tree—an especially giant gingko that had been trained into the shape of a hollow bell. Inside there were rows of branches, organized into pews. The center tree was a governmental gathering point similar in nature, I ascertained, to the church hollow under the old oak in my own mouse village. My female companion informed me that this particular owl city was governed by a democratic oligarchy which was unfortunately not in session. So, I could not see their government at work.

The oldest owl elected to that oligarchy, my companion told me, was currently nineteen years old. Imagine that! *Nineteen*. I was an old mouse already when I turned two, and I will be an old mouse indeed if I make it to three. These owls who prey on us have lives nearly ten times the length of our own. I shudder to think of how many mice an owl must eat to keep its belly full that many years. And, yet, think of the great work that could be done... With only one more year, I could do... oh, so many things. With another ten? Twenty? It is hardly fair to have been born a mouse.

Perhaps that is when my heart began to betray me. I do not know. It may have been later when we visited the fledgling's playground. The branches there had been woven into a floor as well as a ceiling, and the young owls, still learning to fly, could safely practice their new skill. They tumbled through the air, awkwardly scuffling and fumbling as they grew used to their own wings. There was a small owlet, all fuzzy still, who made me think briefly of the runt from my sister's first litter. Only because he was smaller than the rest, mind you. But, still, it was a similarity. Younglings have a way of pulling at the heartstrings.

I think the true moment of horror, though, was in the cathedral, a structure built from a quartet of red-leafed maples, woven into one. The boughs were freshly decorated with white and yellow flowers, but there were also living vines of wisteria and honeysuckle that twisted their way along the ceiling in draping arches. The entire space was lit with the soft glow of fireflies. The adult insects had been domesticated by the owls and trained to dance among the wisteria flowers.

I believe it was a church service I attended, for an owl perched in a hollow of one of the red maple's trunks and preached to us about the importance of stewardship and proper care for the trees, flowers, insects, and all the other small creatures under the owls' dominion. Then a choir of owls sang, and their trilling, cooing voices joined in a mass harmony that touched my very soul. I challenge you to hear that song and *not* lose yourself. I *challenge* you. I truly do. For I was lost when I heard it, and I think I shall never find myself again.

My female companion led me back from Nocturnia in a daze. I could neither get the sound of the owls' song out of my ears nor the sight of those delicately painted portraits of soon-to-die mice from my eyes. I flew with my companion to the cafe built of umbrellas, all the way flapping my wings by rote. A rote I had learned too fast. A rhythm that had too quickly grown familiar and comfortable. The mantle of power I'd borrowed had already settled too easily onto my shoulders, and my emotions waged a war within me.

All my loyalty to mice said I must destroy these owls. Wreak whatever havoc I could on them. But... the sights I'd seen haunted me.

My heart—my own *traitorous* heart—spoke of beauty and value unmeasured. A vibrant and lovely society that cared about the effect they had on my own race. How could that be? In my own eyes, my mouse life was nothing more than grist for the mill of Nocturnia's stomachs. Yet, those stomachs were connected to hearts that loved my kind for our sacrifice. Was I the monster?

Destroying owl society would be as wanton as the destruction I hoped to avenge.

I perched in the umbrella cafe, beside my she-owl

companion, and we listened to the poetry that had been promised. We were part of a crowd, and the poets—amateur authors, I gathered—took turns in the limelight. They perched, one after the other on one of the umbrella handles, hanging from the ceiling. They told their poems in cooing voices, espousing philosophy and waxing eloquent.

My companion had grown bold through the course of our adventures that night and stepped sideways along the branch we shared, until her soft feathers pressed against mine. I felt the tip of her beak at my neck. Enough of my mouse-self was left to panic. I froze. But she only pulled at my feathers lightly, preening and grooming. She fawned over me, brazenly flirtatious, and I could only shudder. Here was death seducing me, and I thought: *I will let her. I will live in this utopia forever.*

If I only could have. But, for all of us, the timer must run out, and mine ran out before dawn.

As quickly as I'd found myself falling through the air, early that evening, I once again found myself in the small, dark space of my cheese-grater cage. My she-owl girlfriend was gone. I wonder if she noticed the difference in me, in the body I'd been wearing, when it was suddenly inhabited by a real owl again?

I'll never know. For I can never go back.

Upon my return, Brielle uncaged me, and then she left, wordlessly terrified by the hours she'd spent keeping watch over the owl doppelganger trapped inside my normal mouse body. Who knows what obscenities he had screamed at her when he realized the trick I'd played on him? What threats he made?

Whatever happened that night, she would not explain it. She took her pay in shards of peppermint candy and packed her few belongings. She left that very morning, her antennae quivering and her six legs stepping falteringly. Her mandibles moved as if to speak to me when she stood, finally, by the door, but she only shook her head and turned away. I think her broken heart—already damaged by the recriminations of her own queen—could not take abuse delivered from the tongue of her only friend. Even if whatever words were spoken were not truly mine.

And so I find myself alone.

I've tried to continue my work, but new experiments don't interest me. What purpose is there to toiling away futilely in this small life I live? The fur on my muzzle is graying. My days are numbered. Yet, I could still do great work *if only I could focus*. Instead, my thoughts return, always, to the owls and their city. Thoughts that nauseate me and make me doubt the meaning of the life of a mouse.

I cannot share my thoughts with my fellow mice. Who would believe me? And those who believed my experiences would yet be unable to understand their significance and enormity. How could they, when I hardly can? More likely though, they'd simply disbelieve.

Sometimes, I doubt my sanity myself. Owls cannot possibly be the gentle titans I imagined on my flight of fancy. Those beings were hardly the nightmares that stalk careless mice from the sky. If only I could go back, just once, to confirm what I saw, perhaps it would give my mind some peace. Perhaps, I could find a way to understand and reconcile that world with my own. *But, no,* I left the light of moral, upright mouse life once, and all too quickly my eyes adjusted to the dark. And it has taken far too long for my eyes to adjust back. If they have. If they ever will.

Besides, Brielle is gone, and I have no one to free me from the cage. No one to aid in my safe return home. And, yet, I cannot bring myself to get rid of the feather...

5

THE OTTER'S MERMAID

The air turned salty in Arlow's whiskers as he pedaled his watercycle out of the shade and protection of the thick rainforest trees. He squinted down the river, but he couldn't see the ocean yet. The river curved around rolling grass knolls and disappeared behind a thicket of coastal brush. Arlow pedaled harder with all four paws and felt the cool water slip even faster around his body, pressing his clothes against his fur.

The spinning turbine at the back of the watercycle and the smaller one at its nose, propelled Arlow forward. Two ski-like buoys kept the entire contraption skimming along at the water's surface. The river's current was in his favor, and while otters swim fast, a watercycle is faster.

Arlow was eager to round that bend and, hopefully, catch his first view of the ocean just beyond. His whole life, Arlow had dreamed of leaving his small hometown on the banks of the river and traveling downstream. He'd heard thrilling tales from retired sailors of the ocean. And the beautiful sirens who lived there.

Around the bend, Arlow found another bend and, after that, another. The sun began to set, filling the sky with an amber red glow. When he gritted his teeth in frustration that he'd have to spend another night camping on the riverbank, Arlow realized that—so slowly he hadn't even noticed—the quiet rhythmic roar of the ocean had crept into his rounded ears.

Arlow redoubled his efforts.

He didn't make it to the ocean that night, but he did make it to civilization. It had been many days since he set out from his home village on the watercycle, so, although it wasn't the ocean —the pearl of his desire—he was happy to see an inn by the riverside.

Arlow unstrapped himself from his watercycle and left the tangled contraption of turbine wheels, gears, leather straps, and pedals to dry on the ground in the darkening evening outside. He kept his pack of supplies on his back and went to the front door of the inn. The door was cracked open, so he stepped inside and greeted the pudgy, puff-furred otter lady he found bustling about the small diner-like front room.

"Goodness!" she exclaimed, dusting off her frilly apron and sizing up the sleek, young specimen of otterdom before her. "A river boy! We don't get too many of you down here. My name's Florentine, and this is my inn." She had a pleasant matronly nature.

"I'm on my way to the ocean," Arlow said. "Do you know how close it is?"

The apron-clad woman made her way to a desk at the side of the room near the door Arlow entered by. There was a small bell on the desk and an open registry where patrons of the inn signed for their rooms. "You're quite close," she said. "Though, you won't find a better inn between here and there. We have a room available tonight and a homemade breakfast in the morning."

Arlow looked around the small front room that served as both restaurant and office. There were stairs in the back, presumably leading to bedrooms upstairs, and another door that must lead to the kitchen.

"I don't have much money," Arlow said. "In fact, I have none." He could see the otter lady's whiskers droop as she pondered whether she could turn away a tired young traveler simply because he couldn't pay when there were perfectly good rooms going empty upstairs.

"Never mind that then," she said, recovering her composure and putting on a cheerful grin for him. "Just sign your name on the registry here, and you can make yourself at home in the room at the end of the hall upstairs. But, mind you," she pointed a well-manicured claw at him, "you'll be expected to help cook breakfast in the morning."

Arlow's pride stung at the idea of anyone taking pity on him. "I appreciate your kindness," he said, keeping his voice level, "but I believe I can earn my keep a little better than by merely helping out in the kitchen."

"Is that so?" Florentine said, looking Arlow up and down. He was a skinny river otter boy on his way to find out that sailing on the high seas wasn't all big adventures and fighting pirates. She'd seen his kind before. Arrogant. Ready for a fall. "Well, then, what makes you so special?"

"I'm an inventor," Arlow said.

"Fancy!" she exclaimed. "Well, I don't think we have need for any inventing just now, but some help peeling the potatoes in the morning would be nice. Now, I'll leave you to yourself," she said. "There are extra blankets in the closet under the stairs."

Arlow grumbled to himself, *"Everyone needs inventing,"* but the older otter woman clearly wasn't paying attention. She'd bustled her way back to the dining tables and was gathering up table settings, most likely left over from dinner. *Never mind,* Arlow thought. He needn't convince her of the invaluable nature of invention with mere words. If an automated potato-peeling machine awaited her in the morning, that would be far more persuasive.

And so it was.

After a comfortable night of sleep, Arlow woke up early the next morning and brought his pack of supplies down to the kitchen with him. He found the potatoes in a bin by the back door, and he set about designing a peeler for them. First, he carved a chute that was the right size for the potatoes to roll down, using some young tree bark from a sapling outside. Then, he built grips from nuts and screws to affix the chute to one of the bowls he found in the kitchen and created a slotted, hinged arm to hold one of Florentine's paring knives. He was careful to make sure that the bowl and knife would still be removable, in case Florentine wanted to use them for something else.

Except for the borrowed bowl and knife, all of Arlow's supplies were either carved out of the stand of young trees behind the inn or pulled from his backpack, where he stored many sizes of nuts and bolts, and other small gadgets and widgets. The final touch was to take a piece of slender, flexible pipe from his pack and affix it to the nose of the kitchen tea kettle. When he put the kettle on the stove and heated it, the steam from its nose flowed through the pipe, and into the potato peeler, where it powered the entire contraption.

The little machine was peeling away with a merrily flashing blade when Florentine entered her kitchen. "Lordy!" she exclaimed. What have you done to my best mixing bowl?"

Arlow dropped the potatoes, one at a time, down the bark chute into the mixing bowl where they danced around getting peeled. "Don't worry. It's all reversible," Arlow said. "Here, you try one."

Arlow held a potato out to the sea otter lady, and she took it reluctantly. But, when the potato emerged all smooth and slimy, perfectly peeled, she clapped her paws. "My, my," she said. "I guess you are an inventor."

Arlow was pleased. His own mother hadn't reacted nearly as well when he'd built inventions out of her kitchen utensils. Of course, he'd been younger then, and the inventions had been less reversible.

Just to show off, Arlow took Florentine out front and showed her the watercycle he'd invented for his ride down the river. When they went back inside, she made a delightful pair of chowders out of the potatoes he'd peeled—clam chowder for them and corn chowder for the herbivores staying at the inn.

The other tenants came down and joined them for breakfast. There was a beaver couple, come to the coast to see the woodcraft at the harbor, and a tourist squirrel who chittered energetically through the whole meal about what a treat Arlow was in for—*visiting the coast for the first time! Oh the sights to see at the sea!*

Arlow, however, was only interested in one sight: the sea lion caves. And, before he set out, he made sure to get directions from Florentine to find them. She also packed a lunch of fish cakes for him and entreated him to return and build more "clever contraptions" for her.

* * *

The last of the ride down the river was pleasant and smooth. He passed slowly through the harbor town, enjoying the sights it had to offer and waving at the various figures he saw on shore. Most of them were puffy-furred sea otters like Florentine.

When the ocean finally opened up before him, Arlow was stunned by the long line of water-filled horizon, broken only by the various sailing ships moored in the bay. His paws stopped pedaling, and he drifted along in the current with his mouth agape. He'd never seen so much water. The whole world was blue from the tip top of the sky all the way down to the water he floated in. He wondered idly if he swam far enough out into the ocean if it would meet the sky, and he could watercycle his way upward to the sun and moon.

Eventually, Arlow started pushing the pedals again. He rode out of the bay and pedaled against the surf to a stretch of golden beach where he shed his watercycle, backpack, and clothing on the sand. He danced barefurred in the breaking waves, cold as they were, like a tiny pup. Then he swam in their swelling undertow, flirting with its strong pull outward, into the inexhaustible vastness of the ocean.

By the time Arlow tired of reveling in the exhilarating power of the ocean's edge, the sun was high in the sky. He lay in the noonday heat, eating his fishcakes and wishing he'd been born by the ocean instead of deep in the forest. The fishcakes were good, and Arlow decided he would return to Florentine's inn that night. Perhaps he would make his home there for a while. He had a lot of ideas for improving her kitchen and record-keeping. He could turn that bedroom into his workroom and live in an inn beside the sea.

Arlow stayed stretched out on the sand until his thick fur was thoroughly dried. Then, he threw on his shorts and jerkin, strapped on his pack and watercycle, and delved into the water again, enjoying the delicious transition from being dry to being thoroughly wet.

This time, Arlow didn't intend to stop until he'd pedaled his watercycle all the way to the sea lion caves.

The ocean was calm, just out past the waves. Arlow watched the golden beach pass by on his right as he cycled north. The farther he went, the rockier the shore became until the whole beach was interrupted by a sheer cliff side. Arlow made sure to stay safely past the wave's pull for he had no wish to be dashed against the rocky cliffs. However, the cliff side opened into a deep, wide cavern. Exactly as Florentine had described.

Arlow stopped pedaling and floated in the calm beyond the waves, watching the wide cave. There were brightly colored cloth banners—mostly yellows, oranges, and reds—dangling and flapping in the breeze. Funny buildings made from cloth hung over wooden frames clustered along the edges of the cave, built in the range of rocky floor that served as the tidally fluctuating dividing line between dry land and ocean's water.

Arlow saw the canvas walls of the small buildings billow softly in the wind. Some of their walls trailed in the water; others clearly would when the high tide came in. Farther into the cave, where the rock looked to be usually dry, there was a giant bonfire and strings of fish smoking in the air above it.

Most importantly, though, there were sea lions—those mythical creatures halfway between otter and dolphin. Arlow felt his heart skip beats as he looked at them. A group of sea lion ladies bathed in the sun that shone down on the edge of the cave. They lay on the sun-soaked rock, dressed only in the barest slips of colorful silk. Their fur was sleek and shiny; their muzzles were long and elegant; and, the smooth curve of their bodies into hydrodynamic flippers and fins was a revelation of reality. They were beautiful sirens. He had found his mermaids.

Other sea lions—both men and women—moved around the small town, stoking the fire, hanging strings of fish, and otherwise facing the chores of daily life. They kept mostly to the border between the worlds of hard land and deep water, but when they ventured farther out onto the rocky floor of the giant cave, the sea lion men and women pulled themselves with their strong arms, dragging their flippered tails behind them.

Arlow was so absorbed in watching the sea lion village that he didn't notice one of its denizens approach him.

"Hello traveler," said a husky, sonorous woman's voice from behind Arlow. He turned to see her, but the speaker was gone before he arranged himself and his watercycle to face the right way.

The voice laughed, from behind Arlow again, and he began turning back. Another laugh kept him pedaling, and soon Arlow was turning in awkward circles.

"You're not very dexterous in that thing," the voice said, still full of laughter. "What's its purpose? Can't you swim without it?"

Frustrated, Arlow exclaimed, "Of course I can! I *am* an otter." Then he gave up paddling and flipped his tail, angrily splashing the surface of the water.

"There's no need to be angry," the voice said, finally

floating lazily into Arlow's view. She was a sea lion with the narrow, earless face of her species and the long, wide neck. Her head tilted, and her neck arched elegantly. While the sea lions in the village looked strange and awkward pulling themselves along land, this sea lion woman looked utterly natural. She was in her proper element, bobbing at the surface of the sea. "So, what's it for?" she asked Arlow again. "What is it?"

Arlow couldn't stay angry while staring a mermaid in her beautifully whiskered face. "It's a watercycle," he said plainly. "It's for speed."

The sea lion's eyes sparkled. "I'll race you," she barked, floating onto her back. The pink silk of her slip, wet with sea water, plastered against her belly and narrow hips. Beneath the water, Arlow could see her hips slim down to where they ended in a long, brown-furred flipper tail.

"All right," Arlow said, enjoying the idea of impressing a mermaid. He was confident in his invention's abilities. And his own.

The sea lion girl pointed with a long flippery hand to a rocky outcropping farther down the shore, about a mile away. She counted to three, and before Arlow had his watercycle properly positioned, she was off, swimming away.

The sea lion girl's first burst of speed was breathtaking. As Arlow pedaled after her, he felt his heart in his throat at the sheer unbridled joy of his situation: *he was chasing a mermaid!* Oh, she was fast. The curve of her head and back kept breaking the surface of the water; sometimes, Arlow could see the serrated line of the tip of her tail.

The harder he paddled, the faster the mermaid seemed to swim. Arlow reconciled himself to losing the race. It would be disappointing, to be sure. But, at least, when he reached the rocky outcropping, there would be a mermaid waiting for him.

Yet, as the race progressed, Arlow's speed stayed steady, and the sea lion's burst of energy wore off.

Arlow passed her by, not long before they reached the rocky outcropping. He back-peddled, bringing his watercycle to a stop just in time for the front turbine to bump gently against the rough rock. He turned his watercycle and watched the sea lion girl swimming toward him.

Arlow was surprised to find as he watched her that she swam by pulling herself forward with her flippers rather than by swishing her tail. Her long body cut through the water toward him, flying straight like an arrow. *To his heart*, he thought. Arlow was smitten before he even learned her name.

* * *

ANGELICA, for that was his mermaid's name, spent the rest of the afternoon showing Arlow around the sea lion village. She teased and flirted with Arlow, splashing him like a bratty young pup one moment and then locking eyes with him, only to glance away, shy and mysterious in the next. As the evening approached, Angelica asked if he would stay for dinner, but Arlow's heart was already faint from a day filled with so much fantasy. So, instead, he promised to return on the morrow and retreated to the safe haven of Florentine's inn.

As the days passed, Arlow and Angelica fell into a comfortable pattern. They swam together every morning as soon as Arlow arrived from his night at the inn. Sometimes their morning swims took them north up the coast; sometimes they swam straight out to sea, losing themselves in the featureless, flowing landscape of the sea. Always they talked and played, sharing the sweet nothings of their pasts mixed in with games of chase that ended, more and more often, in an embrace.

Arlow told Angelica about his many failed attempts at invention as a young pup. He'd burned many bridges in his hometown before learning to put his clever ideas to useful purposes instead of devilish pastimes like catapults for his mother's silverware. For her part, Angelica made a guessing game of her past for Arlow. He learned about her parents and siblings by answering riddles. She infuriated him by making him guess who among all the young men in the caves with them was her first love. He guessed nearly every male in the village who wasn't related to Angelica before discovering, with many hints, that the answer was himself.

In the afternoons, Arlow helped Angelica with the crafts and jewelry she made and sold to the tourist shops in town. Arlow had no eye for artistry himself, but he could string shells and beads in the patterns Angelica instructed him to—though, much more slowly than she herself did. In spite of her long, webbed, flippery fingers, Angelica was quite deft with the delicate beadwork of the jewelry and the complex braiding of seaweed baskets. Arlow couldn't master the basketwork at all.

While he helped with the beads, Arlow thought about the ways that his inventions could help Angelica and the other townsfolk in the sea lion village. When he finished modernizing Florentine's inn, he fully planned to make the sea lion village his next project.

Arlow split his evening meals between the sea lion village with Angelica and the cozy dining room of Florentine's inn. Whether he stayed with Angelica for dinner or not, though, he always returned to the inn to work on his inventions for the remainder of the evening.

By the end of a month's time, Florentine's kitchen was an engineer's dream of Rube Goldbergian innovation. Gears turned; steam whistled; clockwork machinery tick tocked; and it was almost entirely automated. To make dinner, all Florentine had to do was buy fish at the market, dig up vegetables from the garden, and set the kitchen contraptions in motion. Delicious steaming meals prepared themselves, and, after the inn's guests finished eating, the automated kitchen even washed the dishes. As far as Florentine was concerned, Arlow had paid for room and board at her inn permanently.

If Arlow had been interested in selling his inventions to other merchants around the town, he could have made a tidy sum. However, what truly interested Arlow was the challenge of new creations. So, while he didn't mind other animals from the town poking around his inventions, seeing if they could figure out how to copy them, Arlow had little interest in re-building a machine he'd already finished simply to turn a profit.

Instead, Arlow's sights turned to different goals.

· * * *

THE FIRST INVENTION that Arlow brought Angelica was a beadwork loom. The wooden loom was small and light enough that Arlow was able to transport it, strapped to the back of his watercycle. Though... just barely.

Given beads organized into different compartments in its boxy belly, the loom could grab and string the beads into any pattern that Angelica typed onto a primitive keyboard at the loom's base similar to a miniature church organ. The different keys symbolized the different compartments, except for one key that symbolized the end of a string and told the loom to tie off the beading thread.

Angelica laughed when she saw Arlow cycling his way toward the village with the loom strapped behind him. "This invention doesn't help you swim faster," Angelica said. "That's for sure!"

She kept laughing as he untied the boxy contraption from his cycle and began shaking the water out. Arlow wasn't bothered by her laughter. He didn't take teasing well from most people, but Angelica's whiskery smile melted his heart every time and her jabs rolled harmlessly over him. Besides, he knew she would be impressed when he showed her what it could do.

"No," he said. "It is for speed though. Just a different kind of speed."

Angelica looked at Arlow quizzically with her head cocked to the side.

"It'll work better after the sun dries its innards a bit," Arlow said. "C'mon, let's go for our swim." He reached his paw out to grab her slender flipper, pulling his beloved mermaid toward the water.

"All right," Angelica said. "But, I have a different direction I'd like to swim this time."

Now it was Arlow's turn to look at Angelica quizzically. He thought they'd swum together in just about every direction there was. Angelica showed him he'd been wrong.

Arlow followed Angelica lazily along the surface of the water, swishing his powerful tail to push himself backward as he lay staring up at the sky. Angelica swam with much more energy, but she hadn't dragged a heavy piece of machinery in from the town that morning. As the fog set in over the ocean around them, Angelica bobbed her head under the surface. A moment later, the flip of her tail splashed salt water on Arlow's face. He blinked the drops out of his eyes, and, suddenly, the meaning of her words made sense to him.

With a rising sense of excitement, Arlow rolled over and pointed his nose *downward*. His ears and nostrils clamped shut against the water as he submerged and swam after Angelica. All he could see of her was the graceful serration at the tip of her tail and the trail of turmoil she left in the water. Arlow swam deeper and deeper, feeling the same exhilaration he'd known on the first day they'd raced together. He was chasing a mermaid again! He would chase her until his lungs gave out and his body burned for air.

Angelica didn't make him wait that long. Her body twisted around and she came back to meet him. They swirled around each other, feeling each other's motion in the currents of the water they shared. They danced a slow spiraling dance. Then their whiskery faces met in a kiss.

Arlow wondered how deep they were. When Angelica broke away from his embrace, Arlow looked around and saw the ocean landscape around him. Kelp forests swayed between rocky outcroppings beneath him. He could see deep crevasses in the rock formations. Their depths disappeared into the darkening blue and the thickening of the kelp. Suddenly, Arlow was less curious about how deep he was now and much more curious about how deep the crevasses went. There was an entire world to explore down here! But the pressure in his lungs was growing...

Arlow breached the surface to great gulps of air. Angelica appeared beside him a minute later, barely out of breath.

"Holy mackerel," Arlow gasped. "How long could you have stayed down there?"

"Not much longer," Angelica replied. "Though, apparently longer than you." Her black eyes sparkled.

Arlow ignored the jab. It was only fair that a mermaid could swim deeper underwater than him, a normal otter. Though... He wasn't a completely normal otter. He was an inventor. Arlow's breathing began to settle, and he asked, "Have you explored those crevasses down there? Do you know how deep they go?"

"I've explored them some," Angelica answered. "But I've never found the bottom."

Arlow's curiosity piqued. Although he knew he couldn't hold his breath as long as Angelica, he had to try. All in all, they made four more dives that morning before Angelica's desire to return and discover the meaning of the machine Arlow had hauled into her village outweighed Arlow's desire to keep swimming stubbornly toward the bottom of the ocean.

The loom's mechanical innards were sufficiently dry by the time Arlow and Angelica made it back to the village. So, Arlow asked Angelica to bring him some of her beads and beading thread. Hesitant at the idea of feeding her precious jewelry supplies into Arlow's strange box, Angelica gave him only the plainest, simplest beads. Arlow assured her they would suffice. For now.

By this time, a number of the other sea lions had gathered around where the loom was set up on the smooth rocky floor of the giant cave. Arlow's chest swelled imaging how pleased Angelica would be with her gift and how jealous all the other sea lions who made jewelry would be.

To begin the demonstration, Arlow cranked a lever at the side of the loom to wind it up, then he took Angelica's slender fingers in his paws and played a pattern on the loom's keys. Their webbed fingers pressed down on the keys together, and the belly of the machine ka-thunked and ker-chunked. Beads slipped onto the thread, visible through an open panel in the box, and the growing bracelet—or necklace, whatever Angelica wanted it to be—came out of the side and dangled down like a tail.

Arlow kept playing the loom until the string of beads hung all the way to the ground. It fell in a coil when he pressed the final key, and Arlow picked it up ceremoniously to present to his lady.

The crowd of sea lions who had watched the performance applauded and congratulated Arlow on the cleverness of his machine. They had all heard about his inventions, but none of them had seen any beyond the watercycle until now. When the crowd lost interest and wandered away, Arlow turned to Angelica and asked, "What do you think?"

"Oh, Arlow," she said, "It's terribly funny."

"Funny?" he repeated in amazement. Her choice of words had him completely flummoxed. Surely she was trying to express the idea *wonderful, amazing, useful,* or *life-changing. Funny* was a strange way to put it.

"I'm sure you were trying to be helpful," she said, "by making this for me... But, I can't possibly use it. Not for the jewelry I actually sell." She went on to explain to Arlow about how much she enjoyed making jewelry by paw and that much of the value in her crafts came from the time and loving care she put into them. It all sounded very backward and superstitious to Arlow, and he, quite honestly, had trouble listening.

Arlow was sure Angelica would realize the value of his gift with time. Besides, he was already busy planning the next machine he meant to make for her: a basket-weaving loom.

*　*　*

As the weeks passed, Angelica showed no further inclination towards using her jewelry loom. It became a toy for the young ones in the village. They could make bracelets and necklaces to play with—jewelry that was discarded when the young ones were done with it; jewelry that no one cried over if it were broken. Arlow was sure that the basket-weaver would be different, except he could never get the baskets to come out quite right.

While the loom-made bracelets and necklaces were indistinguishable from hand-strung versions—to Arlow's eyes, at least—the machine-made baskets were obviously different. The reeds never bent quite right. There were sharp corners where Angelica's baskets were always smooth and round. The tightness of the braids varied, growing loose and sloppy at the ends of reeds. Sure, Arlow could have tinkered with his machine, improving it until the baskets came out right. But the more work he put into it, the more despondent he became. What was the point? The jewelry loom worked perfectly, and Angelica didn't use that.

Instead, Arlow began developing a new passion: He read treatises from the dolphin oligarchy that explored the secrets of the fishes and the nature of the breathable aether. He studied tomes of internal anatomy focusing on the lungs; and he convinced himself he could build an apparatus that would allow him to breathe underwater.

Dolphin physics was strange to Arlow, but if the translations of their science was correct, he needed only to frission the water—summoning breathable aether out of it like an alchemist summons gold from lead. Then, he could stay underwater indefinitely and explore those deep crevasses in the ocean floor.

Angelica encouraged Arlow's new passion, in part because it kept him from building more *useful* machines for her. Florentine was also excited, and she elected herself to become Arlow's lab assistant. With the extra time she had available now that most of her daily chores were automated, Florentine made it her job to gather the supplies Arlow needed for his experiments. She also helped with record keeping—writing down neat columns of the data Arlow collected in a large empty book, much like the register she used for the hotel.

This freed Arlow's paws for the delicate alchemical work necessary of frissioning the aether: pouring fluids from one beaker to another, carefully titrating them, and the like. Arlow enjoyed listening to Florentine's tiny gasps of amazement as she watched him work. He felt that Angelica would better appreciate the importance of his work if she could only see it the way that Florentine did.

For a while, Arlow thought of moving his lab and quarters out to the sea lion cove, but he knew the logistics weren't right. It would be much harder to bring in supplies there. He'd have to cycle in jugs of oil for his work lamps himself, regularly. The sea lions simply lit their nights with the unsteady, flickering glow of bonfires.

Besides, the way that they let high tide rise into their canvas-walled homes was quite comfortable and charming when one was relaxing, but it would destroy any work he tried to do on paper. The more Arlow thought about the primitive state of their lives, the more he wondered if it was really the right environment for his beloved Angelica.

* * *

THE NIGHT when Arlow finished building his breathing apparatus, he proudly displayed the final product to Florentine and her current guests at the inn. It was after dinner, and Florentine was entertaining a troupe of river otters who were her guests with a few hands of gin rummy in the small dining area.

"It's done!" Arlow exclaimed, skipping down the stairs. "Get me a big bucket of water, and I can show you!"

The visiting river otters didn't know about Arlow's

local fame as an inventor, but they were always up for a new game. So, the hands of cards were set aside, and a big bucket, sloshing with water, was fetched from the kitchen and set in the middle of the table. Arlow climbed up on the table beside it.

Arlow strapped on his breathing apparatus—a rubbery, membranous mask that covered the bottom portion of his face. The mask was attached to two bulbous, fist-sized metal canisters that rested at either side of his neck. Arlow tightened the leather strap that held the mask against his face, and then he shoved his head into the bucket.

For a moment, Arlow was afraid to breathe. He knew the apparatus should work, but there was a difference between trusting his calculations and trusting his calculations to protect him from a lungful of water. Still, he could picture Florentine and all her guests staring at him —head already stuck in the bucket. It was too late, for his pride, to back out now.

Arlow drew a deep breath of cool, clear air. Then he pulled his head out of the bucket, hopping and dancing, whooping at his success. At first the other otters misunderstood his actions and thought he was choking on a deep breath of water.

"No, no!" Arlow cried. "It worked! I was able to breathe!"

"But you were only under there for a few seconds," one of the otters objected. "How do we know you aren't making it up?"

"Yeah!" another one said, climbing up on the table beside Arlow. "Stay under there for an hour, and I'll believe it!" The otter guffawed and several of the others joined in. A couple of them were already poking at the apparatus, hanging loosely on the leather strap around Arlow's neck.

Florentine merely stood at the back of the room, her paws raised to cover her face. Arlow was the closest thing she'd known to a son, and she was overcome with amazement and pride in him.

"Here, you can try it," Arlow said, undoing the buckle behind his head and holding the contraption out to the other otter standing on the table.

The other otter pulled the contraption over his head, tightened the straps, and ducked his own head in the bucket. When he emerged with his head dripping to exclaim, "He's right! It works!" the whole group burst into a round of applause. Each otter insisted on a turn at this new game of ducking their heads in the bucket to breathe.

Florentine came forward and hugged Arlow as he stepped down from the table. "You are brilliant," she whispered. "This invention will mean so much to our relationship with the dolphin city out at sea."

Arlow's whiskers prickled with pride, and, despite the fact that there was no music, he whisked Florentine into a clumsy cross between a waltz and a jig. She'd become as much a surrogate mother to him as he'd become a surrogate son to her.

All the other otters—heads dripping from the new

game—joined in the dance, whirling about the room to the padding rhythm of their own webbed feet slapping the wooden floor. It was an almost perfect evening. Only one thing was absent—Angelica.

* * *

AT FLORENTINE'S INSISTENCE, Arlow taught her how to make the completed breathing masks. For himself, he only wanted two. Florentine, however, intended to sell the masks to the local navy yard. She had already discussed their development with one of the ranking officers, and he was eager to begin training an undersea battalion and open diplomatic negotiations for setting up a standing trade agreement with the dolphin oligarchy.

None of that mattered to Arlow, though he admired Florentine's gumption in handling such mundane matters as the distribution of his inventions. She was an invaluable partner.

It was Angelica, however, whom Arlow wanted to share his success with. It was her eyes that he wanted to see shine at him with admiration. And, so, he brought the first two breathing masks with him to the sea lion caves the next day.

"I thought we could swim downward again today," Arlow told Angelica when he found her at the rocky ledge of the cave.

She had a basket in her lap and was working the reeds with her slender flippered hands. She sat with her tail over the edge. The end of her fin trailed into the lapping ocean water. "Why?" she asked, wrinkling her delicate nose.

"I've made a..." Arlow pulled the two masks out, hanging on their leather straps, "I mean, invented..." He found his heart beating too strongly and his throat too thick to speak. The masks simply swayed on their straps in front of him, and he watched Angelica eye them carefully. She tilted her head and looked up at him.

"What does this one let you do quickly?" she asked wryly.

"N-nothing," Arlow stammered. "I mean, they let you stay underwater. Breathing. As long as you want."

Angelica smiled then, and her eyes sparkled. "You want to explore the crevasses," she said.

Arlow nodded, feeling the tightness in his chest release as his mermaid smiled at him. She set the basket she was working on aside, and she slipped off the ledge, sliding smoothly into the water. "All right, then," she said. "Let's explore."

Arlow slipped the mask over Angelica's face, and he reached around her neck to fasten the buckle and gently tighten the straps. Then, he fixed his own mask over the bottom of his face, and he was sure that Angelica laughed at him behind her mask. He could tell by the merriment in her eyes. Seeing her though, he had to admit that he must look silly. If a beautiful mermaid like her could look goofy wearing his breathing mask, he must look absolutely clown-like.

The two of them swam together, side-by-side with her slender flipper clasped in his webbed paw, along the ocean floor. They followed the sandy floor downward, letting the twisting sunlight from the light blue surface above fall away from them as they swam deeper and deeper.

They couldn't talk, but Angelica squeezed his paw when they came to the beginning of the rocky crevasses. Arlow turned to look at her, and the excitement in her eyes told him everything he needed to know. They explored the twilight kelp forests of the rocky crevasses together, stopping each other to point out starfish, intricately patterned coral, and gelatinously tentacled sea anemones.

At the nadir of their journey, Angelica stopped Arlow. She pulled him in close, and then she slipped the mask from her face. For a moment, he panicked—being so far beneath the sea—but, then he remembered how easy it would be to pull the mask back up. So, he let his body relax against hers as she pulled his breathing mask down as well. They kissed at the bottom of the kelp forest, slowly twirling in the dim blue night of the ocean floor. Arlow felt her fin pressed against his legs, and he wrapped his arms around her back.

He was breathless when he pulled the mask over his mouth again. Angelica had already begun swimming back. He followed her, entranced by her magic, all the way up to the surface. Watching her swim, he came up with an idea.

The breathing masks let them explore deep under the ocean together; with the right invention, he could make it possible for them to explore the land together. He wanted Angelica always by his side, and that meant she would need to walk on land.

Arlow would build his mermaid legs.

* * *

The legs needed to be light-weight but strong. They needed to provide support and impetus while still responding to the intentions of whoever wore them. It was a tricky project, and Arlow spent longer in the design phase than was usual. For weeks, he scribbled sketches and tested materials without truly beginning construction.

Arlow kept his work secret from both Angelica and Florentine. He wanted to surprise his beloved, and he didn't want his business partner cheapening the purity of his gift by filling his head with ideas of how to monetize it. No, this was just for Angelica. If she liked it, then she could come tell Florentine herself whether the legs were allowed to become a mass-produced commodity. If she didn't like the gift... Well, that didn't bear thinking about.

Of course, Angelica would be thrilled to come live with Arlow in Florentine's inn. She talked of how she and Arlow should spend more time together constantly. Better yet, the two of them could pack up and travel the world together. Arlow had heard a lot of tales lately about the sunny climes, south down the coast.

Arlow did wish that Angelica would show a little more

interest in his secret work. He wanted to tease her about having to wait until the project was done. He wanted her pleading eyes to overcome him, and he would confess his plans to her.

But only Florentine pleaded with Arlow to tell her about his work. So, the project remained a secret, built entirely behind the closed door of his upstairs laboratory in Florentine's inn. All summer, he slaved in that stuffy room.

The long summer days stretched their waning light late into the evening. Nonetheless, he burned through many jugs of oil, supplementing the natural light with hours of extra work by lamplight.

He cut the framework for the legs from a newly discovered, ultra-light metal called aluminum, and he welded the pieces together into hollow braces. Leather straps held the braces against the sides of his body—for he had only himself to test the legs on. At each hip there was a lever that he could work with his paw. The levers cranked pulleys that ran down the inside of the hollow braces; gears inside the knees amplified any pressure on the levers.

Thus, a light touch at the hip could trigger one of the legs to step. Gyroscopes in the feet kept the entire contraption balanced. With a little practice, Arlow was able to walk about his laboratory quite easily, entirely under the power of his mechanical legs. His own legs dangled unnecessarily, dragging on the wooden floor.

Arlow couldn't wait to see Angelica wearing the

gleaming metal legs. He decorated their smooth silver surfaces with etchings of swirls, hoping to make them pretty enough for her. They would be yet another piece of jewelry for her to wear.

Arlow planned to sneak the legs out of the inn under the cover of breaking dawn once they were finished. He planned to leave for the sea lion caves before Florentine or any of her guests arose. Angelica would be the first to see them.

But in the pale light of early morning, Arlow's resolve faltered. He had put so much of himself into this gift. He needed reassurance. And, so, Florentine found Arlow and his mechanical legs, sitting at the dining table waiting for her, when she came down to start the automated kitchen machinery cooking breakfast.

"What is this!" she cried, clapping her hands and bobbing her head in excitement. "Have you finished your secret project? What is it? What does it do?" Her questions ran together, leaving Arlow little space to answer her until she fell into *oohing* and *ahhing* over the gleaming invention. Her claws traced the patterns of the etchings, and she poked at the joints, trying to ken their functions.

"They're legs," Arlow said simply, certainty and pride returning to puff up his chest.

"I thought they looked like legs!" Florentine exclaimed. "What are they for?"

"I built them for Angelica."

Florentine straightened, her long sinuous spine growing stiff.

"I mean to ask her to marry me," Arlow said, voicing the thought for the first time. "With these legs, she can come live here in the inn with us. Perhaps Angelica and I will travel down the coast for our honeymoon."

Arlow felt more sure of his plans than ever, but Florentine looked worried. That troubled him.

"What's wrong?" he asked. "You don't mind if Angelica lives here, do you?"

"Oh, dear no," Florentine said, looking away from Arlow. "I wouldn't mind at all. But..." Her paws pulled nervously at the fabric of her dress. "You've put a lot of thought into this plan, yes?"

"Oh my, yes!" Arlow exclaimed. "I've been planning it all summer."

"And Angelica likes the idea?" Florentine pressed, looking hopeful. "She wants to come live here?"

"Well..." Arlow said. "The legs are a surprise. She doesn't know yet that she'll be able to walk on land with me. Travel the world. Live here, together."

Florentine nodded. It was a somber nod for a jolly sea otter like her. No matter how Arlow pressed her after that, she would say nothing other than that he needed to go talk to Angelica.

Florentine hoped fervently that Arlow knew his beloved better than she feared he did. Perhaps any sea lion lady who could fall in love with a skinny, quirky river otter inventor like Arlow would in fact be thrilled with the mechanical legs he'd built her. Perhaps Florentine's inn would become home to the first sea lion cyborg as well as an increasingly renowned inventor.

If not... Florentine only hoped that Arlow's heart would not be so broken that he'd move on from this town, taking his laboratory and inventions away from her inn and taking his strange, eccentric energy out of her life.

* * *

ARLOW RODE his watercycle downriver from Florentine's inn, out the bay, and down the coast. He had folded the mechanical legs up in his backpack, and their knees dug into his spine no matter how he shifted his body. The morning air was cold, and the slant of the sun hurt his eyes. But the real pain was impatience.

He couldn't wait to see his mermaid put on the shining mechanical legs he'd built for her. Angelica's elegant, tapered body would float above the ground with the magic of invention holding her up. The delicate curve of her flipper tail—usually hidden under the distorting curtain of the sea—would trail over the ground, revealed by the silken hem of her dress at mid-thigh. She would be glorious.

She was already glorious, but his gift would make her *more*.

It was a relief when he arrived at the rocky ledge at the border between sea and land that was the sea lions' home and comprised the bulk of their world. A few sea lions were already awake and cooking breakfast kippers over small fires, but most of the village was still asleep. Angelica, however, was not among the dreamers. She was threading jewelry on her loom, and Arlow's heart jumped to see her. It was the first time he could recall ever seeing her use it, and he knew that was a good omen.

Arlow dropped his watercycle on a rock that was high enough to be dry on top, and he slipped the backpack off his shoulders. Pulling it by the straps, he rock-hopped over to where Angelica was working. As he got closer though, he could see something was wrong.

"What happened to the loom?" he asked. The loom's keys had been removed and were piled in a basket beside it. "I can help you fix it."

Angelica looked up at Arlow and smiled sadly. "Oh Arlow," she said. "I'm sorry, but I don't want it fixed. Actually, it isn't broken. I'm just taking the keys out."

"W-why?" Arlow stammered. "I thought the children liked it." He didn't add, *even though you clearly don't*.

"They do," she said. "That's the problem. Some of the older ones are refusing to learn how to thread beads the right way. By paw. So, I'm going to hide the keys until they start attending to their lessons better."

Arlow was disappointed that Angelica still didn't like the loom, but he tried to focus on the fact that she wasn't destroying it *permanently*. Just disabling it for a while. It was still a valuable toy for the children, even if she didn't use it the way he'd envisioned.

"What's in your pack?" Angelica asked, pushing the basket and loom further back on the rock. She scootched her body closer to where Arlow stood, and he sat down beside her. He plunked the heavy pack down, feeling very mixed emotions about opening it. The omen of the loom did not speak well of his chances.

A burst of prickly pride swelled through his chest, and Arlow knew that the mechanical legs were different. The loom had been meant to replace an activity in Angelica's life—an activity that she clearly enjoyed. The mechanical legs were not meant to replace anything, merely to supplement.

"Angelica," he said slowly, feeling the shape of her name and savoring the way that it meant *her*. "I've brought you another invention."

The air was tense and silent between them, although wavelets splashed against the rock at their dangling tail and feet.

"This one is to make you faster. *When you walk on land.*" He opened the backpack and pulled the shining legs out. He stood them on the rock between them, and his paws grasped the ankles tightly, all his nervousness squeezing into that one gesture. "I want you to marry me, and we can live in Florentine's inn together. We can travel the world. We can go anywhere." Arlow's eyes drank in every nuance of Angelica's face—the way her dark eyes shifted; how her whiskers pulled closer to her muzzle; and the gentle tilt of her chin, drawing closer to her body.

"Will you marry me?" he asked. "Will you walk beside me for all your days?"

The air was filled with sounds. Arlow could hear other

sea lions waking up and beginning their days. Gulls cawed in the distance, and waves continued to crash. But Angelica was silent, and that was unbearable.

"Why do you ask me both questions together?" she said, her voice soft enough that it was almost lost in the sound of the waves.

"What do you mean?" Arlow asked.

Angelica reached out and touched the mechanical legs with her slender flipper. She traced the swirling etched patterns much as Florentine had, but the gesture felt completely different. It was filled with sadness. Arlow didn't understand.

"These would let me walk," Angelica said. It wasn't a question, but Arlow nodded anyway. "I've never wanted to walk." Her voice was distant, and Arlow wanted more than anything to pull her back close to him.

"Will you try them on?" Arlow asked, hoping that when she took her first steps that the feeling would set her free. Her heart would fly to him.

Instead, she dashed his hopes against the rocks like the slapping waves: "No," she said.

Angelica shook her head fiercely. Arlow could see tears in her eyes. Then she rolled to her side, pushing herself off the rock they sat on. For the first time she felt awkward and lurching, maneuvering herself off of the land by the power of her arms. By giving her legs, Arlow had made her *less*.

Angelica swam away from the sea lion caves, straight out to sea. Arlow hesitated a moment, nursing the pain in his heart and the wound to his pride. The pain in his heart was stronger though, and he had to chase his mermaid. He followed her along the surface, unable to catch her or even keep up. Yet, he chased her all the way out to where she dove down toward the rocky crevasses and kelp forests that they'd explored together with his breathing masks.

Arlow dove down too, but Angelica's lithe form had already faded into a mermaid shaped shadow, rapidly disappearing into the eternally twilit water. He lost her there. Although, he swam through the ocean for hours, diving until his lungs ached, peering through squinted eyes and imagining her shadow everywhere—in the waving kelp fronds, in the shapes of the rocks, and in the inscrutable, endless blue.

He finally gave up and returned to the sea lion caves. She had to return to her home sometime, so he would wait in her tent for her. When he drew the burlap doorhanging back though, he found Angelica already inside, leaning against a rush-woven ottoman with her flipper tail stretched out before her. She held a necklace in her hands.

Arlow hardly knew what he was saying, but he burbled apologies one after another. He had to win her love back. It was what made his life complete, grounding him in reality. Without his time with her, he would be lost entirely in the whimsical, unreal climes of invention.

"Stop, stop apologizing!" she said, cutting him off without even looking up. "I won't walk beside you." Her words were sad and bitter, as if she was balling up all the hurt he'd caused her and trying to throw it away all at once. "But the other question..."

She lifted the necklace up, and somehow Arlow knew that she meant to give it to him. He knelt down and lowered his head; she placed the beaded necklace over his head, letting the heavy pendant fall on his chest.

Arlow touched the detailed beadwork. Blue and purple bits of shell alternated with each other, and a mother of pearl pendant hung in the center. He'd watched her work on this piece. It had taken many days of concentrated work, and all those hours of his mermaid's time were now strung around his neck, surrounding him with her and serving as a reminder of those happy hours together. He finally understood why Angelica insisted on making the necklaces and bracelets herself.

"The other question is the only one I really want answered," Arlow said. He touched her face, and traced the long curve of her neck with a gentle claw. She looked up at him, but then she glanced away shyly, reminding him of the looks she'd given him the first day they'd met.

"If you will come live with me here in these caves," Angelica said, "share my home with me... then, I will marry you."

"My work-" Arlow began to say, but he knew that was wrong from Angelica's frown.

"Keep your laboratory in Florentine's inn," she said. "But sleep in the caves, and wake to the sound of waves echoing off their walls."

And the feel of his mermaid sleeping in his arms.

Arlow considered this new proposal. He had imagined grand adventures, traveling along the coast and exploring the world with Angelica. The life she suggested was much smaller. It was the life he was already living. Only better.

Arlow thought about the life he'd imagined. Did he really care about adventures? He wasn't sure he did. He cared about inventing, and he cared about Angelica. He was happy with his life here.

"You'll need a bigger tent," he said, looking around the small chambers, "if we're both to live in it."

Angelica's eyes shone, and she cried out in happiness. Arlow pulled her into his arms, feeling her body press against him. He lifted her up and spun around. In his arms, she floated above the ground.

When he put her back down, lying down on the floor of her tent beside her, Angelica rushed to tell him that sea lions had a tradition of building larger tents for newly married couples. It was part of the wedding preparations and had to be done a very specific way. She didn't want Arlow getting any ideas about mechanized tent-building monsters with long pulleys and metallic spider-like legs.

She needn't have worried. He was already imagining a way to increase the speed of his watercycle, so he'd have a faster commute between the sea lion caves and Florentine's inn. And, although he didn't know it yet, Florentine was writing out a list of inventions that she wanted them to work on together. It would keep him busy for a long time.

6
THE CANOE RACE
WRITTEN WITH DANIEL LOWD

THE LAST CAMPER HAD LEFT. The cabins had been swept clean of the dirt from the tramping feet of a hundred teenagers. The dining hall had been swept and scrubbed free from the grease of a summer's worth of meals. The canoes had been pulled in from the lake and stowed in the boat house for winter. The fire pit had been emptied of ash. The gate on the road leading to Camp Riverwind had been locked.

It was finally time.

It started with a lone squirrel. Then another. Then a third, a fourth, and ten more leaped from the trees and skittered across the roofs of the cabins and dining hall. Finding no signs of humans, they moved to the ground, peered through the windows, and searched every nook and cranny before converging at the fire pit.

"All clear!" the squirrel band chittered in unison. The signal carried throughout the valley to the ears of raccoons, beavers, birds, bobcats, a moose, and a black bear.

The raccoons did not have to be told twice. They knew from years of experience that campers sometimes leave bits of food or, even better, shiny things to covet and fondle. The best treasures go to the quickest and cleverest raccoons. This year, the trash cans had been emptied, but not perfectly. The first raccoon found a few broken pieces of candy. The next found their shimmering wrappers. A third found craft beads in the dust beneath the picnic tables—one bead to slip on each claw, making her the most fashionable raccoon of the season. Having lost the race to the prime outdoor locations, the last two raccoons stationed themselves in front of the dining hall and waited for the beavers.

The two beavers waddled out of the lake and got to work. The trick to the dining hall was to gnaw a small hole in the corner of one door, just large enough for a squirrel to squeeze through in order to open the door from the inside. Once in, a careful search of the kitchen revealed a large collection of keys. After the two raccoons in the dining hall finished arguing over who saw the colander first, they used their nimble hands to help unlock the rest of the camp.

The scrub jays watched as the growing throng of critters raided the camp and declared victory over the previous inhabitants. But they were too busy making snide remarks to join in the celebration, cawing that they had been flying around camp all summer, and it was really no big deal. Besides, why celebrate the end of a camping season that had brought them so many seeds and other delectable scraps to enjoy? They did this every year.

When the others converged on the fireless fire pit and started singing songs, the birds decided it wouldn't hurt to watch the fools for a few minutes, other entertainment being scarce. And by the time the critters around the fire pit started singing, "Oh My Darling, Avian," even the grumpiest of jays couldn't resist joining in. Even the most superior bird must have some respect for the classics.

Everyone gave the two bobcats their space when they entered. No matter how playful and sweet a bobcat seems, no squirrel will ever trust a creature with claws that sharp and an appetite that carnivorous. The bobcats took their space towards one end of the rough semi-circle of animals, singing for some songs, and merely tapping their claws during the others.

The moose and bear were so late that they almost missed the entire opening jamboree. The larger creatures had learned, for their survival, to be somewhat more cautious around humans. Being big means being unable to scurry under a bush or up a tree at the sound of trouble. And humans could cause a lot of trouble. So they waited until dusk before making their way through the woods to the back of the gathering.

Animal noises are well-known to humans, but, apart from the ostentatious warblings of songbirds, few of their songs have ever reached human ears. The magnificent bellow of a bull moose is nothing compared to his sweet, rhythmic baritone when he rumbles, "Old Moose River." And, unlike chipmunk song, four-part squirrel harmony is always smooth and never squeaky. Raccoons are masterful crooners, but they have trouble agreeing with each other long enough to sing unison. The growly voices of bears and bobcats don't suit every song. But for a song like "On Top of Old Smokey," the punctuated roars are essential. Beavertail percussion completes the ensemble. The forest had never known sweeter songs.

Darkness came, the singers tired, and one by one they adjourned to the cabins for sleep. The raccoons, squirrels, and beavers shared one cabin, sleepy piles of fur too tired to fuss or fight. The bear had her own cabin, due to her bulk. The bobcats had a separate cabin as well, due to their claws and tempers. The moose and jays were most comfortable outside. All slept soundly, dreaming of the adventures this week had in store.

* * *

THE CAMPERS ROSE bright and early to descend upon the dining hall. Two raccoons did most of the cooking, with some help from an assistant spice-squirrel. From the mix they found in the pantry, they cooked seedy pancakes for the birds and squirrels; bark-mulch pancakes for the moose and beavers; and fresh fish pancakes for the raccoons, bobcats, and bear. All had berries on top, but the bobcats insisted on smearing theirs around to make the pancakes look less like bread and more like meat.

After breakfast, each animal picked an activity of his or her fancy. The birds were suckers for macrame, weaving long strands of colorful fibers into sturdy ropes and bracelets. The squirrels joined them at the craft tables, but preferred to thread beads to make tiny necklaces.

Raccoons tried their hands at archery, as they did every year. In a rare feat of cooperation, two of them held the bow, two pulled the string, and one notched the arrow and aimed. The first five times, the bow knocked them down and tangled them up, but the sixth time: <u>success!</u> The arrow sailed through the air and almost hit the hay bale target. This was an all-time camp record. The raccoons chattered with impish glee, eager to boast of their victory to the other animals. But they almost lost themselves to squabbling when none could agree which one of them was most responsible for the perfect shot.

Meanwhile, the beavers took a tour of the camp, analyzing the architecture from every angle. The cabins were built simply, using techniques the beavers had mastered long ago. The dining hall, on the other hand, was a never-ending source of inspiration: vaulted ceilings with exposed rafters, large windows with wooden shutters, a stone hearth in the center, and beautiful wood trim in every corner. The moose meandered along behind them, nodding his head from time to time. He understood very little of their shop talk, but enjoyed the company and pretended to follow along.

Suddenly, a feline scream rang out from the nearby hills. The bear and a bevy of birds hurried to help. When they arrived at the source of the sounds, they found two bobcats high in the treetops, fluffed up to twice their normal sizes. Apparently, they had taken the zip-line and found it more thrilling than anticipated. The scrub jays danced along the innocuous cable, cawing and cackling at the predators' misfortune. Eventually, the cats climbed down and spent the rest of the afternoon sulking over their hurt pride. The bear waited until they had left to take her turn.

*　*　*

THE NEXT DAY brought more of the same. The raccoons tried to convince the moose they could shoot an arrow between his antlers. The bobcats played with macrame string while trying to look dignified. And the squirrels and bear played hide-and-seek.

There aren't many places for a bear to hide. Trees provide little cover when the seeker is a squirrel. Buildings with large windows provide no cover at all. But the boat house was large, dark, and filled with canoes. It was worth a shot.

A minute passed and the bear had not been discovered. Then five minutes. Then ten. Twice, she heard the scratching of little paws racing by. Once, she was sure she heard the "it" squirrel open the door and peer inside, but he gave up before checking all the corners. It wasn't until half an hour had passed that the bear was finally discovered.

All the squirrels were impressed at her ingenuity. They hadn't believed a bear would fit between all of the canoes. They counted ten—no, twelve—canoes in total.

And then one squirrel got an idea. It's hard to say which one said it first. Ideas spread among squirrels faster than gossip among scrub jays. In an instant, the boat house was filled with the chittering of fifteen squirrels, all saying one thing: "Canoe race."

The animals had seen canoes on the lake every year, but never thought to float in them. The animals who liked to swim saw boats as unnecessary, and the animals who did not preferred to stay closer to the shore. But, the squirrels argued, practicality was hardly the point of camp. Archery and crafts were equally ridiculous, yet plenty of fun.

After the squirrels made their case at the evening fire pit circle, a brief but noisy discussion ensued. Who would be the judge? How would they propel the canoes, lacking human arms to paddle? In the end, they agreed that participants would be allowed to use whatever strategies they could devise, and the bear and moose would serve as judges. The rest of the animals formed teams by their species. Only the bobcats declined to participate.

The race would take place the following afternoon.

* * *

BREAKFAST the next morning was brief. Each team was eager to start preparing for the competition. The squirrels were sure they would win, since they came up with the idea in the first place. Squirrel logic. The raccoons were confident in their wealth of shiny objects, which could surely buy victory. The scrub jays claimed not to care about the contest at all. Birds shouldn't have to prove their obvious superiority to the flightless folks. But since the other animals needed a reminder, they would oblige. The beavers refrained from boasting almost entirely. They considered it unprofessional, and this contest was clearly a serious endeavor. Boats were, of course, merely a specialized kind of architecture.

By early afternoon, the entire camp had gathered at the waterfront. Four canoes were resting halfway in the water with their respective teams around them, having been dragged there earlier by the moose and the bear. The moose reviewed the rules. The first team to move their canoe to the center of the lake, as marked by an old buoy, and then return it to shore would be the winners. The bear let out a starting roar, and the race was on.

The first team to make progress was the squirrels. Half of the squirrels dragged a strange contraption of sticks and cloth into the canoe, while the rest pushed the canoe further into the water and climbed aboard. Once afloat, the contraption unfurled to reveal a bed sheet sail hanging from a tree branch mast. Bead necklaces secured the mast to a seat in the middle of the canoe. Crude though it was, the sail caught enough of the afternoon breeze to propel the squirrel team to an early lead. The squirrels cheered and congratulated themselves repeatedly on their cooperation and ingenuity.

The jays were prepared as well. They used long ropes of macrame to harness themselves to their canoe so they could pull it like a team of flying horses. At least, that was the plan. In practice, the canoe was heavy, and the birds were small. So, upon reaching the end of the rope, each bird met with a sudden jolt from the mass of the canoe and plummeted downward. Catching themselves mid-fall, they rose up again, gave the canoe a second tug, and the process repeated itself. Bit by bit, the canoe inched forward as the birds performed their strange, lurching dance.

The raccoons had brought no equipment, only currency: fourteen foil candy wrappers, thirty-six glass beads, and eight smooth, round stones that fit in a raccoon's paw just so. Since bribing the judges would be unsportsmanlike, the raccoons decided to hire the bobcats to push them. Half of the treasure would be paid in advance, and the rest would be awarded after the raccoons took first place. The bobcats, however, had no interest in raccoon trinkets and even less interest in approaching the water. Swimming was for fish, and fish were for eating. Not for emulating. The bobcats motioned to the dead fish they had brought for snacks. While the raccoons furiously defended the value of their goods and the worthiness of boat-pushing as a feline career option, their canoe sat motionless in the sand.

The beaver canoe was also motionless, and the two

beavers were nowhere in sight. After some time, they reappeared dragging a second canoe from the boat house. The bear and moose looked at each other, but nothing in the rules prohibited multiple canoes. After placing the second canoe next to the first, the beavers disappeared into the woods. When they returned, they brought a carefully measured log, which they positioned between the two canoes. The next step was to fetch discarded planks of wood from the firewood pile, which slowly came together to form a platform on top of the log and canoes. The traditional cement for beaver construction was mud and rocks, but this project called for something stronger and lighter: fitted wooden joints. By gnawing grooves in the boards, the beavers created a rough approximation of the techniques they had seen in the dining hall ceiling.

Not far from the beaver construction zone, tensions between the five raccoons and two bobcats had gotten out of control. The raccoons had utterly failed to persuade the bobcats to help them. Since shiny objects and clever rhetoric had both failed, the raccoons resorted to theft and violence. Simultaneously. They grabbed the bobcats' fish and began to swing them wildly, slapping the confused bobcats repeatedly. The bobcats were stunned. This was their first time being fish-slapped by a frustrated gang of raccoons. Once they overcame their amazement, they slashed the fish to pieces and chased the raccoons all around the camp. The canoe remained motionless.

The harnessed team of birds continued to make slow

but steady progress. To coordinate the rhythm of their tug-and-fall strategy, they began a squawking chant. To cope with the extremely strenuous task of hauling a large canoe through water, they worked out a rotation scheme for birds to sit on the boat and rest before returning to duty.

The squirrel racing team was the first to reach the buoy in the center of the lake, well ahead of the birds. For the return trip, however, the wind was against them, and the squirrels had no experience sailing into the wind. They tried facing the other direction and thinking really hard about the shore, but to no avail. Running around the canoe also had little effect. In an increasingly frantic attempt to turn around, they began to spin and swing the mast wildly. Surely some angle would make their boat go the other way!

Instead, the wild swinging made the canoe rock until it fell over, tossing the fifteen miniature sailors overboard. Squirrels are known neither for swimming nor for staying calm in an emergency. Each thrashed around desperately and ineffectually.

The birds didn't notice—they were lost in their chanting. The beavers, of course, were lost in their woodworking. And the bobcats and raccoons were busy chasing and being chased, respectively.

The moose saw the scene unfold and knew what had to be done. He waded into the water, deeper and deeper, until his hooves no longer felt the gravelly lakebed. Then his powerful legs began to kick in long, strong, cyclic strokes to propel him through the water. He was unintentionally majestic.

The drowning squirrels had just enough sense to climb on the shoulders and antlers of their savior when he arrived. It was a crowded ride back to the beach, but none of the squirrels complained. The black bear met them with sheets, curtains, and other stolen scraps of cloth that could serve as towels.

In the end, the birds were the first and only team to finish the race.

The awards ceremony was held on the floating platform that the beavers had built, where all of the animals fit comfortably, except for the moose who stood nearby. The bear awarded colorful ribbons to the scrub jays for placing first in the contest. Their victory caws were loud and long. When the caws died down, the squirrels stepped forward to present a special award of valor to the moose. The trophy was a wreath of tender branches taken from high in the trees and woven into a circlet. Finally, the raccoons presented themselves with a special award for Most Masterful Survival of an Encounter with Angry Bobcats. Their self-given prize was the very baubles they had originally offered to the bobcats as payment. The bobcats glared but said nothing. The beavers considered the sound construction and successful launch of their platform ship to be reward enough.

When the ceremonies were over, the squirrels began to dance. Bushy tails waved and twirled as the squirrels jumped and spun. Several of them joined paws in a circle and marched around one way, then the other, then into the middle and back out again. Each step was punctuated by high-pitched chitters of glee.

The raccoons were in a mood to celebrate, too. Two of them began to dance a foxtrot around the platform. Not to be outdone, another two started to tango. The fifth raccoon had no dance partner, but she had other skills. She picked up three smooth stones from the raccoon prize pile and juggled them. The bobcats soon found themselves covetously mesmerized by the movements of the very stones they'd spurned before.

The scrub jays were still tired from their extreme exertion during the race, but not too tired to show off a little. They took to the sky in vee- and star-shaped formations, ascending and then descending into loops and barrel rolls. Without a canoe weighing them down, they felt lighter and freer than ever before.

The beavers just sat back and enjoyed the show, proud of their handiwork that had made this floating party possible.

***

THE MORNING of the final day of camp was spent cleaning up from the previous days of mischief and fun. The beavers disassembled their canoe platform. The bear and moose returned the boats to the boat house. The jays re-hung the curtains in the cabins. The squirrels picked up every piece of litter they could find. The raccoons grabbed brooms and swept the buildings clean of mud, fur, and feathers. Even the bobcats helped out, in their way, by sleeping on each of the beds a final time to make sure they'd all been returned to their original, comfortable conditions. Finally, the raccoons locked the doors, returned the keys, and camp was closed once again.

The animals met at the fire pit one last time, for the beginning of their annual parade. They had seen humans hold parades many times, marching along the forest trails almost every day of the summer. The animals didn't know what made these trails more special than the rest of the forest where the humans didn't walk, but clearly they were important. So, once a year, on the last day of camp, the animals held a parade of their own.

The moose led the way, stately and regal as he ambled among the trees. The squirrels scurried close behind, trying to keep ahead of the others while playing tag at the same time. The raccoons walked awkwardly with their arms full of treasures. The scrub jays flitted about above the throng, laughing at the idea of walking so far. The beavers discussed trail maintenance and erosion prevention methods. The bobcats argued about whether or not rocks became alive when juggled, and what one should do about it. The bear brought up the rear, soaking up the cheerful, lively sounds of her companions' conversation.

When they reached a clearing at the top of the highest hill, they sang a final song: "Kum-bear-ya." Then it was time to part ways, until next year.

7
FOX IN THE HEN HOUSE

THE EGGS NEVER HATCHED. Henrietta and all her coopmates laid eggs every day, and every day the Coopmaster came and took the eggs away. No baby chicks. Henrietta had so much love in her feathered breast and no one to spend it on.

Only nine inches below the slatted floor of the coop, a cold and hungry litter of fox kits waited for their mother to return. One by one, the kits closed their eyes and fell into a patient sleep. Their breathing slowed. Their hearts slowed too. Still, the mother did not return.

But one kit was not patient. His heart beat fast, and his nose twitched at the smells that drifted down to him from between the wooden slats. The musty, dusty, warm-blooded smell of chickens tantalized him, filling his nostrils.

While his littermates waited for a mother that would never return, losing themselves into the sleep that becomes death, the impatient kit followed his nose out from their den and into the chicken coop above. There, he found a new mother.

Neither Henrietta nor any of the other chickens in her coop had seen a fox before. Chickens don't often live long after seeing a fox, and the last massacre of that particular hen house had left no survivors to tell the tale. The Coopmaster had ordered replacements from the local feed store and raised them from eggs. None of them knew the haunted history of their home. Thus, when Henrietta saw a small, pointy, red-furred face peek into the coop, she wasn't frightened. In fact, her first thought was, "Why, what lovely plumage! I do believe it's exactly the same shade of red as my own!"

Henrietta was smitten. She was the only red hen in her coop; all the others sported black, white, or checkered feathers. Clearly, she and this little creature were meant for each other. She would call him Henry.

And so Henry became a chicken. He was invited into Henrietta's nest where she sat on him, keeping him warm with her thick, soft feathers. All the hens doted on him and offered him all the grain a growing chick could want. But Henry wasn't a chick, and he didn't want grain. He wanted eggs.

The eggs weren't serving any better purpose—in fact, none of the chickens knew why they laid them. Day after day, they laid the mysterious, pearlescent objects, and day after day the Coopmaster came to take them away. So, when Henrietta's little red-furred chick began to crack eggs and lick out their viscous, slimy insides, none of the hens begrudged him. Better, they thought, that Henry eat the eggs than that the Coopmaster steal them. That dirty thief!

The chickens treasured Henry and hid him carefully from the Coopmaster. If the Coopmaster stole their eggs, there was no telling what else he might steal, and they couldn't stand to lose their baby.

For his part, Henry reveled in the attention from his coop full of clucking new mothers. He loved the warm pressure of Henrietta's weight perched on top of him, pressing him safely into the nest as he slept. He enjoyed the gentle tugs and tickles as various chickens took turns preening his fur with their beaks. His life was a blur of warmth and touch and safe, comfortable smells. And, of course, the eggs were delicious.

As Henry grew, the chickens began to speculate about him. He looked so different from the rest of them. He hadn't changed shape as he grew, sprouting wings and talons like they'd expected. He'd merely grown larger and sleeker. His smell was sharp and dangerous. Terribly exciting! Why, it made their hearts flutter!

Eventually, one of the youngest hens—Calliope with the loveliest, downiest, white feathers—suggested that Henry might not be a hen. He might be a rooster.

All the hens were atwitter at the idea. A rooster! In their hen house! Oh my! Some of the more romantically minded hens had dreamed of meeting a big, strong rooster some day.

A black-checkered hen named Dorrit, the fattest in the coop, swooned at the very idea. The other hens had to fan her with their wings until she recovered, rousing from her faint only to exclaim, "Oh Henry! You are the handsomest young rooster I could imagine!" Then she turned all shy and hid in her own nest with her head tucked under her wing for the rest of the day.

After that, the chickens began to court their young squire. Some sang songs to him in warbling voices; others followed him around, plying him with eager compliments. As always, Henry loved the attention.

Dorrit plucked flowers from the garden to bring Henry. He was quite flattered, but he had no use for flowers.

Calliope dug up worms for Henry. Those tasted funny and squirmy in his mouth. They weren't rich and yolky like the eggs, but their flesh burst satisfyingly under his teeth. Henry approved and asked Calliope to teach him worm-hunting. As the two of them spent more and more of their afternoons together, hunting worms and gossiping, it became clear to all the hens that Calliope had gained Henry's favor.

At a word from Henrietta, the other hens stopped courting her son. If he'd chosen Calliope, there was no need to confuse the young couple. No, indeed, it was time to give them space to get better acquainted. And time to prepare the wedding!

The big day was set for a week hence. Under Dorrit's direction, the chickens plucked flowers and vines from the garden to decorate the coop appropriately. At Calliope's suggestion, they gathered worms for a special feast. And Henrietta arranged for them to build a new, larger nest for Henry and Calliope to share, discreetly hidden at the back of the coop, behind a screen she wove out of straw.

While the rest of the hens worked industriously on the wedding, Calliope strolled with her handsome husband-to-be around the edges of the farmyard. His presence close beside her made Calliope nervous, and her presence close beside him made Henry's heart pound with anticipation.

Calliope's white-feathered body was plump and tempting; her neck slender and appealing. Henry felt an urge, deep in the pit of his stomach, to nuzzle her neck, caress that plump body with his muzzle. He didn't understand the feelings, but they were strong and exciting.

On the night before the wedding, Henry confessed his confusion to Henrietta. As any good mother should do, Henrietta assured her son that his feelings were completely normal. On the morrow, it would all make sense. "Don't worry," she said. "I know you love Calliope, and you'll make her a good husband. As you are a good son. And a good rooster. Just follow your instincts, and let your feelings for Calliope be your guide."

Henry was reassured. He did love Calliope. She was far and away the cleverest of the chickens in the coop. On their walks, she'd told him many stories, sharing her insights on the world and on the political intrigue between different chickens in the coop that Henry had never noticed before. He could listen to her musical voice cluck away, filling his ears with ideas and stories, forever.

The wedding was a solemn affair. All the chickens arranged themselves in a circle around Calliope and Henry. Each and every one of them had prepared a few words to say. Chickens have a lot to say. And they all got their turns—wishing Henry and Calliope happiness, reminiscing about old times, and making promises to support the two of them in their future together. And, of course, hoping for them to have many children.

Then the newlyweds went inside to enjoy their newfound marital bliss while all the other chickens stayed outside, to give them their privacy.

The new nest was made from the freshest straw and had been lined with fragrant flower petals. It was plenty large. Calliope roosted in the middle, nervously preening her neck feathers, and Henry curled his body around hers.

"My bride," he said, pressing his muzzle against her breast.

"My love," she clucked, tracing the tip of her beak down the curve of his ears. A tingle of excitement shot through him at the touch.

Henry opened his mouth a little and breathed softly against her. Calliope's feathers ruffled under his breath. He touched his teeth to her neck in a touch as soft as hers. He nipped lightly, playfully at her like the kit he used to be, and he felt her heart race under the breast pressed against him.

Calliope, suddenly, held herself very still. She didn't understand the feelings racing inside of her. She expected to feel love for her husband. Instead, she felt only fear.

Henry, however, was unaware of the change in his bride's feelings. His own feelings were running high, and everything in him said to press himself harder against his wife. He tightened the grip of his jaw, feeling his teeth press into her plumage. A hunger inside Henry roared for him to bite harder against her tender, delicate neck in his mouth. Overwhelmed with love for his bride, Henry followed his instincts.

Calliope began to struggle, but then her body shuddered and fell still. A satisfying crack between his teeth and the hot flow of blood into his mouth told Henry that he was doing what was right. Nothing could feel more right than the glorious taste that exploded in his mouth. He felt himself overcome with a blind urge to rampage and ravage, working his jaws until white feathers flew around him.

Henry had never eaten a meal so amazing, so succulent, so filling. Immediately, afterward, Henry fell into a deep, contented sleep.

In that sleep of satiation, Henry dreamed a disturbing dream. He was a tiny kit again, nestled under his mother hen's feet, and he was watching all the hens in the coop fly about in a crazed, frightened flurry. "Where is Calliope? Where is Calliope! Where has she gone?" they all clucked. Every chicken was in a tizzy, and Henry felt guilty. Though, he didn't know why.

The clucking changed, as chickens began to bock, "She's dead! She's gone! Someone has killed her!"

Then Dorrit squawked and flapped her wings, commanding the attention of all the chickens in the coop. They roosted around her, settling down and quieting themselves to hear what Dorrit had to say. She turned to the assembled crowd and announced, "The killer is none other than..."

Henry awoke in a fever. Although he'd lost himself in his passion, Henry knew what he had done. He'd eaten his beloved. His wife. His Calliope. His tender, tasty, delicious Calliope... Henry's mouth watered at the memory of her flesh on his tongue. He felt power surging inside him, as if he'd finally realized who he was. He had woken up into himself for the first time and all his life was like a mad play.

Henry wanted to share his insight with Calliope, but the feelings that welled up in him at the thought of her were complex and shifting. Love. Regret. Hunger. And an insatiable desire to feel her hot blood pumping onto his tongue.

Faster than he could think, Henry's feet carried him out of the chicken coop and into the yard. His eyes shone with a mad light as he looked, blinded with bloodlust, at the chickens who'd raised him. Loving clucks turned to screeches of horror as Henry flew at the hens.

Feathers flew in the air.

Henry tasted blood again and again, until there were no more chickens. Only a mad fox, shaking limp carcasses in his mouth, mere feathered bags of flesh and broken bones. His belly was too full to eat anymore but his tongue still screamed for the taste of hot blood.

When finally the Coopmaster came with a gun, Henry darted into the forest behind the farm. He ran through the underbrush, haphazardly dashing without knowing his way. The speckled light filtered down through the trees, dappling his red coat. And, only now, did his sight begin to clear. Only now did he realize: Calliope, Henrietta, all the chickens... were gone.

Henry found a hollow, rotting log, smelling of earth and wood like the place he was born, the place his littermates had died. He knew what he was now. And what he had never been.

The next few weeks were hard. Henry was used to living in a warm hen house, eating eggs, and listening to the friendly clucking of the hens. He was used to the feel of soft feathers and the gentle preening of careful beaks. He wasn't used to working his paws numb, scratching out hollows in the cold dirt ground; or hunting for his food; or falling asleep to melancholy silence alone.

Henry was like the kit he had been before he found the warmth of the hen house and Henrietta had named him. Except, now he was grown, and he could take care of himself. He could find his way through the forest. He was lean and strong, a deadly predator. He was a fox again.

But he missed his chickens.

8
FRANKENSTEIN'S GRYPHON

Igor the arctic fox lurched across the tundra, limping from the deadened feeling in his left hindpaw. That paw had never fully woken up when Frankie Mouse reanimated him. The electric surge from the lightning bolt hadn't made it that far, but Igor was still grateful to Frankie. Without his kindness, Igor would still be lying in an unmarked grave, forgotten and unmourned. Instead, Igor adventured across the tundra on glorious missions in service to the most magnificent mouse throughout the land.

Frankie Mouse's castle rose above the frozen wasteland like a dream. The hewn-ice masonry of the towering turrets and soaring spires gleamed in the waning winter sunlight, a constant reminder of the fealty Igor owed Frankie.

Two more miles and Igor would reach the motley collection of freshly dug graves that served as a memorial to Dusky Dillon, a snow leopard who had recently emigrated from Asia to northern Russia and set herself up as a murderous gangster queen. Her reign of terror had ended in a blood bath that concluded her own and a dozen other lives.

Frankie Mouse wanted her body. There were no others like it in northern Russia. Her broad back, large paws, and wide muzzle—all put together with a feminine, feline grace—meant she cut the ideal figure for a bodyguard and warrior minion for Frankie. He wanted her body, and he wanted it fresh. He needed it fresh enough to resurrect her.

Igor had questioned whether a murderous villain like Dusky Dillon would truly make the best, most trustworthy body guard, but Igor assured him that everyone— even Dusky Dillon—deserved a second chance. Besides, Frankie had pointed out, Igor had done his share of villainous deeds before his own resurrection.

Igor couldn't remember *before* his resurrection, but he felt bad for questioning Frankie Mouse. Frankie was so wise and patient with him. Igor would make up for doubting him by bringing Dusky Dillon's body back to the lab before sunrise the next morning. That would make Frankie Mouse happy with him.

Under the blanket of dusk, Igor limped into the haphazard graveyard. Flowers in small bouquets, mostly the yellow and white blooms of arctic poppies and snow buttercups, and other tokens such as handmade dolls or tiny flags marked most of the graves. The largest patch of freshly overturned dirt, though, bore no markings—no tokens of love. It had to be the grave of Dusky Dillon.

Igor set to work on the cold dirt with his bare claws, scratching and scraping with his front paws; kicking the loose soil away with his hind paws. Dusk deepened to night, and the hole beneath Igor's paws deepened toward the inanimate feline body buried there. Owls hooted in the distance, and Igor pushed himself to dig faster, harder. He didn't want to be caught grave-robbing. He ignored the numbness in his paws.

Igor's claws sank, finally, into flesh, cold and dead but soft compared to the hard packed dirt. A villain like Dusky Dillon didn't rate a coffin, only dirt and good riddance. Igor excavated gently around the dead limbs to avoid damaging the body. Frankie Mouse would prefer it that way.

The smell of death filled Igor's nostrils. It took all of his willpower to continue digging, and, once he finished, it took all of his strength to drag the dead bulk of Dusky Dillon's body out of her grave. The jumble of cold limbs and dirt-caked fur did not bespeak value to Igor, but his heart swelled knowing that he held in his arms an object that his master dearly desired.

Igor draped the leopard body, much larger than his own fox self, over his back and began limping out of the graveyard. Dusky Dillon's hind paws and tail dragged on the ground behind him.

Igor set his eyes on the glowing torchlight along the turrets of Frankie's castle in the distance. He imagined the grand gala dances and feasts that Frankie must enjoy in the ballrooms. He pictured mice, voles, and hares in regal dress waltzing together, toasting Frankie with spiced wine, laughing and singing inside the ice-hewn halls. Someday, perhaps, Igor would be invited to join them. For now, he let his imagination propel him forward, lightening the weight of Dusky Dillon on his back.

Igor plodded toward Frankie's laboratory, an underground structure, outside the castle walls. One paw in front of the other, he dragged himself onward. When he was nearly there, an owl called from the sky, "*Whoooo goes there?*"

A second owl called, "That's the body of Dusky Dillon! Whoooo do you think you are? Take that corpse back to the graveyard!"

Igor heard the owls' wings flap as they circled above. If they knew he was working for Frankie Mouse, they'd leave him alone, but Frankie Mouse had sworn him to secrecy. No one was to know of his plans for Dusky Dillon.

One of owls shrieked inarticulately, and then Igor felt the owl's body slam into the corpse on his back. He stumbled forward under the added weight and lost his hold on Dusky Dillon's arms. Tangled in dead limbs, Igor slammed into the ground, knocking the air out of his chest. Igor struggled to right himself, but he was flustered by the flurry of snowy owl wings that filled the dark air around him.

"Stop it! Stop it!" one owl cried to the other. "Get a

hold of yourself! We must get this body back to the graveyard."

The other owl tore at the dead leopard's head with sharp, angry talons. "Murderer! You killed my hatchmate!" the owl screamed at the dead body, completely forgetting the fox beneath it.

Igor pulled himself out from the fray, but then he realized the damage the owl was doing to Frankie Mouse's prize. "Nooooo!" he howled. A blood rage filled him, and before thinking he lunged and snapped his jaw of razor sharp teeth on the crazed owl's neck. One more lunge, and the second owl went down.

Igor found himself, dazed, sitting on his tail on the tundra, surrounded by three disfigured and dead bodies. Dusky Dillon's formerly perfect feline head was savaged beyond repair. Frankie Mouse would be so disappointed in him. If he were a kit, he would have cried.

Instead, Igor pulled himself together, hoisted Dusky Dillon's body onto his back again, and dragged it the last mile to Frankie's laboratory. All the way, the twinkling lights that played on the ice walls of Frankie's castle mocked him. He would never be allowed inside with the civilized mice, voles, and hares. He murdered owls and robbed graves. He belonged hidden in Frankie's underground laboratory forever.

Igor descended the stone stairs into Frankie's basement laboratory feeling like he was crawling into his own grave. His master wasn't in evidence, so he laid Dusky Dillon's body out on the largest work table.

Igor didn't feel right leaving the two dead owls lying on the open tundra to rot, so he headed back out into the night. Another two trips across that last mile of tundra brought the steadily stiffening owl bodies into Frankie's lab as well. Igor laid their winged bodies on the large work table, draped over Dusky Dillon. Then he waited in the corner, wringing his paws and waiting for his master to appear.

At the stroke of midnight, the heavy, wooden door into the lab opened. A small figure with large, round ears stood silhouetted by the torchlight from outside. "Did you bring me the snow leopard?" he squeaked.

Igor, shaking, pointed at the pile of bodies on the work table.

The mouse approached, twitching his whiskers. He examined the leopard's ruined face. Frankie's own frown seemed nearly as terrible to Igor as the unnatural scowl torn into Dusky Dillon's face by the enraged owl.

Frankie lifted one of the owl's wings and then another. Of the four wings, two were torn and bloodied; two looked all right.

"This isn't what I wanted," Frankie squeaked. "But I can work with it."

"I'm sorry, Master," Igor blubbered, still huddling in the corner, paws clenched tightly together. He had no one else to hold his paw, so he held his own.

"Come here, Igor," Frankie said. "We have more work to do than I expected."

"We do?"

"Yes. We have to dismember these bodies. Then we must do a lot of sewing." Frankie looked the bodies over with an appraising eye again. "We're going to make a gryphon."

Igor worked diligently under Frankie's direction. He made precise cuts, severing the wings from one of the owls and the head from the other. Frankie admonished him constantly to hold the knife steady and avoid damaging the feathers.

When they finished with the owls, Igor came face to face again with his failure to bring back a perfect deceased leopard for his master. Carefully, Igor sank Frankie's sharpest knife into Dusky Dillon's neck, sawing through muscle and bone. He removed her disfigured head, rendering her feline body once again perfect but headless.

"Now sew the wings on—" With his paw, Frankie traced two lines along Dusky Dillon's spotted back. "Here and here. You need to cut into the leopard back and sew the muscles together before sewing together the skin. That way, the wings will still be usable."

"Yes, Master," Igor said.

"I have work to do with the heads." Frankie took the severed owl head and Dusky Dillon's head to a smaller work table. "I need to combine the brains," he said. "This new creature must be able to operate both owl and leopard body parts."

Igor and his master worked through the dark hours of night and into the pale hours of early morning. With careful paws, Igor pushed and pulled a tiny, crescent-shaped needle through dead muscle, leaving a straight, dashed line of stitches. He used a thicker needle on Dusky Dillon's spotted pelt, joining it to the owl's feathered skin. He had to work the needle around the feather quills, leaving a jagged line of stitches. But the feathers would cover it.

When Igor finished, he left the newly be-winged leopard body, headless, on the table. He approached his master, quietly so as not to disturb him, and stood behind his shoulder. Frankie's work with the two brains must have been complicated, because he was still poking with tiny forceps at the mass of crenellated, pink flesh inside the open leopard skull.

Igor saw a gleam amidst the bloody pink. Between two folds of the brain flesh, Frankie's forceps held a small green square traced with intricate right-angled patterns in silver lines and minuscule gold rectangles.

"What's that?" Igor asked.

Frankie held the forceps with one paw; his other paw deftly stitched the pink flesh around the green square. The strange object disappeared into a pocket of Dusky Dillon's brain.

"Never you mind," Frankie said. "You're done with the wings?" He looked over his shoulder and saw the newly made gryphon body lying on the table. "Very good. I'm nearly done with the brains. I'll need you to mend the bone and sew the skull shut."

"Then sew the head on to the body?" Igor asked, feeling clever.

"Yes. I'll prepare the resurrection machine."

Igor took the skull from Frankie. To repair the bone, he replaced the oval fragment that Frankie had cut free and sealed the crack around it with an amber-colored resin. When the resin hardened, it would be even stronger than the original bone. At least, that's what Frankie had told him when they'd reconstructed a mangled mouse corpse the week before. Her bones may have been strong when the resurrection machine woke her up, but she'd been dead too long. Her brain never recovered.

As Igor sewed Dusky Dillon's new avian head in place, he wondered whether this gryphon would really be Dusky Dillon anymore. Her head was the owl's head; perhaps, her name should be the owl's name? But Igor didn't know the name of the owl who'd attacked him.

He finished stitching the line around Dusky Dillon's neck, and then he put the needles, thread, and resin away. He could hear the powerful, electric whir of the resurrection machine now and the howling wind outside. The tundra had been calm only a few hours ago, but Frankie had the power to summon storms.

A series of wind turbines above ground whipped the atmosphere into a low pressure frenzy, drawing down nimbus clouds and inviting lightning to strike their conducting rods. Frankie controlled the turbines from a panel of levers and switches on the side of the resurrection machine. A giant, tangled mess of wires and gears trailed down from the ceiling, hooked into Frankie's control panel, and clumped around a simple wooden chair. Igor had awoken to his new life in that chair. Soon, Dusky Dillon would awake there as well.

"Bring over the body," Frankie squeaked.

Igor grabbed Dusky Dillon by her leopard arms and draped her newly reconfigured body over his back as he had before. He dragged her across the room on his back, turned himself around, and awkwardly settled her corpse onto the wooden chair. She slumped forward when he disentangled himself, but she stayed on the chair.

"Wire her up," Frankie said.

Igor lashed Dusky Dillon's complicated frame to the chair using thick, black cords. He made sure not to crush her wings. He'd spent so much time carefully sewing them in place. Then he pulled down a skullcap from the tangle of wires above the chair. He affixed the cap, trailing all its wires, to her head and held it on with a leather strap looped under her new owl beak. Other wires hanging from the tangle above had metal cuffs at their ends. Igor tightened the cuffs around Dusky Dillon's leopard arms and legs at intervals—ankle, calf, thigh, and wrist, forearm, bicep.

"Done!" Igor said. He could hardly wait for Dusky Dillon to wake up. Once Frankie had another assistant, Igor wouldn't have to sleep alone in the lab at night. He'd already fixed a cot up for her, next to his in the supply room. He could teach her how Frankie liked his assistants to behave—label alchemical supplies fastidiously; disinfect everything after working with a corpse; and never, ever go into Frankie's laboratory office. He could talk to her about working for Frankie, and they could wonder together about the marvels in the ice castle and Frankie's royal court.

"Stand back," Frankie squeaked, impatience in his voice.

"I'm sorry, Master," Igor said, flattening his ears and lowering his head. He limped backward, away from Dusky Dillon and the resurrection machine. "I was daydreaming."

"Yes, well, hopefully that glitch will be fixed in this incarnation," Frankie said. Then, he threw the switch that opened the conduits for the lightning.

Sparks of blue fire jumped from the tangle of cords, and an electrical hum built up in the room. The skullcap on Dusky Dillon's head glowed dully then brighter. The entire resurrection machine rattled like a restless spirit was trying to escape. Outside, the winds died down.

"Time to come online," Frankie said.

Igor knew Frankie was speaking to himself but pretended the words were meant for him. "That's right!" he agreed, even though he didn't understand.

Dusky Dillon blinked her yellow, owlish eyes. She clacked her beak, trying it out for the first time. "Master," she said, her voice reedy and growly at the same time as her owl tongue and leopard vocal cords sorted themselves out.

In an uncharacteristic show of glee, Frankie clapped his paws, hopped from one foot to the other in a dance, and whirled around. His long tail spun after him. "Delightful!" he squeaked. "Do you know your name?"

"Dillon," the gryphon answered. Her voice gained strength, but it retained the growly undertone.

"That's right. And what is your job?"

"Bodyguard and loyal servant to the Great Frankie Mouse." Her yellow eyes gleamed.

How did she know that?, Igor wondered. She'd never met Frankie before dying as either owl or leopard. Perhaps, she had heard of him and knew he was the only scientist in the region with the skills to resurrect her, and she guessed that he'd want a strong creature like her to be his bodyguard. That had to be it.

"Very good," Frankie said. "Igor, undo her bindings, and let Dillon out of the machine."

As Igor loosened the metal cuffs around Dillon's limbs, Frankie got his coat from his office.

Dillon stood up and stretched her wings. The snowy white feathers on her head and wings blended beautifully into the thick pelt of white fur, covered in horseshoe patterns of soft gray, over the rest of her body.

"Magnificent," Frankie said. "I guess, sometimes blind luck can work out better than careful design." He stroked his whiskers. Then, muttering to himself, he added, "Though, it will be nice not to rely on it." Raising his voice into a commanding tone for his minions, Frankie said, "Dillon, you're in charge of the lab." He turned to Igor. "You take your orders from Dillon now."

Igor stood in shock. One of Dillon's feathers could have knocked him over. Or, if Frankie meant what he said, Dillon could simply order him to fall over, and he'd have to do it.

"Master!" Igor cried, his canine voice rising into a whine.

Frankie shushed him, dismissing him like an unreasonable child instead of the valuably trained servant he was. "I'm going home for some sleep now."

Igor always marveled at how Frankie could call his giant castle of ice simply "home." He would love to treat the wonderful with such familiarity. He would love to experience the wonderful at all. Instead, he lived in a dank basement laboratory and had been demoted beneath a neophyte who couldn't possibly know how his master liked things run.

To his horror, though, Igor discovered over the following days that Dillon knew everything about running the lab and pleasing Frankie. She knew what Frankie wanted before he told her. In fact, Frankie hardly spoke to her, and he barely acknowledged Igor anymore. At first, Igor resented Dillon for displacing him, but then his lonely, pack animal heart cleaved to her—the only creature available to give him society and solace. His sullen attitude towards her turned solicitous, and he sought her friendship at every turn.

One night as Igor and Dillon were settling into their cots in the supply room, Dillon suddenly froze. Her avian head tilted to the side, and she announced, "There was an accident in Izerberg today—toxic chemicals in the well water killed nearly a dozen mice."

"How do you know that?" Igor asked. He and Dillon had been alone in the lab all day, tending and titrating Frankie's experiments. Neither of them had gone anywhere or had contact with anyone besides each other.

"Does it matter?" Dillon asked. "What matters is that our master wants the bodies. We need to leave now, if we're going to make use of the dark."

Exasperated, Igor wanted to yip at Dillon, *"It does matter! And how can you possibly know that Frankie wants us to go dig up those mice? He hasn't been into the lab in three days. Are you simply guessing?"* Admittedly, it was an easy guess that Frankie would want fresh mouse corpses in perfect condition from a clean death by poison.

Igor held his tongue. Snapping at Dillon wouldn't make her like him. Instead, he tried to be like her and anticipate her needs. A dozen mouse bodies was more than they could carry. "I'll set up the cart."

Igor and Dillon trudged across the tundra, their way lit by two gas lanterns hung on the rickety cart they took turns pulling. Dillon's wings were beautiful, but they weren't strong enough to lift a leopard body. She couldn't fly.

Two hours to Izerberg. Five hours digging, breaking open coffins, and carefully laying out the mouse corpses in a pile on the cart. All the while, an oppressive silence weighed Igor down. He wanted the cheer of companionable chatter, but he feared anything he could say would be met with the judgmental glare of yellow eyes.

After two hours trudging toward home with a heavy cart of dead mice slowing them down, the sun broke above Frankie's castle on the horizon. The parapets and towers glowed pink and crimson. It looked like a castle built from dawn itself.

The lock on Igor's tongue loosened, and he sighed, "I love that castle." Pulling the heavy cart didn't seem so bad when he was pulling it toward heaven. "Some day these mice may be servants and courtiers in that place." He pictured them in ruffled cravats and layers of petticoats, crushed velvet and fine lace. "Frankie is so kind to save them from death and bring them to a new life in his castle."

A long moment passed, and the quality of the silence between Igor and Dillon changed.

"What castle?"

Igor stopped pulling the cart. He turned to stare at Dillon. Her leopard body and half-folded wings dwarfed him, but her owl head looked small.

"What do you mean, *what castle?*" He held out a paw to point at the horizon. He imagined his paw could touch the perfect vision, as if it were only a miniature for him to play with. He sighed. "There's only one castle in all the world as beautiful as Frankie's."

Dillon repeated, "What castle?

"There is only one castle!" Igor said with frustration.

Without frustration or any emotion that Igor could identify, Dillon said, "I see no castle."

Igor's heart fell.

The castle was the most beautiful thing in his world, the center of all his hopes and dreams—and Dillon was blind to it. He couldn't share it with her, and, worse, he feared that her blindness meant there was something wrong with her. Had combining two bodies mangled her soul? Was the castle truly heaven, visible only to the pure of heart? Maybe Dusky Dillon's bad deeds in life—worse than his own, for sure—were enough to sentence her to damnation without the hope of Frankie's castle.

They walked the rest of the way in silence, trading turns at pulling the cart. When they reached the lab, Dillon and Igor unloaded the mouse bodies and arranged them carefully on the work tables like little dolls. Five mice fit easily on the table that had been barely large enough for Dillon's hulking girth on the night Igor brought her in pieces from the graveyard.

"Our master will be here soon to work on them," Dillon said. "We should sleep."

"Work on them?" Igor asked. He looked at the doll-like mice. They were perfect, undamaged by death. "What do they need done to them?"

Owl eyes blinked at him. "We've been up all night. We should sleep. Our master needs us in good condition."

Igor frowned. He felt so little warmth from Dillon. It wasn't that she seemed cold to him... But, perhaps, cold to everything? Frankie had brought her back from the dead, but she still seemed dead inside.

"I think I'll stay up and see Frankie," he said.

"No. You need to sleep." Dillon stared at Igor until he lowered his ears; his tail drooped; and he slunk off to his cot in the supply room. Dillon watched closely as he pulled his thin wool blanket over his fur. He turned his back to her and listened as she got into her own cot. He felt sure that her yellow eyes still watched him.

Igor pretended to sleep but kept himself awake by filling his mind with stories about the mice waiting on the laboratory tables to be resurrected. Two of them, buried in matching coffins beside each other, would awake and embrace, glad to find themselves together again. The littlest corpse would awaken still a child and sentenced to forever be one—she would charm Frankie with her innocent heart, and he would make her his Lady-in-Waiting. She would bring Frankie his fine wines and candied chestnuts, and, unable to resist, he would share the sweets with her.

The lock on the lab door clanked, and the door whined, swinging open. Frankie had come!

Igor's heart pounded with excitement, but he forced himself to creep, slowly and silently, from his cot. Dillon didn't move; she hadn't heard him. Step by painstaking step, Igor placed his padded paws on the stone floor, careful to keep his claws from scraping. By the time he'd closed the door to the supply room behind him, Frankie was already standing over the work table of mouse corpses. Igor approached and saw that Frankie had opened the skull of the child corpse he'd been daydreaming about. Light flashed off a pair of needle-thin metal forceps that Frankie had pressed into the pink flesh of her brain. Igor thought he saw another of the green squares that Frankie had put in Dillon's brain.

"Was her brain damaged by the poison?" Igor asked.

Frankie jumped and squeaked. When he turned and saw Igor, Frankie glared, and his whiskers turned down, trembling in anger. "This is delicate work. You should know better than to startle me." Frankie turned back to the child corpse's open brain and withdrew the forceps. If there had been a green square held in the forceps, it was gone now, lodged in the brain. Frankie folded back the sawn open skull and began applying resin to the seam. "Besides, shouldn't you be sleeping? Dillon told you to, didn't she?" Frankie's tone changed from anger nearly to indifference.

"She did," Igor admitted. "But I'm worried about her." He wasn't sure how much to tell Frankie. Would Frankie hurt Dillon if he knew that her soul might be mangled? Would he take her undeath away? "There may be something wrong with her eyesight—she can't see your castle."

"My castle?" Frankie mused. "Oh, that blighted delusion. Never mind about that. You just do what Dillon tells you, and everything will be fine." He sewed the gray-furred skin together over the mended skull. When he spoke again, his voice changed to a sickly sweet, sing-song tone. "If you remain a faithful servant, then someday I'll know you can be trusted to live in the castle as one of my courtiers." He finished the last stitch, tied off the thread, and put the needle away. "Now go back to sleep. Dillon will have more orders for you this evening."

Igor was not the smartest fox, but he could tell when he was being lied to, especially when his master didn't respect him enough to hide it. "Yes, Master," he said, but his heart screamed in anguish and raced with adrenaline. He meant to go back to his cot, but his paws carried him to the front door of the lab.

He stood outside the lab and stared up at the castle, glittering and glorious in the light of day. He walked beside the icy wall, heading toward the castle's main gate. Steam rose from the glossy vertical surface in the beating of the sun, and his reflection kept him cold company. He was tempted to touch the ice with his paw, but when he reached toward it—courage failed him. Perfect beauty should not be marred with paw prints. That would be hubris.

At the main gate, no one stood guard. There were no mice in armor, but, surely, a strong castle like Frankie's didn't need guards. Ice walls were defense enough.

Igor called out, hoping a sentry inside would hear him: "Ahoy! I'm here on behalf of Frankie Mouse. Open the gate!"

No answer.

Igor called again and again. His cries turned from pleas

for entry into the pouring out of his soul to a closed gate of ice. The sun rose higher in the sky, and Igor's cries gave way to soft whimpering and, finally, curled up on the ground beside the pure beauty of the castle, sleep. He was as tired and in need of sleep as Dillon and Frankie had told him he was.

Igor awoke from incoherent dreams of disappointment and betrayal to a cold wind ruffling his fur. Many hours must have passed while he slept for the sun was much lower in the sky and marred by clouds. The clouds grew and darkened as Igor watched them. Frankie must have been powering up the resurrection machine, ready to bring back to life the poisoned mice.

Igor lifted himself from the cold ground and limped away from the castle gate, shoulders hunched to protect himself from the wind and rain of the growing storm. With dripping fur and raindrops in his whiskers, he descended the stone stairway to the lab and slipped inside as quietly as a gimped fox could. On his way to the supply room and his cot, he stopped to dry himself with an old work rag. As he rubbed down his white fur, Igor saw the blue sparks and dull glow of the resurrection machine coming to life. He moved closer to watch. Shortly afterward, the first of the poisoned mice came to life in it.

Igor meant to go straight to his cot after drying his fur, but he stood mesmerized, watching as Frankie helped the newly resurrected mouse out of the machine. Then, one after another, Frankie resurrected the others until all the corpses on the tables were gone; instead a ring of reanimated mice sat around Frankie, awaiting his commands.

They didn't look like courtiers and ladies-in-waiting in Igor's mind's eye anymore. The tilt of their heads, the bearing in their shoulders, and the stern, grim expressions on their faces... They looked like soldiers. Frankie didn't think they'd be able to see the ice castle either, let alone live, drink, dance, and be merry in it.

Thoroughly shaken, Igor returned to his cot and wondered why Frankie needed an army. He trusted his master and wanted to help, but his master did not trust him. Perhaps Frankie was protecting Igor's feelings, hiding some grave danger from him.

In spite of the adrenaline coursing through his body, Igor must have fallen asleep again for he woke up to Dillon's giant, feline paw on his shoulder.

"Wake up. There are more poisoned mice for us to fetch."

"More?" Igor asked, incredulous. "In Izerberg?"

"No. This time it's Gayton. Similarly far, but in the opposite direction."

For the next ten days, their schedule stayed the same: they robbed graves all night, slept all day, and then Igor awoke to the news of more poisoned mice. The hard work left very little time for speculation, but Igor couldn't help feeling that all the toxic well water couldn't be a coincidence. Was this the danger that Frankie was protecting him from? Had a plague struck the land? Igor didn't know how soldiers could fight a plague, but, by now, Frankie's army was more than one hundred strong, a formidable force and still growing.

Finally, a day came when Igor woke up in his own time. He lay in his cot, relishing the indolence after weeks of constant hard work. He used the time to come to a few decisions. First of all, he needed to figure out how to help Frankie better, and, as little as he liked it, that meant snooping through Frankie's secret office. It was against Frankie's orders, but Frankie had given him no choice. He knew he could help more than as a simple laborer. He would prove that to Frankie, and then Frankie would be grateful.

Secondly, Dillon had to see the castle. It was one thing to miss it at night on the horizon. Surely, in the shining whiteness of daylight on the tundra, standing right beside the castle's walls, she couldn't miss its majestic glory.

Breaking into Frankie's office would be easy. He just needed to get Dillon out of the way so that she wouldn't tell on him.

When Igor got up, he found Dillon hunched over one of the work tables. A re-animated mouse sat beside her, and spread in front of them were piles of green boards and spools of silver and gold wire. Dillon used a utility knife in her giant paws to cut the boards down to tiny squares. The mouse took the tiny squares and soldered intricate patterns onto them with the spools of wire. Their concentration was so complete that Igor considered breaking into Frankie's office right then, but it would be safer if the lab were empty.

"What are you making?" Igor asked. "Frankie put one of those in each of your brains. Do you know what they are?"

Dillon and the mouse looked up.

"Hello," the mouse said. "I'm Svetlana. You must be Igor."

Dillon said, "They're chips, and our master wants us to make more of them."

"Chips? Igor said. "But what do they do?"

Dillon looked at him blankly with her owl eyes. Svetlana wrinkled her nose, rippling her whiskers in amusement. "Why would you want to know what they do? Master wants them. That's all that matters."

"Where are the other mice?" Igor asked. Frankie resurrected new mice every night, and then they disappeared with him. Svetlana was the first one Igor had met after her reanimation.

"Working for Master," Svetlana said, returning to her work.

"Doing what?"

"Building barracks." Svetlana didn't even raise her eyes to look at him while answering.

"Why would Frankie need to build barracks when he has a whole *castle*?" Perhaps Frankie didn't think any of his reanimated acolytes were worthy of entering his castle. Igor had assumed it was just him, because he'd been a bad, villainous fox in his previous life. Although, he couldn't remember any of his villainous deeds. "Have you been to the castle?"

Svetlana didn't answer him. Dillon shook her head, almost imperceptibly. They kept working on the mysterious green chips.

Igor's heart sank as he realized that Svetlana didn't know about the castle either. If a perfectly normal mouse like her wasn't good enough to enter Frankie's castle, what hope was there for him? But even if Frankie wouldn't invite them into his glittering court, Dillon and Svetlana deserved to see it. No one should be denied the sight of heaven, even if they were denied entrance.

"You need to see it," Igor said, swishing his tail agitatedly. "Come with me."

"We're working," Svetlana said.

Svetlana and Dillon might not obey him, but they would obey their master. "Frankie told me to take you there," Igor said.

"You haven't seen our master today," Svetlana said, reasonably.

Igor hazarded a further deception: "He told me the way that he gives orders to you."

Dillon clacked her beak and spoke with clipped words. "I don't think so."

"Why not?" Igor cried in outrage. What special connection did Dillon share with Frankie that Igor had no part of?

"Your mind isn't linked," Dillon said.

Igor didn't know what that meant, but he could see his deception was getting him nowhere. Words fall behind actions. Igor sized up the situation: Dillon was much larger than him, but he could outrun her with the head start afforded by surprise. He rushed around the table, grabbed Svetlana with one arm around her middle, and ran with her under that arm for the lab's door. To slow Dillon down, he slammed the door behind him before rushing up the stone stairs and into the bright, white tundra day.

"There!" he screamed, pointing with his free paw. "There's the castle!" He threw Svetlana at the snowy ground at the base of the castle wall.

She whimpered, but Igor couldn't make out the words.

"What?" he snarled, showing his sharp, canine teeth.

"I see nothing!" she squeaked before hiding her face in her paws.

Dillon arrived and stepped up beside Igor on massive, leopard paws with her owl wings spread wide enough to make her look even bigger and more menacing. "There's nothing here, crazy fox."

In desperation, Igor threw himself at the castle wall, needing to feel its solid, smooth ice against his paws. As his body reached the wall, a bright flash blinded him. He felt nothing with his paws, but his body rushed forward into empty space; unbalanced, he toppled and slammed into the ground.

All around him, all he saw was white—uniform and blinding. He reached up, trying to discover anything but emptiness and the ground under him, but his paws felt nothing, and, worse, he couldn't even see his paws.

"What happened? Am I in the castle?" It must have

been a trap door in the ice wall, a secret entrance. "Am I inside?" His excitement rose. He could hear Svetlana and Dillon behind him. "Come in! Tell me what you can see!" The glory of the castle was too great for his poor eyes, but, surely, a blameless mouse like Svetlana, a mere victim of a poisoned well, would be able to see.

Igor stood up, held his paws in front of him, and carefully walked forward. He took small, shuffling steps. He felt Svetlana come up beside him and take one of his paws in her delicate mouse hands.

"If you keep walking this way," she said, "you'll fall into the quarry. Come back."

"Quarry?" Igor asked.

"The old marble quarry," Svetlana said.

"That's what you see? Describe it to me."

Svetlana described the angular gashes cut into the Earth, the rubble, and the dingy, haphazard barracks being built by the reanimated mice way down on the quarry's floor. She didn't see heaven; her eyes saw a bleak, labor-filled hell.

"That can't be right," Igor said. "Where are the dancing mice? The hares playing music? The fancy-dressed voles?" But he let Svetlana lead him away, back toward the lab. Suddenly, his vision returned. When he looked over his shoulder, the glittering castle wall towered behind him.

For the rest of the day, Igor lay on his cot, staring at the gray ceiling, listening to Dillon and Svetlana construct chips in the lab, and remembering the bright whiteness that had filled his eyes inside Frankie's castle. When night came, Svetlana left the lab, presumably to join the other reanimated mice at the barracks she'd described. Or in the castle she couldn't see. Dillon joined Igor in the supply room.

"Our master will expect you to return to work tomorrow," she said, settling on her cot. She pulled the thin wool blanket over her folded wings. "He needs herbs gathered. Check the canisters to see which ones are low in the morning, and you can begin at first light."

Igor intoned dully, "Yes, Dillon." Then he waited until he heard her breathing slow into sleep. Igor had failed to show Dillon the castle, but he could still break into Frankie's office. Perhaps he could find answers to the castle mystery there, as well as clues to Frankie's plans.

Igor moved slowly and silently. He had all night, and he couldn't risk Dillon hearing him. He worked his way through the lab in the dark, not daring to risk turning the lights on. The darkness reminded him of the whiteness inside the castle, and he pretended that he was there— perhaps in the kitchen, preparing a secret meal for Frankie to surprise him.

Igor felt blindly through the small drawers in the work tables until he found the set of needles. He selected the heavy, curved needle that he'd used to sew Dillon's wings on and a thin, metal rod. Then, he made his way to Frankie's office door. He inserted the metal rod and needle in the lock and patiently wiggled the needle until he heard a tiny click, then another, then four more. He turned the rod, and he was in.

Once the door was safely shut behind him, Igor reached up and felt above him for a pull string. He found one, pulled it, and the small room filled with light. Igor stared in confusion at the single chair, desk, and contraption on the desk. Frankie had wired a typewriter up to a large metal box with a black glass window on one side. Several smaller boxes on the desk, wired into the typewriter as well, blinked at Igor with tiny colored lights in red and green.

Tentatively, Igor approached the desk and sat in the chair. He put his paws to the keys of the typewriter, and, as if the contraption had sensed his presence, the black glass window leapt to life with scrolling, white text. Igor knew how to read, but a lot of the letters on the black glass didn't make real words. Though, he recognized his name as well as Dillon's and Svetlana's, and a bunch of other names that must be the other reanimated mice. Intrigued, he hunted out the letters of his own name on the typewriter—*I, G, O, R.*

As soon as he pressed the "R" key, the writing on the glass changed completely. Most of it, he didn't understand this time, but buried in the jumble of nonsense words, he saw the word "CASTLE." With rising excitement, he typed that word, too. Again, the writing on the glass changed. This time, he understood a lot of it—*ICE, SPARKLING, GLITTERING, DANCING, MUSIC, FEAST, VELVET, RUFFLES.*

These words described everything that he knew

existed but couldn't see. Everything that Dillon and Svetlana didn't even believe in.

For several minutes, Igor simply stared at the black glass, dreaming about Frankie's castle. He hadn't learned anything yet about Frankie's plans, but Igor knew that what he had discovered was important. He just didn't know how.

Eventually, the glamour of the words on the black glass window wore off, and Frankie opened all the drawers in the desk, hoping to find something more clearly useful.

Instead, he found broken wind-up toys, a brush for Frankie's fur, a hidden stash of chocolate, and a bunch of crumpled wrappers—all the useless debris of a long-used, rarely cleaned desk. In the bottom drawer, he found a stash of papers. Most of them were maps. A few looked like ancient letters Frankie had written and never sent. But one was a cryptic list of words. That caught Igor's attention.

Much like the words on the black glass window, the words written on this list didn't quite make sense, and many of them were mixed with strange symbols he didn't recognize. Though, looking at the typewriter, he saw that each of the strange symbols could be found on one of the keys. He decided to try typing a few of the words and see what happened. The words that most appealed to him were: *COPY SCREEN* and *UNIVERSAL OVERWRITE.*

After he typed COPY SCREEN, the white text describing Frankie's castle flashed into reverse letters—

each letter a little white box with blackness in the shape of the letter inside. It made Igor think of the whiteness inside Frankie's castle again, and he felt sure that what he was doing must be right.

He typed UNIVERSAL OVERWRITE, and suddenly the list of names from before began streaming over the glass. The red and green lights on one of the metal boxes wired into the side of the typewriter began blinking furiously, and Igor heard a sound like an electronic nightingale choking to death. He turned back his ears to dim the offensive noise.

Unsure what any of the contraption's behavior meant, Igor returned to studying the papers he'd found in Frankie's desk. Several of the maps were marked up with red circles, arrows, and lines. Perhaps they indicated plans for an impending battle with a neighboring province. The largest map indicated that a moose king inhabited a castle to the north, and Igor lost himself poring over the strange squiggles that Frankie had drawn there. He didn't like the idea of going to war with a kingdom of moose; they were literal giants compared to mice and even foxes. But it would explain why Frankie needed so many reanimated followers.

"What are you doing!" Frankie Mouse squeaked behind him.

Igor's ears flattened in surprise and shame. He hadn't heard the door open; he'd been too lost in the maps. Igor turned to face Frankie. "You wouldn't let me help you."

"So you broke into my office?!"

If Frankie had been larger, Igor felt sure the mouse would have struck him. Fury and outrage burned in his rodent eyes.

Igor stood from the chair to show his full height. Frankie might be his master, but loyalty should earn respect. And Igor had never been anything but loyal. "Are we at war with the moose king?" Igor asked.

"Not yet, thank goodness," Frankie squeaked. "I can't imagine how much havoc your little trick would have wreaked in the middle of a battle."

"My trick?"

"All my minions are dancing! Singing and dancing, pouring each other imaginary goblets of wine, and feasting on air."

Frankie continued ranting, but Igor hardly heard him. He couldn't shake the image Frankie had described from his head. Was it possible that Frankie couldn't see his own castle?

"You mean..." Igor choked out. "You mean, that the mice are dancing in the *quarry*? Among the barracks? Not in the *castle*?"

"You and your damned obsession with that castle!" Frankie squeaked. "I'd have deleted it from your programming ages ago if your chip wasn't an infernal prototype with all the software hardwired."

Mouse and fox stared at each other, each lost in a deep well of emotions. Igor hadn't realized there was a chip in his brain as well. He didn't know what to make of that.

Finally, Frankie sighed and said, "I know you mean

well. You can't know any better. Now, please, get out of my way so I can fix what you've done."

Igor's paws clenched into fists and his tail swished. "No," he said, heart racing at the thought that he was defying his master. "The castle is real." There was nothing else he believed so firmly. "And if the mice are dancing, then they can finally see it. I won't let you take it away from them." More importantly, Igor realized, he needed to make Frankie see the castle as well.

At the sight of an angry fox, Frankie began, instinctively, to back away. "Dillon!" he squeaked, calling to his bodyguard. Moments later, the hulking form of the leopard gryphon appeared in the doorway behind him. "Grab Igor," Frankie demanded. "And keep him out of my way."

Dillon stepped forward, but before she laid a paw on Igor, the fox cried, "Do you believe in the castle now?"

Dillon stopped. Her owl face was inscrutable as ever, but her spotted tail twitched in agitation. After a moment, she said, "I don't know why I didn't believe in it before."

Igor's heart swelled. Finally, Dillon understood him and could be the companion he'd hoped she would be. Urgently, he said, "Frankie can't see his own castle."

The look of sadness on Dillon's face transcended her avian features. She clearly felt deeply the tragedy of any impairment that would deny her master the experience of his shining, glittering castle of ice.

"I think we can help him," Igor said.

"We *must*." Dillon's voice grew husky with emotion.

Frankie tried to move away from the two predators, his faithful minions, who had him cornered, but Dillon's leopard bulk and spread wings blocked the door, and the office was small.

"It's the chips that he puts in our brains," Igor said. "They let us see the castle. We need to put one in Frankie's brain, too."

"No!" Frankie screamed, launching himself toward his desk. Briefly, his mouse paws brushed the keys of the typewriter, but leopard paws grabbed him firmly around the waist.

"Bring him to a work table," Igor said.

Dillon carried Frankie, kicking and squeaking, into the main room of the lab. She flapped her wings as she shoved him down on a work table.

"You can't do this!" Frankie squeaked. "I'm not dead!"

"Neither were the mice that you poisoned," Igor said. "Not at first."

The look in Frankie's eyes as Dillon held him down on the table told Igor he was right. Frankie had poisoned those wells.

"I'm your master," Frankie said. His voice was frantic, terrified. "You love me." He looked from Igor to Dillon, appealing to both, but Dillon believed in the castle now. She would follow Igor.

Igor's eyes turned soft, and he came close enough to take Frankie's small paw in his larger one. He clasped it firmly; fox paw and mouse hand intertwined as one.

"Of course, I love you," Igor said.

Dillon continued to restrain him with her heavy feline paws, yet, for a moment, Frankie looked relieved. Then, Igor let go of his paw and picked up a bone saw.

"Opening my skull will kill me!" Frankie squeaked.

"Don't worry," Dillon said. "I'm your bodyguard. I'd never let anyone hurt you." Then, she looked at the resurrection machine with its wires draping down from the ceiling in all their glory. "Igor will bring you back."

Frankie continued to squeak: "Do you think that's what it does? Do you remember anything from your lives before?" He stared into Dillon's owl eyes. "You weren't even a gryphon—you were three different animals. Now you're a monster. And you!" He turned his gaze to Igor. "You were a cowardly, thieving fool who couldn't steal enough to feed himself! That fox died! And all you are now is the chip I programmed in your brain!"

All that Igor could think was that his old life didn't sound much like it was worth remembering. Besides, a few memories were a small price to pay for the heavenly vision of Frankie's ice castle. Frankie would understand that soon. Then, they could get back to the important work of bringing Frankie's vision to all the other creatures—mice, voles, hares, foxes, and someday moose—in their land.

Igor lowered the bone saw toward Frankie's head.

9

THE FREEDOM OF THE QUEEN

AMBER FLUID DRIPPED from the hive, but it wasn't honey. It was thick and gooey and satiated. The amorphous being, gold and honey-like, had infiltrated the hive, feasted on the honey and then on the worker bees who'd made the honey; then the drones who the worker bees had waited on; and finally, on the delectable morsels of unfinished dough that were the eggs and pupae.

But not the queen.

The amber fluid coalesced, reforming itself on the ground under the hollowed-out hive. A golden pool, reflecting the blue sky, broken up by branches above. The queen looked down from her branch, wings trembling from disuse and rage and fear. She could see bits and pieces of her children—broken segments of leg or antennae—mixed into the amber swirls. She had been large once—moments ago. A lifetime ago. She had been generations of magnificent daughters and loafing sons, a thriving colony.

Now she was alone. Singular.

"Why did you leave me alive?" the queen bee buzzed at the honey look-alike, puddled under her tree. "Why didn't you eat me too?"

The amber goo stretched upward, forming the shape of a bee's face, mandibles wide and antennae flailing. It spoke in a sticky buzz: "I love you. I idolize you. I freed you from your chains."

"My five generations of daughters and four generations of sons were not chains!" the queen buzzed, her body so light with wrath that she could have almost floated away without flapping her translucent wings. "And destroying the things someone loves is not love."

"Perhaps," the goo buzzed, sounding even more sticky as its bee-face melted back into the formless pool. "Perrrhaaaaps…" the puddle slurred, beginning to flow away. The honey-clone poured across the flat ground like water flowing downstream, trickling away from the queen until it was nothing but a golden line, an illusory shimmer in the distance. Off to cause more damage, eat more hives, leave more bereft queens.

The queen watched. The queen waited. Then she returned to the empty halls of her hive. The hexagonal chambers echoed now, echoed with silence. She couldn't bear the suffocating sound. So she took to the sky, straining and stretching her disused wings.

But as she flew, she remembered. She remembered the

peaceful feeling of losing herself in the deep blue sky. The peaceful feeling of being alone.

Perhaps she would lay new eggs, start a new hive, start again.

Perhaps...

She wouldn't.

Perhaps it was time for a new kind of life.

* * *

Behind her, the hive continued to buzz with puzzled workers and bewildered drones, wondering what hallucinatory vision—what dawning madness in the dusk of her life—had drawn their aging queen away, causing her to seek the freedom of adolescence again.

They would always honor her, and the legacy she'd left behind. But among the ranks of workers, a new queen was already on the rise.

10

HIDE THE HONEY

The bear's paws were covered with honey. It dripped from her claws in sticky, amber droplets. It clumped her thick brown fur together between her paw pads. Everything she touched, her paw came away leaving a ghostly paw print behind, a gleaming sheen of sugar where it had been. She could touch nothing without giving herself away.

"Where are you?" the bear's sister cried.

Sandra and Samantha had been playing together, until Sandra found their mother's hidden jar of honey. Now Hide & Seek had become simply "Hide... and hope no one catches her before she finishes eating all the honey."

Sandra had finished eating the honey. The jar lay discarded on the floor, rolling a little on its side. But the evidence. The evidence clung to her paws, and Sandra couldn't shake, scrape, or smear it off. Though, she'd tried, and left rainbows of shiny sugar smears all around the kitchen.

It was all her mother's fault. Mother should have known better than to hide the sugar so poorly. Behind the boxes of cereal in the cereal cupboard? Really? Even little Samantha could reach that cupboard. So, it was hardly Sandra's fault if she'd found the hidden stash, and once you find a hidden stash of honey, you simply must eat it. No other option. None at all.

Sandra snaked her long tongue around her muzzle again, trying to lick off the last vestiges of sugar there. She'd already tried licking the honey off her paws, but it was just too soaked in. Soaked in sugar down to the skin.

Sandra felt like a honey baked ham, ready to be roasted and basted in brown sugar.

Oh goodness, Sandra would love to roll around in brown sugar sauce like the holiday hams her parents cooked. Though, she didn't think she'd so much enjoy getting shoved in the oven, carved into slices, or eaten up beside piles of mashed potatoes afterward.

Just the rolling in sugar part.

Sandra giggled.

She'd never eaten this much honey at once before. Mother always doled it out in small amounts. A little dollop on toast. A few drips in the mint tea. Never mouthfuls. Never a whole jar. Sandra's giggles erupted into full blown belly laughs, as she rolled on the floor beside the empty jar of honey.

Sandra was the jar of honey now, because all the honey was inside her.

Did that make the empty jar Sandra? Had they switched places?

Sandra's laughter quakes quelled down to aftershocks as a shadow stretched out over her. Samantha had found her. "This isn't a very good hiding place," the little sister bear said, paws firmly planted on her hips. If she hadn't been so short and cute, it might have looked intimidating. Instead, it was just funny, and Sandra started up her giggling again.

Samantha rushed off, and when she came back, this time, she had their mother in tow. A much bigger bear who cast a much bigger shadow. Perhaps, this time, Sandra should have been intimidated. She knew she wasn't supposed to have eaten that much honey. But the laughter just kept bubbling up inside her, as if the honey was being converted directly into laughter inside her belly.

Perhaps that's what sugar really is—hilarity in vaguely nutritious form.

"Oh dear," mother bear said. "You're giddy."

"She's eaten all the honey!" Samantha exclaimed, nearly squeaking in outrage. Though, it wasn't clear if she was outraged that Sandra had broken the rules and behaved badly... or if she was just outraged that she hadn't been included.

A little bit of honey probably would have gone a long way in mollifying Sandra's outraged little sister. Ah well.

Sandra didn't need a little sister. She had a belly full of honey! And she felt like she could do anything!

"Let's get you outside," mother bear said, gently placing around Sandra's shoulders and coaxing her up from the floor.

"Sticky..." Sandra complained, managing to force the word out between fits of laughter.

"Yes, you certainly are," mother bear agreed.

"So sticky!" Samantha agreed. Although she hadn't touched Sandra's sticky paws, so what did she know about it? "Too sticky!" Really, she just liked the chance to be included in admonishing her older sister.

Mother bear lifted Sandra up onto the kitchen counter and washed her little paws under the tap, complete with a horrible green gooey soap. Sandra would never touch that stuff if she could avoid it. It was like the most evil opposite of honey. Instead of tasty and golden, it was horrendous and sickly green.

"Ugh," Sandra complained. "I liked it better when they were covered with honey." The horrid soap had quenched her giggles, like throwing a pot full of water on the remnants of a campfire. All the was left was hisses and smoke. The sad remains of what had been a glorious, burning fire of joy and laughter.

Though the aftereffects of the sugar were clearly far from gone. Sandra could feel a twitchiness in her arms and legs, like the sugar had worked its way into them, and she needed to run, climb, crawl, zoom, and generally just move and move and move until she fell down dizzy.

That's probably why mother bear shepherded her outside. Samantha followed, chasing along, trying to pretend as if she had sugar running through her veins as well. She didn't. All she had was envy of her older sister and an absolute determination to keep up, to not be left out, not again.

So, once they got outside, Sandra ran circles around all the nearby trees. She climbed over decorative rock walls in the neighbor's garden that she'd been told—in no uncertain terms—to leave alone and not climb upon. And then she scrambled her way down to the nearby creek bed and hopped from one rock to the next, trying not to get her hind paws too wet. Samantha was less good at climbing; and she wasn't energized by unnatural amounts of sugar, so she ran fewer circles around the trees, followed along beside the decorative rock walls complaining, "Hey! You're not supposed to climb those!" and chased along the bank of the creek, not quite daring to cross over the rushing waters to the big rocks that Sandra kept hopping on.

By the end of the hour—or however much time had passed; bear cubs aren't very good at keeping time—Samantha was totally exhausted, and Sandra was still buzzing from the sugar in her belly, as if the honey had turned back to bees inside her, and all of them kept stinging her over and over again, insisting that she keep moving, keep climbing, keep rock-hopping, and keep giggling at every stray thought that passed through her head.

It was exhausting. Fun, exhilarating, the best thing that had ever happened to her during her short bear cub life so far... but...

Exhausting.

Mother bear, with a tired little sister bear riding on her shoulders, found Sandra at the edge of the creek, staring at her own reflection, eyes as glassy as the clear surface of the water.

"Well, you look beat, little one," mother bear said.

"Beat," Sandra agree. Saying the single word felt like a huge effort. The honey was long gone from her tongue, but it felt heavy and sticky anyway. Even moving her tongue felt too hard now that she'd run all of her sugar rush off.

"Sugar crashing is no fun, is it?" mother bear asked in a leading tone, as if she thought there was any chance Sandra might learn a positive lesson from this experience.

Sandra hadn't. She wouldn't. She would absolutely, definitely, definitively refuse to learn a positive lesson. The honey had tasted good on her tongue, had bubbled up as joy and laughter inside her belly, and had filled her limbs with restless energy. She'd had more fun this afternoon, filled to the brim with honey, than she'd had during whole weeks of her life lived on a scrimping, measly, reasonable amount of sugar per day.

"No," Sandra insisted. "It's fun. It's all fun. Everything about eating honey is fun." It was a lot of words for a little bear who felt like her arms, legs, neck, and yes, tongue had all fallen asleep. But she would stand by those words any day.

"I see," mother bear said.

"I want a jar of honey," Samantha complained. It seemed fair. Only reasonable—if one sister ate a whole jar of honey and ran around like a maniac until she slumped over in a grumpy funk by the side of a creek, then certainly the other sister was owed an equal amount of honey. It could hardly be fair for only one sister to get such a valuable learning opportunity that she planned to completely refuse to learn from.

Mother bear sighed. Some lessons can't be learned by being told. Some lessons can't even be learned from experience. Some lessons... just can't be learned. Because unfortunately, having a bear cub hopped up on ungodly amounts of sugar is far harder on her mother than on the bear cub herself.

Mother bear scooped Sandra up in her paws and trudged back home with two tired bear cubs draped over her, thinking all the way back about a better place to hide the honey.

11

JELLYFISH FOR DINNER

When Arlene and Angelica married, they never expected to have children. Arlene was a river otter inventor; Angelica was a sea lion artist. And they were very happy together, sharing their lives and their passions, but theirs was the kind of union that bore fruit of the mind, not the kind of union that produced children.

Then Arlene's business partner, a sea otter named Florentine, found an orphaned river otter child hiding out behind her inn, digging through the rubbish for scraps of food. The poor thing needed love and attention, a new home, and parents to care for him. He was so young, he only spoke a few words and couldn't even swim yet. Angelica named him Elijah, and Arlene found herself unaccountably delighted to be raising a little fellow who looked just like she had at that age.

Arlene hadn't realized—with how much time she spent

surrounded by sea lions and sea otters—how much she missed the company of another river otter. She'd left her hometown along the side of the great river many, many moons before (back when she still lived under the name Arlow), and she'd never looked back. Yet, when she looked in Elijah's little round, whiskered face, it was like she seeing all the way back to her own childhood, and she discovered an entirely new joy in life, beyond the joys of inventing and her love for Angelica: she loved being a mother.

Elijah was accepted by and played with the other children in the island village where Arlene and Angelica lived —a small, satellite village of the larger town on the mainland where Florentine kept her inn. Their village was a village of sea lions, and all the other children were sea lions. The sea lion children accepted Elijah as easily as the adults had accepted Arlene, perhaps more easily, since he wasn't constantly pestering them with inventions they didn't have any need for.

The sea lion village—Angelica's hometown, and where she'd lived her whole life—was a small place, unchanged by the passing of time. The larger town where Florentine kept her inn, just a mile down the coast, had installed water wheels along the nearest river that powered street lights, cold boxes for keeping food fresh, and even heated water for luxurious bathing and more effective laundry. It was an exciting time to be an otter inventor, full of change and innovation.

Even so, Arlene chose to live in Angelica's small town where the nights were lit and warmed by nothing more than bonfires and community connection. Sometimes, she felt strange, choosing a life that forewent so many of her own creations, as Arlene had indeed been responsible for many of the technological improvements to the larger town. However, she never truly regretted her choice—she worked with Florentine on her inventions, but her life and heart were with Angelica in the sea lion village.

Nonetheless, as much as Arlene had accepted that the village where she lived was entirely disinterested in her creations, she had no intention of raising her adopted child in ignorance of them. The sea lions of the village gave Arlene strange looks—even Angelica did—as she taught the little, wide-eyed river otter child about the loom she'd invented for stringing beads onto bracelets and necklaces. They tutted and tsked as young Elijah delighted over being able to create beadwork jewelry for himself by playing the keys on the loom like a piano.

Elijah made himself necklaces and bracelets far more easily than the other children his age who were still stringing them painstakingly by hand, the way it had always been done. His creations, of course, were clunky things—yes, functional, but the patterns and color combinations he chose were haphazard and aesthetically questionable. The choices of a small child, not a true artist. The adults were not impressed. Some of the younger sea lion children, though, were thrilled to play with Elijah's pieces, dressing up in them and trading them amongst themselves.

As Elijah got a little older, Arlene started taking him for rides out to sea on her watercycle. With the child perched on her lap, Arlene could pedal the watercycle for hours, riding up and down the coastal waters, just beyond the reckless crashing of the surf. Arlene could let her mind wander, and Elijah watched the seagulls flying above, or the pattern of the trees and shrubs along the shore, or simply stared up at the clouds in the sky. It was a peaceful way to keep a tired child busy, letting them both get some rest. Sometimes, it made Alene feel like she was pretending to be a sea otter with the way they floated lazily on their backs, keeping their children on their bellies. As a river otter, she was less suited to that. She liked to feel the wind in her whiskers as her watercycle whisked its way down the coast. She wanted to be always moving, always going somewhere, always accomplishing something, even if watching a small, sleepy child who insisted they weren't really tired sometimes meant that all she could really accomplish was keeping the child soothed.

It was a peaceful time, and Arlene grew to love it. Of course, like every phase of parenthood, it didn't last, and soon, Elijah was too restless and wiggly to be kept busy in such a passive way. He wanted to stay back at the island and play with his sea lion friends, splashing about in the water around the island.

With both regret and relief, Arlene transitioned away from spending most of her days holding her new child, almost a dual creature with two separate bodies fused into one conjoined being, and back to working on her wacky ideas for inventions. She would scribble thoughts in a notebook while sitting back and watching Elijah play.

* * *

THEN ONE DAY, some of Elijah's friends—several sea lions close to his age—got into a competition with each other, trying to swim under an arch of rocks under the ocean, not far from the island's shore. It was a common game among the children of the village. Angelica had played it during her own childhood. None of the village's children, however, had ever been a river otter before, and river otters can't hold their breath as long as sea lions. That's simply a biological fact. Their lungs aren't built for it.

But Elijah didn't know that. And the little river otter child could be terribly competitive.

Elijah could swim now, but he didn't practice very much. He preferred riding with Arlene on her watercycle, skimming along the surface of the water instead venturing underneath it. So, even though he made it down to the stone arch and halfway under it, Elijah got turned around in the depths. Suddenly, all the water looked the same, and the light from the sky was too diffused and dappled from being strained through the long, green ribbons of the neighboring kelp forest to help him find his way up. Elijah swam about in circles, lost and confused, until his little lungs gave out.

Elijah sank. River otters aren't meant to sink, but the young otter sank. None of the sea lion children noticed, because they'd moved on to a game of chase through the green snakes of kelp, far too busy to notice one of their flock had gone missing.

Elijah surely would have died if Arlene hadn't been watching the group of children play with half her attention. Even while working on her latest invention—a kind of mechanical arm for helping catch jellyfish—there was a sort of clock ticking down in her mind, keeping track of how long it had been since she'd last seen Elijah surface. And suddenly, Arlene dropped her work, feeling like it had been too long.

Arlene dived down, uncertain if she was panicking for no reason, being overly protective and foolish... then she saw her child floating far under the surface, limp and unmoving.

Arlene had never swum faster, nor felt like she was swimming slower, than as she powered her way through the water to save Elijah. The surface had never seemed farther away than when Arlene swept the drowning bundle of fur that was her child—*and needed to stay her child, needed to stay alive*—into her short arms and, clutching him tightly, turned to begin swimming back toward the surface.

With each stroke, the surface came closer, but it felt as far away as ever because even one stroke left was too far, if Elijah's little body gave up trying. Until Arlene's head burst through the surface and Elijah's body began shaking, convulsing, coughing up water, she didn't know... She didn't know if she'd still have a child, or if that was going to be the moment her life branched horribly, irrevocably down a path she didn't want to follow.

Both river otters were horribly shaken by the experience. Even though the uncertainty and terror had only lasted a few minutes, the effects of those minutes struck down to the cores of both of their hearts. Over the coming days, Arlene found they had both been altered, and not for the better.

Arlene already second-guessed her own parenting all the time and had to struggle to ignore the sidelong looks all the sea lions gave her for choosing to do strange things like ride around on a watercycle, but now those looks pierced right through the armor she'd built up against them. And Elijah—poor little soul—learned to be afraid of water. A terrible fear to have if you happen to be a river otter who lives beside the ocean with a bunch of sea lions.

For the next few weeks, Elijah kept his little webbed paws firmly on solid ground, no small feat given that he lived on an island and all his playmates were sea lions who did most of their playing in the water. Sure, Elijah would splash along the shoreline. He wasn't afraid of getting his paws wet, but he had no intention of letting his head go fully under the water ever again.

At first, no one noticed, even though Arlene and

Angelica watched their young ward closely. He was very good at making up excuses—"*Oh, we need that special seashell I found earlier to use as a magic treasure in our game—I'll just run and get it!*" or "*Nah, I want to pretend to be a sandworm and burrow through the sand. Don't you like the way it feels all funny and grainy against your fur?*" or even just a simple "*Race you to the other side of the island! And no, it's not cheating to run across the middle instead of swimming around—it's just clever!*"

Elijah was clever. In fact, he was so clever, he even managed to hide most of his fear of water from himself.

But Arlene loved that little river otter like she'd been given a chance to live two lives—one as herself and one as this wonderful little mirror of herself who made bizarre, wildly different choices from the ones she'd have ever made. And so, even if Elijah could hide his fear from himself, his friends, and even his doting sea lion mother, Arlene eventually saw through the facade.

* * *

"WHY DON'T WE GO SWIMMING?" Arlene asked Elijah one day, leaving no room for the child to avoid the concept.

Except river otter children are slippery, wily little things, so Elijah smiled brightly and said, "Love to! As soon as I'm done making this bead necklace for Aurora."

Aurora was one of the sea lion children, and she had genuinely been begging Elijah for one of his beaded necklaces.

"You can finish that later," Arlene suggested, but the little otter shook his whiskered head firmly.

"I've been promising it to her for AGES, and I can't put it off anymore."

Arlene looked at the length of stringed beads. It was barely started, just a few blue and green beads in an erratic pattern. Still, Elijah made necklaces faster than any of the other children, since he used the mechanical loom Arlene had designed for that purpose, and she didn't want to make him feel like she was pressuring him to swim. "I'll wait," Arlene said, settling down to watch with her full attention.

Arlene generally stayed fairly close to Elijah during the day, keeping one eye on him while keeping the other to her work. She would daydream inventions and tinker with blueprints while glancing up every now and then. But now, she kept her whole attention on Elijah. The two otters talked while the little one strung beads together using the loom. Elijah told his otter-mother all about an ongoing pretend game he'd been playing with some of the sea lion kids. All the while, he kept stringing on beads and then changing his mind about the colors he'd chosen, needing to unstring them—which invariably took twice as long as stringing them in the first place—and then redo the work from scratch with a different color of bead.

When the necklace was finally close to done, Elijah somehow managed to jam the loom, breaking it. Arlene had been watching closely, and she still missed exactly how it had been done. Of course, this meant the loom needed fixing before any swimming could possibly happen, as it was clearly an urgent disaster for one of Elijah's favorite toys to be broken.

Elijah strung Arlene along like this for several days—never actually saying 'no' to swimming, but always coming up with ways to avoid it that seemed so natural for an easily distractible child that his mother couldn't quite call the boy on it. If he'd still been a little younger, Arlene could have forced the matter more easily, but Elijah had grown into himself enough at this point that he had to be reasoned and reckoned with like a full person... even when he was being driven by a childish phobia no more mature than fearing the dark.

At night, after the young otter was curled up in his bed in his own small tent, Arlene and Angelica whispered together in their larger, neighboring tent, trying to work out how to handle him and his new fear. Angelica felt strongly that they shouldn't push the boy, and they shouldn't force him to admit to his fear, because that might just cement it further, making it become part of his identity instead of allowing it to dissipate naturally. She was convinced that if his fear were left alone, it would eventually melt away as easily as morning dew.

As a sea lion, Angelica didn't see how a child could possibly do anything but grow out of such a troubling phase. Sea lions and otters are both built for the water.

But Arlene knew that an otter has more choice in the matter. For a sea lion to become a creature of the land, they'd have to severely limit themselves or else build clever contraptions like the mechanical legs she had once built for Angelica. (The sea lion had soundly rejected them, completely uninterested in trading her ease in the ocean for a gimmicky life on land.) Whereas, a river otter could easily forgo the ocean and even rivers, simply becoming like an oddly stout ferret or weasel with a preference for seafood.

Arlene feared that Elijah's new phobia would lead to him growing up and moving far away, deep inland, away from any large source of water. It was a rational enough fear for an otter who had, herself, moved far away from the riverside colony where she'd been raised, choosing the wide ocean over a narrow river. She knew this situation was different, but she couldn't shake the fear.

Children grow up and make their own choices, and sometimes they leave. It's what they do. But Arlene wanted Elijah to grow up and find a life for himself somewhere nearby enough that they could stay close to each other. She never wanted to find herself picking between staying with her wife or following her child. She honestly wasn't sure which choice she would make, and that was a strange discovery for an otter who had already built her whole world around the sea lion caves in order to stay with Angelica.

Arlene was happy with the sea lions. She wanted Elijah to have a chance of being happy among them too. The ocean was too big a part of their lives for the young otter to turn his back upon it now. There was too much left for him to explore.

Even so, Arlene knew that pushing the child might only make the situation worse—and would certainly upset Angelica—so she needed to take a different approach. The carrot instead of the stick. Or perhaps, in this situation, the chewy, deep sea jellyfish.

Arlene would bribe and lure her child back into swimming. That was her plan.

But she would take it one step at a time. The first step was to get Elijah back into the water at all. And even that required patience. So much patience that, as the days stretched into weeks, Arlene started to doubt herself, and the words she'd brushed off, so easily when said in others' voices started to appear in her mind, spoken with her own internal voice. A voice she was accustomed to listening to and taking very seriously, because it was the voice that told her wonderful things like how to build a watercycle and power street lights and cold boxes with the energy from water wheels installed in the river.

But now the voice in her head betrayed her, and it started repeating the words of sea lions who had scornfully scolded, *"You shouldn't coddle that child with all those complicated contraptions."* She evolved their tired complaints, taking them further, all the way to accusations: *"The watercycle is why Elijah won't get in the water anymore. You spoiled him with machines as a toddler, and now he'll never grow into a proper swimmer, never really belong in the ocean."*

Arlene found no defense even when she tried to imagine the words of those who actually liked her inventions—even Florentine, her business associate and biggest proponent would most likely respond to her situation by asking, "Why do you care so much about keeping Elijah on that island anyway? There's plenty of world further inland." Arlene hadn't met any otters—or really anyone—who understood how she'd become a part of the sea lion village at all.

Arlene was an otter standing between two worlds, and her son was the only otter who stood there with her. She would have to figure this out on her own. So, she let the voices in her mind scream and complain and criticize, but she didn't let them change her. She didn't seek out help from people who she knew would just let her down. She relied on herself, put aside her inventions, and focused her entire attention on following Elijah around every day, waiting for the opportunities when she could gently cajole or lure him into the wavelets that lapped at the island's shore. It made Arlene feel mad, losing the part of herself that worked on inventions, but she knew it was only temporary. Only until she got Elijah past this rough patch.

Sometimes, Arlene wanted to sit her son down on his rudder tail and just yell at him, force him to admit that he was afraid of the water, and then demand he get over it. But that would just drive a wall between them. So, she waited, softly cajoling, gently pushing, until she could reliably convince Elijah to splash around in the shallows with her again, simply enjoying the floating feel of the water lifting him off his paws, or maybe even buoying him up as he floated on his back—but never, ever rising higher than he could escape in two shakes of his rudder tail—before even trying to proceed to the next step of her plan.

The next step was controversial. Even Angelica was skeptical, and she mostly went along with Arlene's plans. But sometimes, you have to make the right move for your child, even when no one else around you understands it. And Arlene was sure that she understood Elijah better than anyone else did. He was an otter surrounded by sea lions; she knew what that was like. She knew what it was like to be unusual—nearly unique even—until Elijah came along. And even now, she sometimes felt like no one would ever really understand her. Except maybe, someday, her son, if she parented him properly.

It's a strange thing—parenting while being observed. You see yourself reflected in the eyes of others, and you know how it looks, but you can't let it stop you from doing what's right, even when it's something that looks wrong.

And so, Arlene enacted the next step of her plan: she invited Elijah to come with her on a dive to gather deep sea jellyfish, far beneath the ocean's surface, way out beyond the kelp forest.

* * *

As soon as Arlene began to introduce the idea, Elijah immediately looked stricken, his rounded ears twisting backwards and his long, elegant, white whiskers flattening tightly against his face. But then, Arlene explained the twist:

"Of course," Arlene said, as casually as she could, "we will have to wear breathing masks, if we're to dive down that deep."

"B-b-breathing... masks?" Elijah asked, consternation wrinkling the fur of his brow between his bright eyes.

"It's one of my inventions," Arlene said. She knew that her son loved her inventions, and he would be intrigued.

"Do they... let you breathe the water?" Elijah's ears had twisted back forward now. He looked excited. She was offering him a rope that would let him climb out of the hole of his phobia, and even if he wouldn't admit to his crippling fear, he still recognized and desperately wanted a path away from it.

It doesn't feel good to be afraid.

"Not exactly," Arlene said. The little otter deflated at her words, but she rushed on. "But they do filter oxygen out of the water, so you can keep breathing air even while you're under the surface."

Now Elijah truly looked delighted. Arlene could see on his little face that he was imagining getting his webbed paws on a breathing mask and never taking it off, never having to fear the water again. This was exactly why the sea lions—who were already skeptical of Arlene's inventions—would have disapproved of her offering one of them to her son as a crutch. It was a very real risk that he would never want to give it up.

But the sea lions already disapproved.

And Elijah already wouldn't swim.

So, as much as Arlene felt the imaginary eyes of others judging her—and it caused her to judge herself too—she knew rationally that this step couldn't actually make things any worse. And it might provide a path for Elijah to finally heal.

Arlene dug her breathing masks out of the wooden chest in the back of their family tent where she'd been storing them. She hadn't used them for a while, but back when she'd first invented them, she'd had a marvelous time exploring the depths of the kelp forest with Angelica. This would be a very different kind of dive. Instead of a romantic adventure with her beloved, carefree and playful, it would be a stressful journey, constantly keeping an eye on Elijah, worrying about her young son. Because he wasn't the only one afraid of him swimming. For all that Arlene had been pushing Elijah back towards the water, she still vividly remembered the limp feel of his small body in her arms as she swam desperately towards the surface, unsure if she would make it in time.

But she couldn't show her fear.

Sometimes, it helps to share your fears with your children and show them adults can be frightened too. But sometimes... Sometimes there's only room for the child's feelings, and it's your job as the parent to become a pillar of strength they can lean upon. Strong and blank. Nothing but supportive. And this was going to be one of those moments for Arlene and Elijah.

The breathing masks were rubbery where they fit over

an otter's face, fitted into place with leather straps and buckles that let Arlene cinch them up tightly around their heads, and then on either side of the face was a silvery canister. Elijah was delighted with how funny his otter mother looked wearing one, and as soon as his was fitted snugly on his face, he scampered, quick as can be, to the nearest tidepool hoping to catch a glimpse of his own face. His giggles at the sight of himself wearing the silly-looking thing came out as funny, gasping hiccups from underneath rubbery the mask, and Arlene found she couldn't help but laugh too.

All suited-up, the only thing left to do was for Arlene to arm herself with a special net she'd designed for safely catching jellyfish. It looked a lot like a butterfly net. In fact, it probably would have worked perfectly well on butterflies too, but otters are a lot less interested in eating those. She strapped the long handle of the net onto an empty backpack she was wearing, ready to be filled with the delicious flesh of shimmery, translucent jellyfish before the day was done.

When Arlene and her son stepped into the lapping waves at the edge of the island, she was surprised to see Elijah rush past her, straight into the water. After weeks of avoiding the water, the little otter dove straight in, obviously eager to swim again. His fear had been holding him back, but he was an otter. He still loved the feel of the water all around him, buoying him up, tossing him about, and freeing him to do what comes most naturally to otters —*swim*.

Arlene's heart swelled at the sight. She knew his love of swimming was still somewhere in there. All she had to do was give Elijah a chance to feel safe again, and he'd find his way back to how he was supposed to be. She followed him into the watery world of the ocean's edge.

* * *

THE TWO RIVER OTTERS—MOTHER and son—swam past the rocky protrusions around the island and into the surrounding kelp forest. Arlene wished she could see Elijah's face better behind his mask, because everything in his posture spoke of delight. She would have enjoyed seeing his smile, but alas, it was hidden.

Elijah swam jerkily with inefficient movements, more excited than skilled, as he wove his way between strands of kelp. But skill would come with practice. And furthermore, the skills he did have were rusty and mostly honed for swimming near the surface, not navigating the depths.

As the long green strands of kelp rose above them like knotted up tangles of ribbons, Elijah realized for the first time: this was the deepest he'd ever swum, and for a moment, panic shivered down his spine. But Arlene was keeping a close eye on her ward. The last thing she wanted was for this adventure to make Elijah's fears worse, so she was staying very close beside him and caught hold of his small webbed paw at the first sign of his impending panic.

With gestures, Arlene indicated for Elijah to grab onto

the straps of her backpack and ride along on her back. That way, the two otters were able to travel much faster through the kelp forest toward the deep crevasse where Arlene intended for them to do their hunting.

Arlene swam deeper and deeper, until everything around them was greenish-blue, dark and murky. The sun was too far away, buried beneath a thick layer of ocean, to help much here. Arlene still instinctively felt which direction led up and which way was down, but she wasn't sure she could have explained how, given the diffuse, dim light and the way that the water pressed inward from all around. It would be very easy to get lost in the crevasse. But then, soft circles of light began to speckle the water in the distance.

Moon jellyfish.

Each jellyfish sported the outlines of four circles in the middle of its translucent bell that made Arlene think of the shape of four leaf clovers. *Lucky.* It was time to catch some of that luck.

Arlene pulled the net off of her backpack, and as she did so, Elijah let go of his grip on the backpacks straps. The young otter floated where he was while his mother twisted around and then held the net out to him. They held it together, and she helped him swoop it through the water, easily catching two moon jellies on their very first try.

Jellyfish aren't exactly difficult prey. They don't run away. They don't seem to know they're in danger at all. The one trick is that you want to avoid getting stung by their ribbon-like arms, so Arlene used a pair of tongs that she had stored in the backpack to safely pull the two moon jellies out of the net and stuff them in the backpack instead.

Once the net was empty, she handed it to Elijah to operate on his own, and then she followed him around, emptying the net whenever he caught a jellyfish or several. She couldn't see the expression on her son's muzzle, hidden beneath the mask, but his eyes sparkled with sheer delight. He was having the time of his life. And even better, he'd return home a hero.

Everyone in the village loved a good jellyfish feast, but mostly, they were a rare treat for brave, stubborn individuals who ventured into the crevasse just long enough to catch one or two for themself before needing to return to the surface for air. If more of the sea lions were willing to use Arlene's breathing masks, that situation would change. But for now, a backpack crammed full with enough jellyfish to feed the whole village was going to get Elijah a lot of positive attention from all his friends.

Most of the jellyfish they caught were moon jellies, but they also found a patch of beautiful, orange sea nettles with long, trailing arms like ruffles. They even ran into a gigantic, gorgeous lion's mane jellyfish that could probably have eaten them, if they'd been foolish enough to get themselves tangled up in its stinging tentacles. But in spite of Elijah's enthusiastic interest in the giant pulsing blob with all its trailing strings and strands, Arlene insisted they keep a wide berth from that one.

By the time the backpack was stuffed so full of jellyfish that Arlene couldn't possibly cram another one in, Elijah was swimming about much more smoothly, twisting and corkscrewing in the water like he'd never taken a months-long break from swimming at all. But the backpack was full, and filled as it was with jellies, it was heavy. The jellyfish looked lighter than air as they floated through the water, but balled up into a backpack, the weight of their rubbery flesh added up. So, Arlene put the backpack on again, affixed the net to it, and gestured for Elijah to start swimming skyward.

Anytime the young otter looked confused about which direction to take, he looked back at Arlene, and she pointed where she wanted him to go. Out of the crevasse, through the kelp forest. It wasn't the most efficient way to travel, but there was absolutely no way that Arlene was leaving her son behind her, trusting him to follow her, as she swam on blithely ahead.

Elijah might look like his fears had been cured—at least so long as he was wearing a breathing mask—but Arlene was still deeply afraid of losing him to the water. She'd never been afraid of water before Elijah almost drowned. It was a strange thing to be afraid of something so prevalent, so all-surrounding. She'd always seen the water as a safe place, as long as she could remember, until it threatened to take her child away. Now... She wouldn't turn her back on it.

Arlene wondered how long her own fears would outlive Elijah's. Maybe that's just part of being a parent, she thought. Carrying your children's fears for them, so they don't have to. If you're older and stronger, you can take the weights off their backs that would crush them, and it'll only hold you back a little.

A little isn't too much, is it?

* * *

Arlene and Elijah emerged on from the ocean and walked straight to the central bonfires where sea lions were always cooking something. Giant cauldrons bubbled with fishy stew, and strings of fish hung above the fires, cooking in the heat and curing in the smoke.

Arlene handed the heavy backpack to her son, and Elijah's narrow river otter chest puffed up with pride as he poured the gelatinous, rubbery, translucent contents out on a cooking mat. The jellyfish tumbled and sprawled over each other, tentacles tangling and bells squishing. Utterly delectable. Begging to be eaten.

Sea lions pulled their way closer, gathering around, until the otter boy was surrounded by cheering and clapping. He hadn't just overcome his fear and swum deeper than he'd ever swum before, he'd returned to praise and applause for it.

Tired but satisfied, Arlene sat nearby and watched, while warming herself in the glow of the fire. The sky above darkened and stars came out, twinkling across the distance of space like deep sea jellyfish luminescing in the deep. Far and bright. Tantalizing.

Arlene didn't take part in cooking the jellyfish. She'd done her work for the day. But she watched Angelica teach Elijah and some of the sea lion children how to prepare the glass-clear flesh in a variety of ways. Coated in spices and grilled; stewed along with other fish in a savory soup; and some of it was simply snacked upon—raw and slippery, chewy and salty-sweet in its freshness—while the rest of it was more laboriously prepared.

Arlene didn't know how many trips to the jellyfish crevasse it might take before Elijah would lose his fear of the water entirely, but she knew they were on the right track. He would grow up braver for learning to face his fears, even if she'd had to trick him into coming at it sideways. Fears aren't always best faced straight on. But he would overcome this one. Arlene was sure of it.

As she watched her son's face, she basked in the reflected glow of his own pride in his accomplishment. She didn't always know who she was anymore. Raising Elijah had become such a big, unexpected part of her life. Sometimes, it felt like he'd entirely eclipsed the person she'd been before he came along. The person she would have been without him—an otter inventor, completely focused on her work.

But even eclipses pass, and when they do, the world is a little more magical because they happened. Arlene wasn't glad that Elijah had almost drowned, but she was glad of the way that helping him overcome it had brought them even closer together, forcing her to put aside her work and focus completely on him.

"Can we go hunting for jellyfish again tomorrow?" Elijah asked eagerly as Arlene tucked him into his bed of blankets and pillows in his tent that night.

"Not tomorrow," Arlene answered, still tired from the long day and all the long days before it. "We still have jellyfish stew and steaks enough to last for several meals."

"But when we run out?" Elijah pressed.

"Yes," Arlene agreed, realizing that in spite of her tiredness, she was already looking forward to it. "When we run out, we can go hunting together again."

12
ONE SHEEP

THERE WAS ONCE a sheep that could have been a sheep with fifteen other sheep, all living on a farm. But, one day, a man came and invited that sheep to live at the petting zoo with the pygmy goats, pigs, rabbits, and Shetland ponies there. So, that one sheep joined the petting zoo.

Then, there were fifteen sheep left.

But, one day, a woman came from the circus. She needed one sheep to jump through hoops, one sheep to balance on a giant ball, and one sheep to fly on the trapeze for her circus act. So, three sheep—who could have been three sheep with twelve other sheep—ran away to join the circus.

Then, there were twelve sheep left.

But two of the sheep were restless. They'd heard about the sun and sand in California, and they wanted to learn to surf. So, instead of being two sheep with ten other sheep, they caught the next train to the coast. They bought surfboards and lived on the beach.

Then, there were ten sheep left.

Until the ten sheep got a letter from their two beach bum friends. Apparently, there was a used submarine for sale on their beach, and it was a real bargain. To successfully run a submarine, you need a captain, a pilot, a navigator, and a galley chef. So, four of the sheep pooled all their money together and went to buy the submarine. Now they were four sheep in a submarine, instead of four sheep with six other sheep on a farm.

Then, there were six sheep left.

Only, four of those sheep had some real talent. One of them played the drums and another played guitar. A third played the keyboards and sang. The last played flugelhorn. When they jammed together, the music they made was absolutely smokin'. So, they decided to leave the farm and go on tour as a rock'n'roll band. Besides, on the farm, they were just four sheep with two other sheep. On tour, they were four sheep with millions of screaming fans.

So, then, there were two sheep left.

"We'd better stick together," the one sheep said to the other, but, as she said it, a big, shiny, flashy object came flying down from the sky.

"Maybe it's our four friends in their submarine," the other sheep said.

But it was not a submarine; it was a spaceship. And when it landed, an alien came out and invited the second to last sheep to join the other aliens in their spaceship, exploring other planets and star systems in space. What sheep could refuse? So, instead of being one sheep with one other sheep on a farm, the second to last sheep became the first sheep into space.

Then, there was one sheep left.

Only one sheep. And, that sheep got what she had wanted all along. She stayed and ran the farm.

13

SARAH FLOWERMANE AND THE UNICORN

The lion cub hid among the rushes and narcissus flowers at the edge of the lake and watched her father, King of the Jungle, meet and talk with the shining white unicorn who presided over the deep dark woods adjacent to the lions' sunny savannah home.

Sarah thought the unicorn's forest looked more like a jungle than their savannah did, and she wanted to tell the unicorn that... but she'd promised her father to hide quietly during his meeting. He only brought one cub with him at a time to these meetings, and given her plethora of sisters, brothers, half-siblings, and cousins, Sarah's turn to accompany her father didn't turn up very often. She wanted to prove she could be a good little cub, so she stayed quiet as a mouse.

Sarah batted her paw at the lake water and watched ripples spread across the reflective surface, twisting and warping the image of her face. She imagined herself with a twisting pearlescent horn rising out of her forehead like the unicorn's, and the thought made her smile. She wanted to tell the unicorn about that too... but again, she kept it to herself.

Sarah had a lot of practice keeping her thoughts to herself. Again, with so many siblings and other cubs her age, it was easy to get lost in the chaos. Someone was always begging to play a different game or arguing for a larger share of dinner or pleading for more stories at twilight while the adults were trying to convince the cubs to all drift off to sleep. Sarah didn't feel like fighting to be heard.

What Sarah did like doing was fixing the stories her mothers and aunts told in her head while she listened to them—she'd add extra details, subplots, bits of intrigue, side characters and backstories. She'd embroider and weave her own ideas into the stories her mother and aunts told until the stories were hardly the same anymore. More her own than the original storyteller's.

Sarah wondered if the unicorn liked stories. She looked up from the ripples in the lake and, for a while, watched the ripples in the unicorn's mane instead. Silver and white, pale and glowing, like the moon when it's full or the snowfall that only ever happened when the traveling fairies came past the lions' village and cast magic spells to delight everyone.

When her father was done with his meeting, the unicorn disappeared into her deep dark forest like mist melting in the morning. Sarah sighed at the sight of such beauty disappearing from her sight.

"You look lovestruck, little one," King Edmund pronounced. He never just said something. In his voice, even a simple observation sounded like a pronouncement.

Sarah turned shy and shrugged.

"The unicorn is very beautiful, isn't she?" King Edmund asked.

Sarah nodded. Then—trying to be very brave, because she knew her father was brave, and she wanted to be like him—she said, "I'd like to speak to her too sometime."

King Edmund laughed fondly and said, "Maybe someday."

Feeling very brave now that her father had encouraged her, Sarah hazarded, "Maybe I could even tell her one of my stories."

King Edmund laughed again, less fondly and more like he actually thought his daughter was very funny. "You're not as special as you think you are, little one." He laughed again, as if he were sharing a good joke with himself. Then he shook his head, making his golden mane ripple, and said to himself, "Telling tales to unicorns." He said it with wonder... but not the kind of wonder Sarah would have liked to inspire. Not awe at her inventiveness and ambition and bravery... more bemusement at her foolhardiness.

Sarah felt like a fool. And she followed her father back to their village with her tufted tail hung low. Her father's words echoed in Sarah's head for many days after that. She struggled with shame and embarrassment at first, figuring she must have done something very wrong in order to make him say something so cruel. But when she tentatively told the story of her father's words to a frog who she liked to hang out with at the local watering hole, the frog's reaction of horror told her that it couldn't have been her fault. Those were simply words a father should have no reason to say to his daughter.

Sarah decided she would prove herself. She would show King Edmund exactly how special she was. She just needed to figure out a way to do that.

Sarah knew she was special, because her mind sparkled with stories and ideas that were much more interesting than the plain savannah around her. She stared at waving gold grasses, and she saw more than just the grasses—she imagined the rise and fall of entire dynasties among the tiny ants crawling among the grasses' roots. She imagined the blue sky above was another plain of waving grasses where blue lion cubs gamboled and played in an upside-down world. She imagined the golden grass was secretly the fur of a giant lioness curled up beneath their paws—a lioness so large that she was the entire world, and all the smaller lions like Sarah and her family merely lived upon her back.

No one else in her village told stories like those. So, Sarah, determined to prove herself to her father, started telling them herself. Instead of keeping her stories inside, she waited until the other cubs were busy gnawing on their dinners, mouths too full for them to interrupt, and then she began whispering the words of her tales. The other cubs' eyes turned to her, and even as their mouths emptied, all the food resting in their bellies now, they stayed quiet, raptly listening to her whispered tales.

As the days passed, Sarah's confidence grew, and she began telling the stories louder and more often. The other cubs stopped bickering and bantering when they heard her start to speak and settled down to listen.

After less than a week, she was the most beloved story teller in the village, much preferred to her mother and aunts. Her mother and aunts were proud.

Then finally, one day, King Edmund walked by while she had all the other cubs circled around her, listening raptly. She puffed out her chest, sat very tall, and made sure to add extra sparkly details to the tale she was telling of a frog warrior seeking treasure in the hidden caverns behind a waterfall.

King Edmund stayed and listened. When the story was through, he looked at Sarah fondly and said, "You'll make a good aunt and mother someday."

"My stories aren't for putting cubs to sleep!" Sarah roared in her tiny cub's voice.

"What do you think they're for?" King Edmund asked around his laughter. "Telling to unicorns?"

It wasn't really a question. Just an indictment. And Sarah's ears flattened in fury.

She would tell her stories to the unicorn one day. She was sure of it. Her father would see. She would do it in spite of him. She'd do it specifically to spite him.

King Edmund's cruel and dismissive words chased

themselves in circles through Sarah's head for the following weeks. She stopped telling stories to the other cubs and was dismayed to find they hardly seemed to notice, let alone care. None of them pleaded with her to tell them what happened to the frog warrior next. None of them begged her to make up new stories. They just went back to their games and squabbling, as if she'd never told them stories at all.

Sarah was stunned. It felt a little like she didn't even exist, because the parts of herself that she valued the most seemed to be invisible... or at least irrelevant to everyone around her. She wanted to make them visible. Telling stories hadn't done that, so maybe she needed to do it in a more material, visceral, physical, literally visible kind of way.

Her brothers, half-brothers, and male cousins of about her age had begun growing longer fur on their heads and chests. Their manes were coming in, making them look more like miniature versions of King Edmund than Sarah ever would.

Sarah didn't want to be a male lion, but she did feel the curdling of envy in her breast when the male lions of her age cohort acted boastful and bragging about their new manes.

Sarah decided she would outdo them. She would make herself a mane. A better mane. Since she couldn't grow longer fur by simply wishing (and why would she want to? what was so great about some extra fur anyway?) she came up with a plan. The first step involved consulting the fairies the next time they came through the lions' village.

The last troupe of fairies to fly through the village had been black-and-orange monarchs, flying by day, as bright and cheerful as summer sun filtered through the trees. But they wouldn't return for a long while. The next troupe to fly through the region came at night—they had long-tailed green wings, pale and edged in gentle pink. Sarah had to sneak out of the village after the other cubs were asleep to meet with the Luna moth fairies without the watchful eyes and interference of her aunts and mother in the way.

The traveling fairies had settled on flower heads and curved blades of grass beside the edge of the pond. The frog choir was singing for them. Sarah settled quietly on a bare patch of dirt beside the lake, careful not to disturb any of the fairies or the singing frogs.

When the concert was done, Sarah's friend—the frog who had reacted with horror to the story of King Edmund's cruelty—hopped his way over to her.

"What brings the gentlest princess of the savannah to our carnival of the night?" the frog, whose name was Jiggy, asked her. She was the only lion cub who could have crept up on the frog choir and Luna moth audience without causing the smaller creatures to scatter out of fear. Most of the other lion cubs would have rushed and pounced and caused trouble. But all the small creatures of the lake knew Sarah. They knew she was different. She could be trusted.

"I want to ask a favor of the fairies," Sarah said,

keeping her voice as low and soft as a lion could. "I need their help."

One of the Luna moths fluttered off of the flower where she'd been perched, flapped and floated her way closer, and landed on the ground beside Sarah.

"What kind of help—" the Luna moth sang, for fairies always sing, it's simply how their voices sound, "—does such a powerful young lioness think we humble fairies of the night can provide?"

"I want to grow a mane," Sarah stated simply. "A mane of flowers. I know you have magic. Can you help me?"

The Luna moth smoothed her feathery antenna with her front-most talons while her middle pair of arms crossed across her fuzzy white breast. Her green wings flapped slowly, ponderously. "We do not truly have magic," she said eventually, her proboscis singing the words with the clarity and bell-like resonance of a flute. "But for you, I think I can help with this plan."

Sarah was skeptical about the idea that the fairies didn't have magic—she'd told enough stories about them granting wishes and casting spells with their tiny, minuscule hands that she'd started to believe them herself. But she wasn't about to argue with a fairy who sounded willing to grant her wish. So, she simply lowered her head, keeping her eyes respectfully on the ground right in front of the beautiful fairy, and said, "I would be ever so grateful for your help."

The fairy flapped her wings and took flight. She floated like a dream over the bent savannah grasses, and other Luna moths joined her, drifting together like a constellation of stars moving across the sky as the seasons passed.

Sarah watched them, deeply impatient inside herself, but showing only the most stolid patience on the outside.

The group of moths flew across the lake, fluttered on the far side for a while in the darkness where Sarah could barely make them out, and then returned, carrying a broken piece of foliage stretched between them. It was a small yellow flower with a dangling piece of stem that straggled out into a bit of torn up root. It had no leaves. It wasn't a fancy flower—a very simple, common dandelion.

The group of fairies flew up to the lion cub who had entreated them to grant her wish and hovered in front of her. One of them spoke—Sarah suspected it was the same fairy who had spoken to her before, but she couldn't tell for sure—and said, "Do you see the ladybug among us?"

Sarah's eyes narrowed, trying to make out what she was expected to see—at first she saw nothing, but then, yes, hovering just beside the golden petals of the dandelion was a tiny, red ladybug with its shell split so its tiny, black, lacy wings underneath could flap furiously enough to keep the small beetle aloft.

"I do," Sarah said.

"This is Ruby," the fairy said. As the fairy spoke, the ladybug bobbed in the air, as if making a tiny bow before the daughter of the king. "She is a gardener, and she has agreed to help us fulfill your request, in exchange for safe harbor."

"Safe harbor?" Sarah asked uncertainly. That sounded like what her father had refused to grant to an antelope prince who had come begging for help after a period of political unrest amongst his own people. He'd made a delicious meal for the village. King Edmund had said the antelope prince had requested asylum though, not safe harbor. And he'd said it was a fool's errand to seek it—if you're too weak to defend yourself, then you're better off hiding than advertising it to neighboring kingdoms.

King Edmund could be harsh to more than his own daughter, Sarah realized. She didn't want to be like him. Not at all.

But she still wanted a mane—a mane entirely different from his. A mane built upon the principle of offering safe harbor.

"I don't know entirely what that means," Sarah said, because she was a very honest and direct young lion cub. "But I hope I can offer it."

"All it means," the fairy said, "is that you will let Ruby live among the flowers that she helps to grow on your head. Perhaps, as the garden of your mane grows, you will even allow her to bring friends and family to live among the flowers too. If your mane grows full and glorious, there should be plenty of room."

Sarah's breast puffed up in anticipatory pride at the idea of a full and glorious mane of flowers. "I would like that very much," she said.

And so the fairies took the dandelion carried between them and tucked its root up behind Sarah's left ear, where they used pitch to stick it to her fur. The stem was short, and the flower dangled beneath her pointed ear like a fancy golden earring. Sarah admired her reflection in the water, and if she'd been a human girl who'd read *The Last Unicorn*, she would have thought about Mommy Fortuna's need to put a false horn on a real unicorn so that people could see past their own preconceptions.

But she was only a lion, and she delighted in the fanciness of the first flower that would soon become a full mane.

It took a few months, but flower by flower, the growing colony of ladybugs who lived on Sarah's head grew her mane into a garden. Green moss with little white star-like flowers filled the space between the larger dandelions and daisy blooms. The dandelions were gold, matching Sarah's fur, but the daisies grew in shades of pink from the palest blush to the most electric sunrise. The colorful bouquet of flowers grew all around and between Sarah's rounded ears and all the way down to under her chin. Sometimes, when the wind rustled through her new foliage, the blossoms tickled her, but mostly, the green moss holding it all together felt like a warm, comforting hood.

Sarah's single flower earring grew into a full mane more slowly than she would have liked, but the upside was that it gave her mother, aunts, and fellow cubs time to get used to it. Sure, the other cubs might mock a single dangling dandelion, but it was a mere eccentricity —nothing to worry about. By the time the ladybugs' garden had grown into a full mane, the other cubs had worn out their mockery and the adults had accepted that this was simply Sarah now. She had a flower mane. Sure, it was weird, but that was just Sarah. The weird one.

Sarah didn't see herself as the weird one, though. She was still, in her own eyes, the storyteller. And now, she had an entirely new audience for her stories—the ladybugs who made their home among the flowers growing on her head. Ruby and her kin would perch in front of Sarah's ears where their tiny voices could be heard as they exclaimed in excitement and delight at the stories Sarah made up for them.

Sarah didn't share her stories with the other cubs any more. They hadn't really appreciated them. The ladybugs did. Ruby claimed that she was even transcribing some of the best ones on tiny blades of grass that she kept tucked under the moss beside Sarah's left ear. Sarah had no way to verify that—she could only see the little ladybugs when they flew away from her mane or she watched herself reflected in the lake. And either way, Ruby's writing on the tiny pages made of grass blades would have been far too small for a lion to read. Even a cub with a cub's sharp eyes.

Sarah had always believed her stories were good, because she enjoyed them. It still felt good and affirming that her colony of ladybugs loved them too. It had been lonely being the only person who cared about the imaginary characters who danced through her head—like the frog warrior who was more than a little based on her friend Jiggy.

Jiggy was a brave, bold frog, and in a different world, Sarah could absolutely imagine him donning armor made from the shed shells of nuts and brandishing a sword of sharpened obsidian while fighting his way across the savannah. Instead, he hung out beside the lake, refusing to be frightened by Sarah's rowdy and boisterous kin, always listening to her stories whenever he could, and encouraging her to be brave.

At Jiggy's behest, Sarah finally got up the courage to follow her father, King Edmund, to the edge of the forest, even though he had not invited her to come.

Sarah didn't hide from her father, but neither did she turn back when he asked her to. King Edmund's broad, golden face scrunched sideways when she defied him, but he didn't swat her with his giant paw or roar at her with his booming voice. He simply sighed deeply at his eccentric child and continued on. So she kept following.

Sarah had heard King Edmund argue with her mother late one night over her new mane, and so she knew he didn't like it. But Sarah liked it. And in the end, for better and worse, she wasn't important enough to her father for him to really put his paw down about the issue. Her mother, who wanted her to be happy, had won the fight, and King Edmund had hardly looked at Sarah since then.

Perhaps that would change when she impressed the unicorn. Perhaps then her father would be impressed and understand she was, indeed, special.

When they arrived at the lake by the edge of the forest where King Edmund regularly met with the unicorn, Sarah settled down among the rushes and narcissus flowers beside the water, like she'd done before. After checking that she planned to stay where she was a while, the ladybugs in her mane sent out scouts to see if there were any good flowers to pull up and bring back to plant in their garden. Sarah, meanwhile, struck up a conversation with the local frogs who were excited to hear about the choir Jiggy sang with back at the savannah watering hole. These frogs didn't have a choir, but they did have a few barbershop quartets who wore adorable little hats woven from the rushes and a trio known for covering the songs of the most skilled and sought-after nightingale singer in the woods. They called themselves Frogs-in-the-Dale and promised to give Sarah a private concert the next time she came back to visit.

Sarah became so absorbed talking to the frogs and listening to her ladybugs' periodic reports on the possible flowers they could bring her that she completely missed the end of her father's meeting with the unicorn.

"It's time to go home, silly little one," King Edmund said, looking down at his daughter with an expression that seemed to be composed of equal parts fondness and disgust. It made Sarah feel both loved... and completely invisible at the same time.

"What?!" she cried. "Is the unicorn gone?"

"Trotted back into her forest, just like a good girl," King Edmund said. "Just like it's time for you to trot home with me and your brother." King Edmund had brought one of Sarah's younger half-brothers along. The brother sneered at her, clearly unimpressed that she'd intruded on his special time with their father.

Sarah glared back at both of them. She wasn't ready to leave, and neither were her ladybugs. Ruby had settled on a clover plant to add to the garden-mane—one with a tawny, off-white blossom and the rare, precious trait of four leaves—which she was still busy fetching, along with a whole passel of her relatives. Sarah couldn't possibly abandon them.

"I'm staying," Sarah said defiantly.

King Edmund narrowed his eyes, and his paw twitched. It took everything Sarah had in her to keep flinching. And then she realized, if her father did swat her with his giant paw, he wouldn't just hurt her—he might tear apart her ladybugs' village. As soon as that thought entered her mind, she didn't just flinch, she full-on cowered.

King Edmund stepped back, seemingly startled by the idea that a child of his would actually cower at the sight of his twitching paw. He sighed in definite disgust. "Fine, stay," he said. "You know the way home. I didn't bring you here; I won't be responsible for you getting home."

Sarah's father hadn't touched her with his paw, but his words felt like a slap. She stood by the edge of the lake, too surprised and shocked by his disdain for her to do anything but watch him leave, her brother prancing along proudly beside him.

For a moment, she was scared, but then, one of the frogs in her little rush-woven hat croaked, "You wanted to meet with Glory?"

"Is that... the unicorn?" Sarah asked, struggling to form words as she continued to stare dejectedly in the direction her father and brother had gone. King Edmund had never told her the unicorn's name.

"Yes, that's her," the frog answered. "Would you like us to bring her back?"

"What?" Sarah turned to look down at the frog quizzically. "You can bring her back?"

The frog shrugged and croaked again: "Sure, no problem." She hopped away toward some of the other frogs, and Sarah could practically watch the news travel from one frog to the next across the lake until it reached a pair of nesting quail among a stand of cattails. The quails conferred, and then one flew off toward the forest.

Sarah waited patiently, and while she did, her ladybugs returned carrying their chosen clover between them. It was a small flower, but very large to them. Sarah loved the ladybugs very much for caring enough about her mane—their home—to bring a talisman of good luck back to become a part of it.

Sarah held very still while the ladybugs worked to weave the clover's bits of root under the moss, tucking it up behind her right ear. She was still holding still when Glory arrived.

The unicorn shone like moonlight; her silvery mane rippled like a zephyr playing across water. She was too glorious for Sarah to look at her without staring, so the abashed lion cub lowered her eyes to be polite.

"I hear you wanted to visit with me," Glory said. She didn't sing like the fairies—her voice was more like your mother telling you <u>not to worry, everything will be okay</u>, just as you drift off to sleep and can no longer tell the difference between reality and a dream.

"Yes, m'lady," Sarah said. "I wanted to show you my mane and tell you some of my stories."

The unicorn was silent for a long enough time that Sarah couldn't keep herself from raising her eyes and looking at her again. When she did, Sarah saw the unicorn had tilted her head, seemingly waiting for the lion cub to look at her.

When their eyes met, Glory smiled, a gentle twist of her long, narrow muzzle. "There are your eyes," she said.

Sarah smiled too. "I'm sorry, I was afraid you wouldn't want to see me... my father said..." She couldn't repeat what her father had said about her not being special. Not again. She couldn't hear those words anymore, even said by herself.

"Your father..." Glory began, but she cut herself off with a sigh. "He is not known for his kindness. But you are, aren't you?"

"What do you mean?" Sarah asked, intrigued and perplexed. The unicorn knew of her?

"I've heard your name in the buzzing of dragonflies, the songs of birds, and the croaking of frogs for many months now. 'Sarah Flowermane,' they call you, and they all hope you'll one day rule over the savannah. You're beloved, little lioness, because you're kind."

Sarah hardly knew what to say. Her emotions welled up inside her, too big and confusing to even feel them. But in a good way. They were good feelings, and she almost didn't know what to do with that, not after the long months of feeling ignored and misunderstood, surrounded by lions who looked like her but didn't seem to be anything like her on the inside.

The ladybugs in her ear cheered and told her the unicorn was right. She was *their* Sarah Flowermane, and they were dearly proud of her.

Sarah had thought she needed her father's approval. She had craved it. But now... that craving melted away.

"You look overcome, little one," Glory said, using Sarah's father's pet name for her without realizing it. The name sounded so much better—so much kinder—coming from the unicorn. She didn't mean it to be demeaning; she wasn't trying to put Sarah in her place. She was simply speaking the truth—Sarah was still little. Still a cub. But she was growing, alongside her glorious mane of flowers, and some day, maybe she would rule over the savannah. If she did, she would do it with kindness for everyone, no matter how small or different. Because when it came down to it, it wasn't Sarah's stories or flower mane that made her special—although they did make her different. What made Sarah special was the way that she was kind to everyone, and that's a way that everyone can be special if they choose.

The unicorn settled down on the ground beside Sarah, beside the lake, and said, "You wanted to tell me a story? Is that right? Perhaps, you could start with the story of your mane. I think I would like to hear that one."

Over the coming months, Sarah would visit with Glory many times and tell her many stories, just like she'd dreamed. But right then, right now, she started with this one.

14

AN OTTER'S SOUL

Quiley didn't feel like anything was wrong. She put one paw in front of the other; she kept moving. She kept playing and splashing in the river like an otter is supposed to. But everyone kept saying how sorry they were. How hard it must be. It was almost like they thought they knew something about her and Pia that she hadn't known herself.

Sure, she and Pia had both liked to sunbathe on the same wide rock overlooking the nearby rapids, and they'd gone foraging for blackberries together every summer since they'd both been kits. So what? They each had more of a sweet tooth than most of the rest of the Roaring Blue Bevy. Or they had. Now it was just Quiley who loved blackberries to distraction.

Well, more for her.

She didn't mean that. She knew it was sad—heart-breaking even—that Pia had died so young. And so unnecessarily. The worst part was that the Elders Council hadn't learned their lesson. They hadn't learned any lesson at all, and the dangerous water slide made from felled trees stolen from a beaver family, precariously balanced on a series of boulders as big as grizzly bears, was still under construction.

That beaver family had ties to the mountain lion clan, ever since the unlikely marriage between the beaver prince and the mountain lioness princess. They'd be coming for those felled trees. And they'd be coming with lion claws, not only beaver teeth.

When Quiley thought about it, she felt bleak, like everything was pointless. But surely, every reasonable otter felt that way? Surely, the Elder Council had to come to their senses? Or finally be voted out?

But it hadn't happened yet...

And if Pia's death, crushed under one of the boulders wasn't enough...

Quiley put one paw in front of the other and walked herself away from the riverside, past tree after tree, through the thick underbrush of ferns and blackberry bracken, ignoring the ripe berries as much as she could. She didn't want to admit that every time she saw a perfect one, she automatically looked over her shoulder to call back to Pia and brag about snatching it before her friend could.

But Pia wasn't there, and somehow she'd already forgotten. It was like her mind couldn't understand the idea that she had no friend to brag to about stealing the best blackberries.

Okay, so, they'd been friends. Sure. All the otters in the bevy were friends. Otters are friendly, okay? That didn't mean anything. It didn't mean that losing her was a big deal. Otters die. Everything dies.

Well, except dragonflies, if the legends were to be believed. But who believed those? Only kits and fools, like the Elder Council.

One paw in front of the other, feeling nothing but the soft loam under her paws, the leaves brushing against the fur of her back, and the light breeze in her whiskers promising September would soon be here, she kept walking.

If Pia had to die, why did it have to be right during the height of blackberry season? It was the injustice that bothered her more than anything else.

And really, most of all, she was mad at Pia for being so careless. For dying and leaving her to deal with all these other otters, who didn't know her or understand her like Pia had, trying to console her over something that didn't even make her sad. She wasn't sad.

She wasn't.

But All Encompassing Ocean, it was petty to blame Pia for her own death. Deep in her own heart, Quiley couldn't deny to herself that she was mad at Pia for dying... but it made her feel small that she felt that way. Shouldn't she be bigger than that? Shouldn't the world have been better than to be a place without Pia? How could Pia have lasted for such a short time? She was supposed to live much longer, as long Quiley needed her as a berry picking partner at least. And then, maybe, a few extra seasons after that for good measure.

One paw in front of the other, Quiley's webbed paws led her to the stagnant waters of the Emerald Swamp. Cattails bowed in the breeze, and dragonflies hovered eerily over the troublingly still water.

Water is meant to move, like otters.

Swamps are where water goes to die.

And dragonflies are the souls of the dead.

That's what kits and fools believed.

But somehow, Quiley's paws had led her here, to the dragonflies, looking for Pia. Because she couldn't understand a world without her.

Far away from the other otters who had kept trying to comfort Quiley against her will, finally, tears streamed down the thick fur of her face, catching in her whiskers. She tried blinking them away with her inner eyelids, but the tears kept coming, blurring the already blurry view of the muddy, buzzy, horrid swamp.

But the dragonflies were pretty. The sunlight glinted off of their gossamer wings and jewel-cut eyes. Their long, thin carapaces were as brightly hued as shards of sapphire and polished turquoise. Quiley could almost believe they were souls incarnate, buzzing over the swamp grasses, whiling away their purgatory on this world before ascending to a realm of nothing but waterfalls that fell in loop-de-loops and somersaulting streams.

An afterlife of water slides, where an otter could slide from one stream to the next, never stopping, never losing that rush, never holding still.

And stagnant.

Like this swamp.

Oh, Ocean All Encompassing, how could Pia's soul be stuck here? She would hate it here. She'd smell the blackberry scent on the wind and insist on running and tumbling away from here, through the underbrush, ferns brushing her tawny fur, and a wide grin emblazoned across her cheerful face.

Her cheerful face.

Quiley would never see that grin again.

How had the others known how much Quiley depended on Pia when she hadn't realized it for herself until her friend was already gone?

One of the dragonflies floated through the air toward Quiley, moving in sudden zigs and zags, singing with a droning buzz.

The otter cleared the tears from her eyes, wiping the wetness away with the back of her paw. "I suppose you're Pia's soul," she said to the hovering gemstone of an insect. "Ready and waiting for me, just like all the otters back home would have expected."

"And I suppose you're the sun up in the sky, come down to cool off in the swamp water," the dragonfly buzzed.

"What?" Quiley said, dumbfounded. She almost laughed at the sudden absurdity.

"I don't know the rules of the game we're playing," the dragonfly buzzed, lowering itself to land on the bent-over tip of a long blade of grass.

"We're not playing a game." Quiley's whiskers turned down in a frown.

"And I'm not someone's soul."

Quiley had known that. And yet, like a dumb kit in her first turning of the seasons, she'd walked right up to a dragonfly and called it a soul. "I'm sorry," Quiley said, wiping at her eyes again. "I've lost someone... a friend. It's left me a little loopy."

The dragonfly bent its legs and fluttered its wings, but it didn't take flight. Instead, it stood on the bent grass blade, watching Quiley through eyes that looked like blobs of raw turquoise. "Losing a friend is hard," the dragonfly droned. "Many of the naiads I was friends with under the surface of the swamp didn't survive long enough to molt into their adult forms."

Quiley tilted her head, looking at the dragonfly much more closely. Suddenly, she imagined entire schools of baby dragonflies, living under the water, fleeing from schools of fish. She wondered what they looked like. Were they souls when they hatched? That would mean that naiads who'd been eaten by fish and hadn't survived to fly above the surface wouldn't be available for heartbroken otters who came here seeking solace.

No, it made more sense that when a naiad molted into its adult form, taking on its wings and the gift of flight, that it was also gifted with the soul of a departed otter. Or other mammal presumably. If Quiley had been friends with a raccoon or a beaver, she'd want to believe that their souls would come here too.

Though, perhaps the raccoon or beaver would not want to believe that... Perhaps they had their own beliefs?

Quiley was not a theologian, nor a philosopher, but she was starting to feel like a very foolish young kit. Losing a friend can do that to you. Rip away the years of wisdom and experience you've gained, and leave you as small and sad as any child without metaphorical walls and emotional armor to guard them.

"When otters lose a friend, they comfort each other by saying that the friend's soul has become a dragonfly," Quiley said. She felt the dragonfly deserved an explanation for the large mammal's intrusion into its life and swamp. Though, she pointedly didn't tell it everything. It wouldn't like the full legend.

"Fascinating!" the dragonfly exclaimed. "So, you hoped you could come here, talk to a dragonfly, and in essence, be getting your old friend back?"

"She wasn't old," Quiley mumbled. "She was much too young to die."

"Do I seem like her?" the dragonfly asked, tilting its small head that was almost entirely composed of its strange eyes.

"No," Quiley said. "Not at all." There was so much bitterness in her voice that even the dragonfly heard it. Quiley could tell. Or else, maybe, she was just feeling so raw and vulnerable right now that she assumed her emotions were bleeding out of her eyes, ears, whiskers, and the tip of her tail. Every part of her was bleeding pain and complicated feelings like loss and regret over things that had never happened. Never would happen.

Pia would not have a litter of kits who the two of them would raise together, ignoring whichever useless male Pia had chosen as the father. The kits would not have unusually tawny, almost golden fur like Pia.

Those were silly dreams. Quiley had never even admitted to them. Never said them out loud. Never talked about them with Pia.

But she couldn't deny the image in her head of golden kits, curled up between the two of them. She had daydreamed that image, and even if she never gave voice to those dreams, the image was there. In her head.

Quiley swallowed, gulping down the feelings and the pain. She knew what she had to do. It didn't make any sense, but it was part of the legend. And as little sense as it made... She was starting to see the appeal.

"I'm sorry I don't seem like your friend," the dragonfly said. "I would have been willing to pretend for you, and we could have chatted. I'd like to help. See, you've already helped me. Dragonflies—we live most of our lives under water, dreaming about the few days we'll spend flying. And my friends who died... they'll never fly. I like the idea that their souls have gone somewhere, even if I don't know where. And I think, I'd like to be friends with you."

Quiley looked out over the swamp. The surface of the water dimpled where stalks of cattails and blades of tall grasses emerged from it. Dragonflies swooped low over the water, causing ripples where the fluttering of their wings disturbed the glassy mirror of sky.

Quiley had never eaten a dragonfly. She'd eaten other insects—crunchy and squishy between her teeth all at once. She preferred the soft sweetness of blackberries.

And it was strange that Pia's soul would come to live inside this creature who had no idea of its own significance. It was nothing more than a vessel; a convenient shape for holding her essence until Quiley could realize how much she needed it.

"Yes," Quiley said, "I think we can help each other." She leaned close to the small creature, feeling her breath quiver through her whiskers and seeing it rustle the translucent wings.

Quiley leaned close as if she were going to tell the dragonfly a secret, perhaps confess her newfound friendship. The dragonfly held perfectly still. And Quiley's teeth chomped fast.

The sapphire carapace crunched, and the turquoise eyes squished. The wings melted on Quiley's tongue. But they weren't sweet. Not the same kind of sweet as blackberries anyway.

When Quiley finished chewing, she sat up on her haunches, looked down her long belly, and sighed. Pia was gone. But also, Pia was part of her now.

Whenever Quiley hunted for blackberries, Pia would be hunting for them too. Whenever Quiley felt the blackberries' sweet juices sliding down her throat, they'd be sliding down to join the essence of Pia, waiting in her belly.

And when Quiley died someday, they'd go to the afterlife of never-ending waterslides together.

Until then, it was time for Quiley to find a new home with a new bevy of otters. Pia had been pushing Quiley to leave for some time, and she'd been almost ready to agree. But then... The boulder. The numbness. Quiley didn't think she'd be brave enough to voyage along the river, looking for a new bevy without Pia. Now she wouldn't have to.

Quiley patted her belly in a sad yet satisfied way. Then she turned tail and left the swamp behind. It was no place for an otter, nor an otter's soul.

15

FROND FAREWELL

POLLEN FLOATED on the unseasonably warm spring breeze like glitter, glinting golden in the late afternoon sun. Each speck a tiny grain of hope, most to be left unfulfilled, for this pollen dispersed from a plant that didn't belong on the mundane plains of the British countryside. It didn't belong anywhere on Earth at all, and its root-mates had already wreaked havoc across all the great cities of Earth, leaving them empty. The cohort of carnivorous plants had been a catastrophe for humanity, but the wilder parts of the world... those hadn't fallen prey to this pollen's particular magic yet.

So far, only cuttings of the original plant had survived, carefully tended and transported by the very humans who became their prey, but with London laid to waste, the optimistic species of flora tried once again to spread by way of the air.

And this time, one speck of golden hope landed in

exactly the right place, on exactly the right flower—a little yellow primrose that had mutated in a way that proved compatible and was now simply waiting to be fertilized. The little yellow blossom, matched with the infinitesimal yellow seed, closed up its petals and began to bulge, fruiting over the slow course of many weeks into a bulbous protrusion with a seam down its middle that served as a hinge.

The bulbous fruit—vaguely clam-shaped and speckled in variegated shades of green—hinged open in a yawn, waking up for the first time as the sun rose on the summer solstice. All around it, fiddlehead fronds uncurled, stretching out to greet the day. It was a glorious little plant—part primrose, part unearthly terror, and entirely hungry—ready to take over this backwater part of the world.

All the little hybrid plant needed now was a snack, a few tasty, meaty morsels to help it grow bigger and stronger. Once it grew big enough, it could send out runners from its roots that would grow siblings for it, and when the throng of them were all truly strong and thriving, then they could release their own pollen, now adapted to be better compatible with the plentiful primroses on these grassy downs.

Fortunately, the little plant was good at waiting. Being rooted to the ground, it didn't have a lot of choice in the matter. What it could do was stretch out its fronds and leaves in an appealing way, hoping to look delectably edible, and sure enough, after a few days of fluttering its leaves just so and curling its fronds compellingly, a hungry rabbit came hippety-hopping along, grazing on the tender green shoots of grass.

Already well-practiced at waiting, all the little plant had to do was hold perfectly still until the rabbit—a rangy thing with fur the color of wet sawdust—cozied up close enough to take a tentative taste of one of mutated primrose's tenderest-looking fiddlehead fronds. The nip sent a jolt of pain along the frond's stalk all the way to the heart of the little plant, letting it know: *it was time to snap!*

The little hybrid primrose made quick work of the gamy sawdust-colored rabbit. Its clamshell mouth was the perfect size for eating rabbits, and since it swallowed them up whole, no traces were left behind to frighten the next rabbit away.

Over the next few weeks, the plant grew slowly larger and kept its belly full by snapping up a foolish, careless rabbit every few days. However, eventually, the word got out among the rabbits on the nearby downs that the particular glade where the hungry little mutant plant was rooted *might* be haunted, since rabbits kept disappearing there.

And rabbits started to stay away. Even the careless, foolish ones.

The mutant primrose began to grow hungry, and it stretched out its fronds and vines, searching for something furry to capture. The little plant didn't have eyes, not exactly, but some of the darkest green speckles on its clamshell mouth were sensitive to light, so it could see a little. It kept hoping to see another fuzzy brown blur, but none arrived. Disappointed, since the rabbits had been so tasty, the mutant plant directed its energies towards growing little yellow primrose blooms at the end of some of its longer vines.

By holding its new blossoms up in the air, the mutant plant was able to attract hummingbird hawk-moths and some other types of insects to munch on. Capturing them was more work, since it involved keeping the yellow flowers in bloom, and insects tasted dusty and meagre compared to the meaty flesh of a rabbit. So, the mutant plant's growth slowed down, and it had to accept that many months might pass before it would gather the energy necessary to send out runners that could grow into more clamshell mouths, or better yet, go to seed and release a new, more potent haze of golden pollen across the downs.

Then one day, a fuzzy shape approached the mutant plant, stepping hesitantly, cautiously through the dew-covered grass. This figure wasn't sawdust brown, or mud puddle brown, or any shade of brown at all. It was startlingly white. Bright white. The mutant primrose thought it looked a little like a tiny sun and felt an immediate, irrational fondness for the fuzzy white shape.

It was an albino rabbit, and the other rabbits in her warren had teased and taunted her for her too-bright fur and blood-red eyes her entire life. She looked like a ghost or vampire to them. Something unearthly. Something haunted. So when she heard about a haunted glade where something unearthly lurked, she knew it must be where she belonged. Other rabbits may have faced horrible fates there, but she had no fear. The other rabbits had already beaten it out of her with their cruel words and cold shoulders.

The albino rabbit stared at the mutant plant with her eerie red eyes. She saw its fronds and leaves quivering, and its speckled clamshell mouth which had grown spiky protuberances like teeth all along its edges worked subtly, opening ever so slowly, too eager at the smell of rabbit on the air to hold still like it should.

"You're unlike any plant I've ever seen," the rabbit said.

"And you're unlike any other rabbit," the plant answered, before it could realize what a foolish idea that was. It should have stayed still. It should have stayed quiet. But the rabbit's forthright address had startled the plant too deeply, and it was too late to turn back now. So, the plant continued and said, admiringly, "You look like a tiny cousin to the sun, come down to Earth."

The rabbit laughed. "Kin to the sun, I like that."

"Then I shall call you Sun's Kin," the plant said proudly, very pleased to have pleased such a bright, glowing creature. "Will you stay and talk with me?"

The mutant plant hadn't realized it was lonely until now. There hadn't been any alternative to solitude until this brave, bright rabbit had wandered up close enough to talk to and inspired an entirely new facet of the little plant's existence. The plant didn't want to lose this new part of itself that the rabbit drew out and quivered with fear all over at the idea of the white rabbit leaving it, once again alone but now aware of it.

Fortunately, Sun's Kin folded her paws under her and settled down, just out of reach of the mutant plant's grasping vines and clamshell mouth. She might be brave, but she was no fool. She would stay and talk to the plant, but she would not let it touch her. "And what shall I call you?" Sun's Kin asked.

The mutant plant hesitated. It seemed only fair that since it had named the rabbit, the rabbit should return the favor and bestow a name—as a sort of gift—on the plant. But the rabbit wasn't offering.

"I don't know," the plant answered. "No one has ever spoken to me before today."

"A shame for them, surely," Sun's Kin said. "You're so poetic. They were missing out. Perhaps I shall call you Poet Plant?"

The name 'Poet Plant' was perhaps not quite so poetic as 'Sun's Kin', but the mutant plant was so delighted to have been gifted with a name that all its fiddlehead fronds curled up and its leaves fluttered joyously. "I am honored to be your Poet Plant," it said, "and I will answer your shining brightness with words that open like the flowers in a garden, always turning toward and worshipping the sun."

And so Poet Plant serenaded Sun's Kin with lyrical soliloquies, finding that metaphors sprang to life from the tip of its leafy green tongue and words wove their way into intricate braids of idea as it spoke. Poet Plant found a purpose beyond eating, growing, and striving towards reproduction. It found meaning in conversing with Sun's Kin and a true sense of identity in the name the kind rabbit had gifted it.

Days passed by, and the two unlikely friends fell into a comfortable rhythm. During the heat of midday, Sun's Kin stretched out on the grass, just out of reach of Poet Plant's grasping vines and snapping clamshell mouth, and they conversed. They talked about everything under the sun, from Sun's Kin's childhood in the rabbit warren to Poet Plant's ancestral memories of worlds beyond the sky where its progenitor had originated. During the cooler times at sundown and dawn, Sun's Kin wandered off to graze for tasty morsels of greenery, since she'd already eaten the choicest shoots and buds in an ever widening circle around Poet Plant.

At night, at first, Sun's Kin returned to the rabbit warren to sleep somewhere safely underground, and Poet Plant did its best to capture enough hummingbird hawk-moths to soothe its hunger while Sun's Kin was away. But as the two creatures—dissimilar in form but sympathetic at heart—grew closer together, Poet Plant found that it had to occasionally risk snapping up a tasty, plump and spicy bumblebee or other insect while Sun's Kin was there to see. The rabbit didn't flinch at the sight of her friend eating insects, so Poet Plant grew bolder. Furthermore, Sun's Kin found herself staying later and later into the night, watching the stars come out, one by one, as she listened to Poet Plant's stories of faraway worlds until one night, she found that she didn't want to return to the warren full of unfriendly rabbits at all.

Sun's Kin labored under no delusions. She knew that Poet Plant must be the predator who haunted this glade, and watching it snap up insects, she knew it could easily eat a rabbit with its toothy clamshell mouth. But she wasn't afraid. She also knew: Poet Plant would not eat her. It would not risk losing its beloved audience. So finally, tired and disaffected from the latest round of teasing from her fellow rabbits, Sun's Kin cozied right up against the carnivorous plant who had become her personal bard, singing stories to her, for only her, that filled her tall ears with music and her red eyes with dancing visions.

Poet Plant could hardly believe it at first. This bright, glowing, little cousin of the sun had curled her warm, fuzzy body against its thick green stalk, right under the chin of its clamshell mouth. Sun's Kin side rose and fell with her breathing, a rhythm that was totally foreign to Poet Plant who didn't need to breathe. Even so, Poet Plant sensed the vulnerability in the regular rhythm of her sleeping breaths. The fragility of a body that needs to breathe.

Sun's Kin trusted the carnivorous plant to protect her from other, less-known predators, and Poet Plant felt so honored by the tenuous trust that it barely dared move a leaf or frond all night long for fear of interrupting that gentle rising, falling rhythm, doubled by a second, much faster, more thrumming rhythm of the rabbit's heartbeat. Equally fragile. Equally vulnerable.

Hummingbird hawk-moths fluttered safely past Poet Plant's clamshell mouth that night, and as dawn finally began to break, it finally risked curling a few of its vines around Sun's Kin in a gentle, fond embrace.

After that night, Sun's Kin always slept wrapped in Poet Plant's vines and fronds, protected from the furry and feathered predators who might otherwise attack a rabbit foolish enough to sleep above ground at night. A few owls did try to snatch the sleeping white rabbit in their talons, but Sun's Kin slept through their attacks undisturbed and Poet Plant learned that it had a taste for the stringy, crunchy meat and bones of owls.

Eventually, Sun's Kin dug a small burrow beside Poet Plant, nestled among its roots, to keep her warm during the coming winter. When the winter was especially harsh, Poet Plant encouraged her to go ahead and nibble at the runners it had been trying to send out to grow itself siblings. All Poet Plant's reproductive plans had been forestalled by its focus on Sun's Kin anyway.

"Won't it hurt you?" Sun's Kin asked, shivering in the cold winter air.

"A little," Poet Plant admitted, "but not as much as watching you suffer. Besides, I'm not sure I want copies of myself to sprout up in the spring anymore. What if they didn't love you the way I do? What if they put you at risk?"

Sun's Kin had never been loved or cared for by her own species in the way she was by Poet Plant. It was a strange feeling, being treated like her health and welfare mattered. She liked it, and it made her feel guilty about the idea of essentially nibbling off Poet Plant's toes, day after day, every time it grew new ones. But the cold was bitter, sharp, and biting. It cut right through her bright, white fur when she was hungry, and so she accepted Poet Plant's invitation.

Sun's Kin began by tentatively nibbling only the tiniest bits of Poet Plant's roots and extra leaves—they tasted so sweet and green!—but by the spring, the two unusual friends had fallen into a new kind of relationship. Sun's Kin pruned Poet Plant, keeping it trim and neat, only leaving the roots and leaves it actually needed to survive alone. Everything else was fair game, and Sun's Kin found it so much easier to live this way, she didn't have to worry about foraging far afield.

By now, Poet Plant knew everything about Sun's Kin's life before they'd met and had, in turn, shared everything it knew about the world beyond the downs. Even so, the rabbit never tired of listening to the carnivorous plant spin wilder and wilder tales—clearly fictional, nearly ridiculous, but each of them delightful. In the stories Poet Plant told, Sun's Kin explored lairs deep underground filled with lava monsters and demons; she flew across the universe in a spaceship grown from tightly woven blackberry bracken; she outsmarted gods and ascended to a throne on the surface of the moon, where she could look down on the entire world below. She lived more lives in Poet Plant's stories than a simple rabbit could ever hope to experience in reality. She was content.

As the years passed though, Poet Plant began to

wonder how long rabbits could live. It wanted to go on this way forever, but it began to see that Sun's Kin hopped more slowly now, and sometimes, she stumbled on her long feet. Her long ears grew less sharp, and she had to ask Poet Plant to speak up or repeat parts of its stories for her.

Time passes and the wishes of rabbits and carnivorous plants can't stop it.

So, one day, as Poet Plant stroked Sun's Kin's white fur —less glossy now than it used to be—with its vines, the carnivorous plant found itself counting the time between the rabbit's breaths, worrying that its friend had slipped away and the gentle rise and fall of her furry side was over. Her breaths had gotten so weak. But Sun's Kin awoke, lifted her head, and shook out her ears as if nothing had changed.

"I want you to eat me," Poet Plant whispered. "Before you die. I don't want to be left alone without you, and if you eat me, then I'll be with you forever. We'll die together."

Sun's Kin blinked her red eyes, glazed over now with cataracts. "But then who would tell me lullabies?" she asked.

"You know all my lullabies by heart."

Sun's Kin shook her head stubbornly. "I could have eaten you, long ago, you know," she said. Her voice shaky and ponderous. "I thought about it. I know that you were planning to take over the downs with your runners, and all of you would have eaten my kind. All except you, maybe. But all your siblings, all your root-mates. They would have eaten the other rabbits from my warren. But I haven't been among my own kind for a very long time."

"You haven't," Poet Plant agreed. It was captivated by the rabbit's words. Their roles had flipped, and all Poet Plant wanted was to know what else Sun's Kin might say.

"You have to outlive me," Sun's Kin insisted. There was a fierceness in the rabbit's voice, the kind of determination that can only come from age, from watching the world pass by and change, from discovering what you actually value and knowing you're willing to fight for it. "Perhaps I should care more about my own kind, but through all of my life, the one thing that has brought me the most hope, joy, and the greatest value... has always been you. When I am gone, I don't care if there are little rabbits hopping across the downs. I care that there are little Poet Plants, nestled among the greenery. I want to know that you finally sent out runners, that you finally released pollen, and that there's more of you, everywhere in the world."

Poet Plant could hardly believe the words it was hearing. It didn't want to live without Sun's Kin, and it didn't care anymore about populating the world. But it did care about its best friend's wishes.

"I will begin sending runners out at once," Poet Plant said. "I will release pollen first thing next spring."

"I'm glad," Sun's Kin said, and she closed her eyes, peacefully. She pictured the coming apocalypse for her kind, and she couldn't be sad about it. She felt only joy at the idea of her beloved Poet Plant filling the world with its silver-tongued offspring. She fell asleep to a lullaby—a new one, improvised that very moment—about how every blade of grass, every scrap of green in the entire world, should one day sing of the tiny sun who had spent a lifetime sleeping in the roots of a grateful plant and would now rise back up to the sky, where anything as bright and shining as her truly belonged.

16

THE BEST PUPPY EVER

The hospital lights flash in my eyes, and a man wearing blue scrubs injects me with a needle. I can't feel my body anymore, and all I can see is his blue-clothed back and the nervous faces of my owners, Geoff and Bree, looking down at me. I can see them holding my paws, reaching to pat my ears, but all the sensations are distant.

None of my friends at the dog park believed me when I told them that my masters had been bringing me to the hospital to have a real doctor check on my puppies.

"The vet, you mean," they said. "They take you to the vet's office."

But my masters had taken me to the vet before, and the doctor was different. That's how I knew my puppies were going to be special.

"They'll take your puppies away," the other dogs at the dog park told me. "They'll let you nurse them for a while, but the humans always sell puppies in the end."

I knew they were right about that. Muffy, Lulabelle, and Susie had each had at least three litters of their own, and not one of them had a puppy left to show for it. But none of them had been taken to a real doctor at the actual hospital. So, I hoped against hope that with my puppies and my masters it would be different. It had to be.

Beneath the hazy, floating sensation, I feel a dull pain pervading the core of my body. I see excitement in my owners' eyes. Bree lets go of my paw with one hand and reaches across to grab one of Geoff's hands. I can see her squeeze it tight. They are such good owners, standing by me, faithfully. They care about me so deeply.

Time drags on forever. I feel like my body will crack open from the pain. Then, I see the blue-clad doctor's back straighten as he stands up from where he bent over me. He's holding my puppy in his hands! It's large, and he wraps it in cloth before handing it to Bree who clasps the bundle to her chest. He doesn't hand any more puppies to her, and I'm a little confused and disappointed. Muffy says her litters are always exactly four puppies, and Lulabelle brags about the time she had a litter of eight!

Still, I can see from the swaddled bundle in Bree's arms that my puppy is quite large. Larger than any of their puppies could have been, as Muffy, Susie, and Lulabelle are all quite small dogs. I'm a Bernese Mountain dog. Large and proud. And it seems my puppy has taken after me.

Bree holds the swaddled bundle toward Geoff, and the two of them coo over it. I'm so exhausted, I can hardly stay awake, but I simply have to see my puppy before falling asleep. A quiet whimper-whine escapes from my jowls, and Bree smiles down at me. She tilts the bundle in her arms so I can see between the folds of fabric.

Golden eyebrows, cherubic pink cheeks, an upturned nose, and wide blue eyes with long, dark lashes.

I can't make sense of what I'm seeing at first. My puppy doesn't look anything like me. Could it look like its father? I can't remember any male dogs that were ever close to me in the way Lulabelle described to me, but she insisted one of the dogs must have been since I was with puppy.

My puppy doesn't look like any dog I've ever seen though.

It looks like Bree. And Geoff.

I hear the doctor speaking, but I don't understand his words—at least not most of them. "What are you going to do with the dog, now? Return it to the company?" he says. "You know, some couples who use goat surrogates will roast the animal on a spit over a bonfire at the baby's christening to serve in a big ceremonial feast."

"Isn't that kind of barbaric?" Geoff asks.

The doctor shrugs and says, "So, you'll give it back to the company then. I'm sure this dog could do several more years of good work as a surrogate."

Bree and Geoff look at each other, but I'm still looking at my puppy. I can tell from her smell that she's female, and, my goodness, the more I think about it, the more I realize that she's the most beautiful, amazing puppy I've ever seen. She's so special that she's transcended from my own race to that of my masters. I couldn't be prouder of her, and I can't wait to feel her nestled at my side. I know my masters will want to keep her, and I plan to spend the rest of my life serving this most wonderful of puppies.

"Actually," Bree says, "we've gotten attached to Gloria over the last nine months."

"Yeah," Geoff adds. "We were thinking of keeping her on as a nanny dog."

"Oh," the doctor says. I still can't understand his words, but he sounds surprised. "Not many couples with a new baby want a dog this large around."

"Surrogate dogs are supposed to be really good with the children they carried. Something about bonding with the babies before they're born," Bree says. "They're supposed to make the best nannies."

"Right," the doctor says. "Well, good luck with that." Then he leaves me, my masters, and my new puppy alone together.

Bree holds the puppy down to me and lets me press my muzzle lightly against her head. I can tell my masters are pleased with my puppy too. They must be jealous that I have such a perfect puppy while they have none, so I reassure them with a quiet woof, "We can share her."

17

EXCERPT FROM PURRIDE AND PURREJUDICE

It is a truth universally acknowledged, that a cat in sight of an empty box, must sit in it.

However little known the feelings or views of such a cat may be on their first encountering an empty box, this truth is so well fixed in the minds of all good cat owners, that all empty boxes are considered as the rightful property of some one or other of their cats.

"My dear Mx. Kitty," said the dog to her one day, "have you heard that the Amazon truck has arrived at last?"

Mx. Kitty replied that she had not.

"But it is," returned he; "I have smelled the cardboard!"

Mx. Kitty made no answer.

"Do not you want to know what is in the boxes?" cried the dog impatiently.

"No, indeed, for how can it affect us?"

This was invitation enough, and the dog detailed every scent he smelled coming from them.

"It will be no use to you if twenty such boxes come," explained the cat.

"You are over-scrupulous, surely. I dare say our owners will be very glad to share."

"Is that their design in ordering them?"

"Design! Nonsense, how can you meow so! But it is very likely that they may fall for my best puppy dog eyes once the boxes are opened."

"Depend upon it my dear, once the boxes are empty, then I will care. I will sit in them all."

18

TREEGADOON

Elijah's small boat rocked with the storming of the ocean. Gusts of wind blew sharply against his thick, dense fur, and his clothes—even though they were made from special quick-drying fabric—were completely soaked. Waves slapped and splashed against the small boat, threatening to overturn him. Elijah didn't mind the idea of swimming home. He was a river otter who had been raised among sea lions on a small island near the coast. He was used to swimming, and he was used to the ocean's whimsy. But he'd spent the pre-dawn hours hunting jellyfish, and now as the sun was about to rise, his little boat was chockfull of delectable delicacies. There were moon jellies, sea nettles, and—even better—he'd finally caught a lion's mane jellyfish. He'd wanted to catch one since he'd been a little fellow, still afraid of the water.

This morning, he'd finally caught one, and the bulbous pile of squishy, orangish flesh was larger than him. If the boat toppled over, he'd have no way of getting it home. And he had wanted to taste lion's mane jellyfish for nearly as long as he could remember. He wanted to return home, show off his trophy, and then tell the tale of how he'd captured it to a rapt audience of sea lions, as they all sipped on lion's mane soup together.

Of course, there wasn't really much to the story—the hardest part about catching the big, peaceful lump of life had been hauling the slippery thing into the boat—but he would embellish it. Turn it into a tall tale. His audience would expect as much, and they'd all have a wonderful time making up songs and singing them until the early morning.

But first, Elijah had to get home, and right now, the ocean was not cooperating. Every direction he looked, all was gray. Gray sky, gray waves, gray rain pouring down. There was no sign of which direction he should steer toward, even if his boat would have cooperated with steering, which right now was unlikely. The boat was bucking and bolting like a wild bronco, trying to throw Elijah and his precious lion's mane jellyfish back into the sea.

Then suddenly, a bolt of light shot across the ocean from the sky, just above the horizon, where the clouds cleared just enough to let the rising golden sun shine through. The sunbeam cut through the grayness and landed on a tussled pile of green like a spotlight. Where it shone, trees rose out of the ocean, as mysterious and unexpected as a shooting star.

Elijah stared at the trees, bewildered. They grew straight out of the tumultuous water without a sign of land beneath them. There must be an island down below, he figured, merely flooded by the storm. As Elijah continued to stare at the towering evergreens, he made out bridges threaded between them, connecting the small forest into a complex network of treehouses. A whole city in the treetops, nestled among the needles.

Reasoning that he could get help from whoever lived in those treetop abodes and weather out the storm there, Elijah began rowing again, and steered his boat toward the nearest tree.

As the early dawn light brightened, the storm also lightened. Elijah almost turned his boat back, but the mystery of the treetop village called to him, and so he continued forward, peering up the trunks of the tall evergreens as he passed by them. Finally, he came to one with wooden stairs built around its wide trunk in a spiral that stretched from a small, damp dock at the level of the ocean, up to the canopy above. Elijah paddled his boat right up to the dock, moored it to part of the railing, and then secured a canvas cover over his precious, gelatinous, jelly-flesh cargo.

Just as Elijah was ready to begin climbing the spiral stairs, a voice called down from above, causing him to stop and peer upward.

A round otter's face stared down intently from a platform several stories above the sea's level. Another river otter, like Elijah. He wasn't sure what another river otter was doing out in the middle of the ocean, let alone way up in a treetop village. "Hallo!" Elijah called up, and in return, he saw the otter woman's round face widen into a beaming smile, bright enough to fight back a storm twice the size of the one that had been tossing him about only minutes ago.

Before Elijah could ascend a single step on the spiral stairs, the other otter was already halfway down to him, fairly flying down the steps, using gravity to bring her down faster than he could possibly climb up them. He wondered what had her so hurried...

Elijah stepped back to make room for the otter woman on the small dock beside him, but as soon as she reached him, she launched herself right into him, wrapping short arms around him and pressing her head into the curve of his neck.

"What?" Elijah squeaked, surprised by the unexpected embrace.

"Oh, Martin!" the otter cried, still pressed closely against him, shaking as if she must be crying or maybe just really scared. She spoke in a muffled rush, "You made it back! The squirrels... they all told me you were gone... Completely gone! Like the storm had taken you away, or maybe taken me away... The whole village even! But either way, they swore I'd never see you again! Where's Little Lee-Lee?"

The otter woman pushed herself away from Elijah and whirled around to look at his boat. Moving quickly, she knelt down beside it and began untying the canvas covering over the pile of jellyfish, continuing to say as she did, "Is he sleeping? That baby can sleep through anything, can't he? Such a good kit. Oh, I'm just so glad to see you again! But where ever did you find this nice little boat in that wild storm?"

Elijah was too stunned to stop her messing with his boat, but she stopped herself when turning back the canvas covering revealed a squishy mound of translucent tangled up tentacles instead of the peacefully sleeping otter baby she was apparently seeking.

The otter woman stared at the tentacles for a long moment before turning reluctantly back toward Elijah. As soon as she saw his face, her eyes sharpened, looking first concerned, then confused, and finally... as horrified as if she were staring at a ghost.

"You're not Martin," the otter woman said, each word like a stone falling into a lake, never to be found again but leaving behind ripples that couldn't be taken back.

"No, I'm sorry," Elijah said, feeling unaccountably guilty for not being a different otter. This otter woman had looked so happy when she thought he was someone else, and Elijah found he wanted to see her happy again.

"Did you see another boat out there?" the woman asked. "A big one? Martin and I were passengers on it when the storm rolled in."

"I didn't see anyone else in the storm," Elijah answered, feeling somewhat confused. It had been dark in the pre-dawn gloom that he'd chosen for his jellyfish hunt, but it hadn't been so dark that he wouldn't have seen a large passenger ship on the horizon. And the ocean had been clear. Completely clear. So clear, in fact, that he hadn't been sure where the sudden storm had rolled in from...

The otter woman frowned, and the fur on her brow creased in consternation. She was looking at Elijah so closely that he felt he should have been self-conscious about it. Like she was scrutinizing him, and why should a random otter woman who he'd only met moments before have the right to scrutinize him like that? But somehow... it felt more natural than it should. Like she was familiar in an unaccountable way.

The otter woman stuck her paw out and said, "My name's Rosalee."

"Elijah." He took her paw, and all the stress of dealing with the sudden storm drained right out of him. "I'm glad to meet you, and I'm sorry I can't be more help about finding..."

"Martin and Lee-Lee," Rosalee supplied, taking her paw back. She looked even more confused now. "They should be out there..." Rosalee stared past the edges of the mysterious forest out at the relentless ocean. It was calm now, almost like the storm had never happened at all.

Storms out at sea didn't usually subside that fast. At least, not in Elijah's experience.

"You mentioned squirrels earlier," Elijah prompted. He glanced up at the village in the trees above them. He was very curious about it. And while, he felt sorry for Rosalee's loss—or potential loss—it wasn't really his problem.

"Yes, they live in the village up there." Rosalee gestured vaguely upward with a paw. "They call it Treegadoon."

The name echoed with portents and power, making Elijah only more curious about it. "Are they friendly to visitors?" he asked.

"Very," Rosalee answered distantly. She had switched from staring out at the calm, flat line of the horizon to eying Elijah's moored boat like she was assessing its exact value and whether she could afford to buy it from him.

"Do you need a ride back to shore?" Elijah asked.

"I want to go looking for my family," Rosalee answered in a clipped tone, still staring at the boat. Her gaze had passed from assessing to possessive, like she might try to steal it if Elijah left it untended.

"Does your Martin know you're here? At Treegadoon?" Elijah asked, hoping to convince Rosalee it would be more effective to stay put than to go gallivanting about and become a moving target for her husband to find.

"We were separated in the storm..." Rosalee tore her gaze away from the boat, clearly catching on that Elijah could see right through her plans to make off with it. She looked at him, and her brown eyes were full of need, but the edge softened a little when he smiled at her.

"We're at the closest thing to a landmark in this stretch of water," Elijah said gently. "Why don't you give Martin a chance to find you here. We can go up, and you can show me around Treegadoon."

"I don't know it very well," Rosalee said. "I've only been here a day, since the storm started yesterday morning."

Elijah frowned. The storm hadn't lasted that long. It had come on very suddenly and dissipated just as quickly once he'd rowed his way into the shelter of the trees of Treegadoon.

Rosalee misinterpreted his frown, thinking Elijah was displeased that she was refusing his plan. So, she decided to compromise: "If we go up, and you get a chance to look around, will you take me with you when you go? And help me look for my husband and son?"

Elijah brightened and said, "Of course. And if don't find them out here, I can take you to the closest coastal village—I live near it—and we can see if there's any news of the ship you were on. That's probably where Martin would end up if he were rescued by someone else or if he ended up swimming to the shore."

"It's close enough to swim to?" Rosalee asked hopefully.

"A long swim, but yes," Elijah agreed. "I came by boat, because I was hunting jellyfish."

"I saw," Rosalee answered with distaste, her wide black nose wrinkling.

Elijah knelt down, reached a paw into the pile of squishy jellyfish, and tore off the end of a tentacle. The rubbery, translucent flesh was about thick and long as a wide noodle. He tore it in half and offered half to Rosalee. "They're delicious." He took a bite of his half and grinned as his teeth sank satisfyingly into the chewy, elastic delicacy.

Rosalee's disgusted look melted away, replaced by laughter, and she said, "All right, I'll give it a try."

The two otters stood on the dock together, chewing away at their surprisingly tough treats like they were pieces of chewing gum. The jellyfish flesh looked almost like water, it was so translucent, but it had a lot more substance than that.

"Okay," Rosalee admitted. "That is pretty good. Salty and subtle."

"It's even better in a stew," Elijah said.

"Jellyfish stew," Rosalee said appraisingly. "I'd like to try that some time." She was trying so hard to get along with Elijah, but she couldn't help glancing out at the ocean again and again. When she did, the look in her eyes clouded over like she was still lost in the storm, even though it had already passed.

Elijah secured the canvas covering over his stockpile of jellyfish again, and then he said, "Come on, let's go check out the village. I bet there are better vantage points up there for looking to see if there are any other boats around."

Rosalee smiled grimly, nodded, and then cooperated by starting back up the spiral stairs first. Elijah wasn't going to leave her behind him. He still didn't trust her not to take off with his boat, and while he wouldn't mind being stranded here—he could still swim home—he didn't want to lose that glorious lion's mane jellyfish. He still planned to feast upon it back at the sea lion village tonight.

*　*　*

Down at sea level, the tree's trunk felt as stable as solid ground—especially after having spent the entire morning on a small boat, rocked by the waves of the sea—but as Elijah ascended the spiral stair, higher and higher up the wide trunk, he became increasingly aware of a gentle, subtle swaying.

The spiral stair ended at a wooden platform that encircled the trunk, surrounded by woven-rope handrail and netting up to the height of Elijah's waist. The platform connected to several bridges—made from wooden planks with the same rope handrails and netting along their sides—which led to other trees with platforms. Those trees, in turn, were connected to even more trees by similar bridges.

Elijah felt like he'd entered an entirely different world—somewhere strange and magical, perhaps mythical. Somewhere never intended for otters.

Elijah had met squirrels before when visiting the seaside town closest to the sea lion village. Although he lived in the sea lion village with his adopted mothers, one of those mothers was a river otter like him, and she'd taken him to the mainland many times. The town there was a crossroads for many species—a real hub of activity, where ships came and went, bringing travelers and cargo shipments. Even so, the squirrels in that port town were generally either outsiders, passing through, or if they had settled in the coastal town, they were likely unusual squirrels who hadn't felt at home in the cities built by their brethren among the trees. Either way, they were individuals, out of their element, surrounded by a city designed by and for more marine animals.

This, on the other paw, was clearly a place made by squirrels and for squirrels. The kind of place that didn't care if a river otter felt a little sick to his stomach at the uncertainty of whether this tree was truly swaying in the air or not. Elijah was used to either solid ground under his paws or the jaunty rocking of the waves. This in-between sensation was not something his body understood at all.

Rosalee saw Elijah's discomfiture and placed a steadying paw on his shoulder. "You get used to it," she said. "I felt a little sick at the sheer height when I first got up here too."

"The height?" Elijah asked, thinking to look down for the first time since beginning his ascent. As he'd climbed, Elijah had kept his eyes on the stairs in front of him or on the threads of bridges woven among the trees above him. Either watching his step or marveling at this mysterious place he was approaching.

It hadn't occurred to him to look down.

The distance between Elijah and the water below came into focus sharply when he did turn his gaze downward, making his already queasy stomach flip and clench inside him. He hadn't realized that they'd climbed so high. Even landing in water, a fall from this height could be permanently disabling. Or fatal.

The pressure of Rosalee's paw on Elijah's shoulder

tightened. "It's okay," she said, and something about her voice soothed him. It made him think of his mother's voice—not Angelica, his sea lion mother, but Arlene, who was also a river otter.

As the two river otters stood together on the platform, several squirrels began approaching from various directions, skipping and tripping along the rickety wooden bridges as easily as a sea lion bobs along with the ocean's waves.

The squirrels were dressed in outfits that seemed to be formed from sewn-together leaves and woven pine needles—all autumn colors like a rusted over sunset. Somehow, the leaves and needles had been treated in a way that kept them supple and soft, even if they had lost their vibrant green hues from when they'd been alive.

The squirrels' fur varied in hue—some were gray, others red, and a few even had a white stripe, lined in black, that ran down their sides, visible in the gaps between their leafy pieces of clothing. On all of them, the russet, autumn tones of the leaf and pine needle fabric complemented the natural shades of their fur beautifully.

"Did you find your husband?" one of the red squirrels asked, when he got close enough to the otters to be heard.

"No," Rosalee said. Then gesturing at Elijah, she added, "This is another traveler—Elijah—he's offered to take me in his boat and help me look for Martin and Lee-Lee, but first, he wants to see your town."

Hearing her describe the situation, Elijah felt a twinge of guilt that he wasn't rushing immediately back out to see to help this woman who had lost her family. But if her husband and child were river otters—which they must be, since she'd mistaken Elijah for Martin at first—then they wouldn't be strangers to swimming. It really was logical to stay here, hoping they'd show up.

The red squirrel who'd spoken before stepped closer. He was a good head shorter than the two river otters, and his tail flicked and flipped like a campfire fluttering against a strong wind. "We told you Rosalee..."

The otter woman glared at the squirrel, and he stopped speaking. "I'm not staying here forever. No matter what you say." Her words were petulant, and she stamped a hind paw, making her seem younger than she likely was. As it was, she only seemed a little older than Elijah, and it seemed strange to him that she already had a spouse and child. Some of Elijah's sea lion friends had already begun falling into romantic entanglements and marrying, but he had never felt his heart flutter at the sight of another, so it all seemed very strange to him.

At least, he never had until now. But there was something quite breathtaking about this squirrel with fur like fire whose eyes sparkled brightly in the early dawn light.

"What do you mean, *stay forever?*" Elijah asked.

The otter woman stared down at the red squirrel. There wasn't fire in her dark brown fur, but there was definitely fire in her eyes. She was larger than the squirrel, but the squirrel had friends. There must've been a dozen or more squirrels gathered around by now, standing on the different bridges between this tree's platform and the adjacent trees. If the squirrels wanted to capture the two otters who had intruded into their lofty, leafy realm, it wouldn't be hard. They were too high to safely dive down, and from the way the squirrels had been skipping and hopping around on these swaying bridges, they could easily outmaneuver a couple of marine mammals.

"If the squirrels are trying to hold you here... why didn't you tell me?" Elijah whispered to Rosalee, urgent and concerned. "We could have escaped easily, if you'd warned me it was dangerous?"

The squirrels close enough to make out Elijah's whispered words began laughing, and Rosalee turned toward him with the goofiest, lopsided grin on her face... an expression that Elijah somehow found familiar.

"They're not holding me prisoner," Rosalee said.

"We would never hold anyone captive against their will," one of the nearest gray squirrels said, sounding rather defensive. "We love visitors, and we do our best to hurry them on their way... before... well... They get trapped."

"Trapped?" Elijah asked.

Rosalee rolled her eyes, as if the squirrel was saying one of the most ridiculous things she'd ever heard.

"Yes," the red squirrel who'd spoken before said. "Trapped by the curse of Treegadoon."

Ominous words, Elijah thought. Yet somehow, the idea didn't frighten him. The wind blew freely through the trees. The water of the ocean splashed freely past their trunks. Nothing could hold an otter here, if he didn't want to stay. Elijah didn't believe in curses.

Yet Rosalee looked fearful. Defiant. Stubborn and ready to fight. But beneath all that, Elijah could sense she was afraid.

Elijah reached a paw out and took one of hers. He squeezed it, and when she looked at him, he said, "We'll look around, and then we'll go. There's no such thing as curses, and if there were, we'd simply break it."

Rosalee smiled and nodded.

The red squirrel said, "You're very welcome to try, and you're more than welcome to look around."

* * *

THE SQUIRREL ONLOOKERS DISPERSED, except for the red squirrel with the captivating eyes. His name was Shaun, and he volunteered to show Elijah and Rosalee around. Although the otter woman had already been in Treegadoon overnight, she'd spent most of her time there fretting, pacing, and watching the storm, intent on spotting any signs of the shipwreck she'd escaped or her lost husband and child as quickly as possible.

The more she followed Shaun and Elijah around though, the more she felt the intensity of her fear and longing for her missing child fade. It had felt like an ache in her arms all night long as she'd stared out at the storm, wondering whether Little Lee-Lee was safe and how soon she'd get to hold him again. She'd felt like a hollow thing, missing the warm heart that was supposed to be a bundle of wiggling, restless fur in her arms. Her eyes had filled with visions of Martin and Lee-Lee tossed by the storm, wrestling with the waves, unable to find solid ground or even tell which direction to swim in. Every way she'd looked, all she could see was what wasn't there—her husband and son.

Perhaps the exhaustion of a sleepless night catching up with her, or maybe the cheerful merriment in Shaun and Elijah's voices as Rosalee followed them on their tour of Treegadoon was infectious, but either way, the nightmarish visions of an otter child lost and crying in the storm began to fade. She was still worried, but the worry felt like a small thing, nibbling at the corner of her mind, tugging at the edge of her sleeve, trying to remind her that she was supposed to be overcome with feelings. But the overwhelming feelings themselves? Those had lifted like the storm. Somehow, she was sure that Little Lee-Lee was safe.

It was an eerie but pleasant sensation, feeling her worries lift away like fog in the morning light. But since there was nothing Rosalee could actually do about her missing child at the moment, she chose to accept the ease that had started unraveling the tightly tangled knots of anxiety in her heart.

With the early morning sun shining through the trees, Treegadoon was an exceptionally beautiful place, and Shaun's chittering voice had a melodic, sing-song quality as he told her and Elijah all about every place he led them.

Most of the structures were built around the trees with trunks growing right up through their middles. Neither Rosalee nor Elijah could imagine how the squirrels ever felt fully secure, knowing there were several stories of empty space beneath the floors of their little houses filled with nothing but breezes. Though, Rosalee had to admit that the less aquatic creatures who'd been on the passenger ship with her, Martin, and Little Lee-Lee had seemed to feel the same sense of unease about the fathoms of water beneath them.

The two otters exchanged meaningful glances often, especially when Shaun said something just so preciously squirrely that they could barely keep from laughing. A few times, Elijah shook his head in a rueful way when Shaun wasn't looking, and there was something so charmingly funny about his expression that Rosalee almost laughed out loud, giving up the game. Instead, she managed to stifle her chuckle, keeping their otterly secret from the squirrel tour guide.

"We really have everything we need up here in the treetops," Shaun explained. "We even grow gardens!"

"You mean that you gather the nuts, leaves, and fruits from the trees?" Elijah asked.

"No," Shaun chittered, leading the two otters up a flight of steps spiraling around a particularly wide tree trunk towards an even higher level of the city. When they arrived at the higher level, Shaun gestured at the verdant scene in front of them—strawberry plants, tomatoes, zucchini, and all sorts of other practical plants had been trained to grow on a giant net that spread between several of the trees like a giant, garden-sized hammock. "We garden," Shaun repeated triumphantly. "Isn't it lovely?"

This was another case where Elijah's expression almost made Rosalee break out in laughter. He had a befuddled, surprised look of astonishment spread across his muzzle, and there was laughter in her eyes. Seeing it made Rosalee happy in a deep, satisfied kind of way that she simply couldn't explain to herself. Somehow, seeing Elijah's reaction to the garden was even more meaningful to her than her own feelings about it, and that simply didn't make sense.

The three of them wandered about the garden for a while, climbing along the swaying net, and picking fresh fruits to sample. Elijah was particularly enamored of a bright purple berry that looked a little like strawberries, but they grew in tighter clusters, were even more heart shaped, and tasted mildly of lavender. Shaun called them joiberries, and Elijah wondered why he'd never heard of them before.

* * *

Having visited the highlights of Treegadoon—the gathering hall with a roof of woven branches, the library filled with scrolls, the bridge of whispers, the carved out heart of the oldest tree, and the acorn treasury—Shaun finally led the otter visitors to a small cafe even higher than the hammock garden. In fact, the little cafe's platform overlooked the garden, giving it an especially lovely view. Neither Rosalee nor Elijah had ever been so high above ground level before, and truth be told, they both found it a little dizzying. Fortunately, there was a railing around the edge of the cafe's platform, and all the chairs—while a little small for river otters—seemed quite secure.

Elijah stared out at the view of the garden and the ocean beyond while Shaun ordered breakfast for all three of them from a squirrel waiter who seemed delighted to be serving otter visitors, and Rosalee stared at Elijah. His face was restful to look at, like as long as he was happy, she knew everything was okay.

"You mentioned a curse earlier," Elijah said to Shaun, still staring out at the sea. He could see farther into the horizon here than he was used to.

"Yes," the red squirrel agreed, toying with the wooden cutlery that the waiter had laid out for them. "The curse of Treegadoon." His pointed face looked more drawn as he spoke of the curse, whiskers slicking back and tufted ears splaying. Even the brightness in his eyes dimmed ruefully. Shaun didn't want to tell them about the curse.

"Tell us, please," Rosalee pressed, realizing that Elijah might let the squirrel get away with avoiding the apparently unpleasant topic. There was a sweet, flirty energy between Elijah and their tour guide, and clearly, he didn't want to upset the pretty red squirrel. But Rosalee was suddenly certain that she desperately needed to hear about this curse.

Elijah looked troubled now, like he had hoped to keep

the visit light and happy, but he could tell Shaun was unhappy. Even so, Rosalee needed to hear what Shaun had to say.

"Long ago," Shaun began, his chittery voice taking on the hallowed tone of a story he'd heard told over and over again before ever telling it aloud himself. "A visitor came to Treegadoon."

"Like us?" Elijah asked brightly, hoping to bring back Shaun's earlier ease with him. It did not work.

"No," Shaun answered. "A giant white bird. An albatross with a broken wing."

The waiter arrived, laden down with many delicious-looking dishes—bowls of nut mash, piping hot pastries, and fresh garden salads for each of them. Hearing the words of a story that they must have recognized, the waiter scurried to lay out all the dishes quickly and then leave them to their tale, as the waiter's own tail flicked nervously behind them.

"How did the albatross break its wing?" Elijah asked, still trying to bring back the bright, easy, give and take that his conversation with Shaun had held earlier.

Again, Elijah failed, and Shaun continued with the story, his tone heavy with portent: "There are many versions of how the albatross came to break her wing and how she came to find our village, but all the versions agree: the albatross begged for help from the people of Treegadoon, saying that if we let her stay in our city and cared for her until her wing healed, fortune would shine upon us."

A cold breeze shivered past their table at the cafe in the sky. Rosalee reminded herself that there would be many such cold breezes so high up here, but she couldn't help feeling like the wind itself was playing along with Shaun's storytelling. "You didn't take the albatross in, did you?"

Discomfited, Shaun took a bite from the bowl of nut mash in front of him before continuing. "I wasn't there," he said, defensively once the bite of nut mash had been swallowed. "This was long before I was born. Before my parents were born. But... no. The squirrels of Treegadoon did not take the albatross in." His voice lowered with shame to a hoarse whisper. "We turned her away the very next morning, giving her only a few meagre provisions and a small, abandoned row boat, telling her to find help at the shore rather than among us in the sky."

"Cold," Elijah observed, finally having gotten caught up in the story.

"To be fair," Shaun argued, "an albatross is a very large kind of bird. I'm sure we had nowhere suitable to keep her and, way back then, perhaps they worried that such a giant would eat right through their stores of food." Even as he defended his ancestors, Shaun's tufted ears stayed low, and he looked ashamed.

"What happened?" Rosalee asked, fearing the answer but knowing she needed to hear it.

"This part... well..." Shaun toyed with the pastry in front of him. It was covered with powdered sugar and flakes of almond. They shouldn't have been able to grow almonds in a place like this, but many of the taller trees had branches from smaller types of trees grafted onto them, allowing the squirrels of Treegadoon to harvest all kinds of nuts and fruits in addition to what they grew in their hammock garden. "Look, this is a legend, right? So, some of it will sound fantastical... even silly... but..."

"But there's often truth in legends, even if the details are made up," Rosalee agreed.

"Right," Shaun looked into her eyes so deeply that it felt like he was trying to apologize in advance for what he was about to say.

"Just tell me, please," Rosalee pressed. She hadn't felt able to eat a single bite of her food since the story of the albatross had begun, even though she hadn't eaten since well before the shipwreck that cast her here last night. And somehow, she was beginning to think that even more time had passed than that. "I need to know."

"So serious..." Elijah muttered, but both of the others ignored him this time.

"You do need to know," Shaun agreed. "Because you are part of Treegadoon now."

Rosalee didn't like the sound of that, but she didn't dare to interrupt.

"When my ancestors pushed off the row boat with the albatross in it, she had barely drifted beyond the bounds of our town before her feathers burst into flame."

Rosalee held back a gasp, and Elijah rolled his eyes. His otter mother was an inventor—a scientist—and he knew better than to believe in fairy stories about phoenixes.

Shaun ignored both of the otters' reactions and continued: "The fire completely consumed the albatross and her small boat, leaving nothing but a pool of gray ash floating on the surface of the calm sea. Then the ash began to rise and reformed itself, once again, into the shape of a bird, this time with feathers as meltingly golden as the sunrise."

Elijah smiled indulgently. At least, it was a pretty fairy story. Rosalee's heart was racing.

"The phoenix who had risen from the ashes of the albatross had no broken wings," Shaun said. He was staring defiantly at his bowl of mash now, refusing to meet Rosalee's eyes. "And she was a powerful magician."

"Of course she was." Elijah laughed. "And she cursed you? I mean, your village?"

"Yes," Shaun agreed, deadly serious, not at all fazed by Elijah's levity. "The phoenix cursed us for our inhospitality, saying that forever forward, Treegadoon would skip across time like a skipping stone across the surface of a lake, and that we could never, ever turn away a visitor again—that, in fact, anyone who ever stayed the night in Treegadoon would become part of Treegadoon and could never..." He faltered, briefly looking up to catch Rosalee's eye before looking away again. Then his voice fell to the softest whisper "*...could never leave again.*"

Elijah smiled. He had been eating his nut mash all through the story, and his bowl was empty now. Before attacking his garden salad, he said, "That's a good story. Very spooky. I guess it's a clever way to tell visitors that they should be on their way before dark. Don't worry though. I wasn't planning on staying the night."

Rosalee had gotten very quiet. She had stayed the night. There hadn't been any choice with the intensity of the storm. More than that, the words "skip across time" were settling in the pit of her stomach like the skipping stone from the squirrel's metaphor. "What do you mean by *skip across time?*" she asked. But as she looked at Elijah —not Shaun, even though her question was directed at him; her eyes were locked on Elijah—she was certain she already knew. She recognized a notch in the webbing of his left front paw.

Rosalee had never seen Elijah's face before—how could she? She'd never met him until today. At least, not like this, not as he was now. But his face looked like her own face, the curve of his grin, the set of his ears... And his face also looked eerily like Martin's.

All put together, Elijah looked exactly like the grown up version of her Little Lee-Lee, right down to the funny notch in the webbing of his front left paw that he'd had since he was born. She remembered discovering it on her brand new, absolutely perfect baby and being distraught for a moment to find an imperfection before simply treasuring him all the more. *Baby Liam, who she'd held in her arms only one day before.* If he were all grown up...

Little Lee-Lee would look like Elijah.

It was as if Rosalee were looking through time itself, and for a moment, she felt like she was falling through time, feeling the power of all she'd lost. The baby in her arms was gone. Her arms were empty, and they'd never hold him tight again. Not as a baby.

But the sensation of falling was strangely counterbalanced by the anchor of Elijah's eyes, looking into her own, questioning her, exactly the way he'd done just yesterday when he'd been cradled in her arms and didn't understand the incoming storm.

Rosalee realized that Shaun had been talking to her, trying to answer her question about time, but she hadn't heard a single word the squirrel had said, and she didn't wait for him to finish. She'd figured it out—enough, anyway—on her own. She spoke to her son, talking right over Shaun, and said, "Elijah, tell me about your parents."

The other otter—who looked almost exactly the same age as Rosalee—seemed troubled by the way she had so rudely interrupted their tour guide with a complete non sequitur, but Shaun shook his head, indicating he didn't mind. He waved a delicate red-furred paw as if to say, "Go on, answer her question," and then picked up his pastry, finally taking a chance to eat. He looked relieved to be let off the hook for a moment, and Rosalee suspected he'd already worked out what was going on—why she was asking such a seemingly random question.

"Well, okay," Elijah said, uncertainly, still out of the loop, "I don't know why you suddenly want to know, but I have two mothers—a river otter inventor, Arlene, and a sea lion artist, Angelica."

A sea lion couldn't be a river otter's biological mother,

but with two mothers, perhaps the river otter inventor could be. Even so, Rosalee didn't think so.

"Were you adopted?" Rosalee pressed, ever more sure of her conclusion in spite of the obvious ridiculousness that this fully grown man of an otter could be the same person as the baby she'd held in her arms only yesterday. His whole childhood had already passed. Without her. She'd seen none of it—only the very beginning, and now... to skip ahead like this? It took her breath away. It knocked the ground out from under her feet.

And yet, her child wasn't lost. Rosalee was looking right at him.

"Well, yes," Elijah admitted, still looking lost and confused. "They adopted me when I was quite small. I couldn't even swim or talk."

It made Rosalee feel old—so very old, to have such a fully grown child—and also very young at the same time. For suddenly, she wasn't the mother of an infant anymore. She wasn't responsible for keeping him alive, raising him, and making sure he turned out okay. All of that had already happened, and she was freed of those weighty responsibilities. It was like skipping back in time to before she'd become a mother, but also like skipping forward. It felt like time was a spool of thread, meant to be neatly wrapped around and around in tight little circles, but it had come all undone and tangled up, crisscrossing wildly in every which way.

"Did they name you Elijah?" Rosalee asked.

"Yes, apparently, I made a babbling sound like 'lee-lee-

lee' when I was very little, and so they thought a name with those sounds would suit me." Elijah smiled fondly as he told the story.

Even if the storm had stolen Little Lee-Lee away from his parents and left him bereft, he'd had a good enough childhood afterwards for it turn his whiskers up with happiness at its remembrance. Rosalee was glad. She reached out and grabbed her grown son's paw with her own.

"Yes, you did make that sound as a baby," Rosalee agreed, her head spinning from the change in tenses from how she would have said the same sentence an hour ago and her voice shaking from the immense fear of rejection she felt as she opened up to this grown man, hoping he would understand who he was to her. *How important.* He was still her baby... even if he didn't know or remember her at all. Even if he had different mothers who'd taught him to swim and talk, thrown birthday parties for him, and comforted him when he'd felt lost.

Elijah looked down at Rosalee's webbed paw clasped around his, bemused, but he didn't pull away.

"It's why your father, Martin, and I named you Liam, and I called you Little Lee-Lee." Rosalee's voice broke on those last words. Little Lee-Lee was gone. Even if he'd grown up to be a fine young man—a man whose eyes looked exactly the same when he was confused—gentle and kind. But the baby was gone, lost to a strange trick of time and a curse cast by a phoenix—a mythical creature who was supposed to stay in storybooks.

"That doesn't make any sense," Elijah said, laughter in his voice. Not harsh laughter. Not mocking. Just confused and amused, but still, gentle. Always gentle.

He had grown up without her, but he had grown up well.

* * *

Elijah understood that Rosalee had undergone a great loss—an unthinkable loss—and so that was probably why she wasn't making any sense. She must be out of her mind with worry over her missing husband and baby. No wonder she would cling to a fantasy story to find a way to get past her fear that her baby had drowned in the night.

Perhaps it had been cruel of Elijah to make her wait through a tour and leisurely breakfast simply to satisfy his own curiosity about the squirrel city before taking her to search for her missing family. He could always have come back again later to Treegadoon. Although, not if Shaun's silly story about the town skipping across time were true, Elijah thought with amusement. If that were true, then Treegadoon wouldn't be here by tomorrow morning.

"Maybe it's time for us to go looking for Martin and Liam," Elijah suggested, arranging his empty dishes and dirty cutlery together in a way that would make them easy for the squirrel waiter to manage.

Rosalee looked like she wanted to object—to press her point that Elijah himself was one and the same as Baby Liam—but instead, she nodded. Whether Elijah was Liam or not, Martin was still missing, and she did want to search for him.

Rosalee turned to Shaun and asked, "Is there any chance that Martin could have skipped through time with us last night? If he didn't..." She glanced uneasily at Elijah, knowing that he didn't share her belief in the curse of Treegadoon and also probably measuring out how much older her husband would be if he'd lived through all those years while she'd lived through only one night. She couldn't have liked how the calculation turned out. Elijah was a grown man. Her husband would be twice her age by now, if he'd lived through that time.

"Martin wouldn't have let our child out of his sight," Rosalee insisted. "He wouldn't have. So, if they got separated, it must have been by the curse." Clearly, she didn't want to say, either he died in the storm, or he's still here, but it was what she was thinking. *"Is there any way he could still be here?"*

Shaun smiled weakly, awkwardly, glancing around himself as if he were wondering why he'd let himself get drawn into the role of tour guide and if there were some other squirrel he could foist the role of town ambassador off to at this late point. "I don't know," Shaun admitted. "I'm not an expert on exactly how the curse works. We haven't had outside visitors for a very long time." He smiled warmly at Elijah, who obviously was the reason he'd let himself be drawn into this awkward position. The romantic tension between the two of them had been palpable since they'd first seen each other.

"Is there someone who is an expert?" Elijah asked wryly. The idea of an expert on a made-up story amused him very much. He wondered what Mama Arlene would think of this place and its superstitions. She was such a devout scientist, she'd probably come up with an explanation for the town-wide delusion about their curse that would make sense of the whole thing. Of course, there was a thought—maybe it was only Shaun who believed this children's story.

"Tell you what," Shaun said, his red tail flicking behind him like a restless bonfire on a windy beach. "You two stay here a little longer, and I'll go ask around, okay?"

Elijah wasn't the one with a husband and child missing, so he looked to Rosalee for her reaction. She seemed unsure but nodded. So, Elijah said, "Sure, we'll wait for you. A few more minutes won't hurt."

Shaun scurried off, away from the cafe, back down the spiral stair that had brought them so high up in a city that already seemed like it floated in the clouds. Treegadoon was plenty magical without make-believe stories about phoenix magicians added to it. At least, that's what Elijah thought. Maybe he would bring Mama Arlene here to see it someday. She'd be fascinated by the architecture. He would bring Mama Angelica too, except a sea lion wouldn't be able to do much more than gaze upwards at the city from sea level.

With her back legs melded together in a mermaid's tail and her greater size—sea lions are much larger than river otters, who are already bigger than squirrels—Mama

Angelica simply wouldn't be able to ascend into this treetop realm at all. Not unless Mama Arlene invented some kind of pulley system or elevator to help lift her into the sky.

See, this is why Elijah didn't need to believe in curses and phoenixes. The world already had mermaids, and the delights Mama Arlene could work with her science and inventions was more than magical enough for him.

Elijah was content to sit and wait in silence, enjoying the view of the sparkling ocean out beyond the verdant garden stretched in front of them on its gently swaying hammock, but he could sense Rosalee's fretfulness.

"Tell me about Martin," Elijah said, knowing that Rosalee would like the idea of him asking about his supposed father (such a laughable idea) and figuring it would make her feel better to talk about him, no matter how this misadventure of hers turned out.

So, Rosalee told Elijah about how she and Martin had met when she'd been traveling along the river from the inland city where she'd grown up, and she'd convinced him to travel with her toward the coast. They'd lived together on the coast for a while before deciding to go on an ocean voyage and further explore the world. The story reminded Elijah of Mama Arlene's story about traveling from her riverside home to the coast when she'd been young. Elijah thought his mother would like this woman, and in fact, he found himself almost unaccountably at ease with her.

Rosalee had a manner that felt unusually easy and

comfortable to him, but then, he was a river otter who had grown up surrounded by sea lions. So, it didn't really surprise him that another person of his own species should feel so much more like him than most of the people he knew or met. Even so, he did find himself looking at her—the glimmer in her brown eyes like sunlight on a puddle, the cheerful roundness of her cheeks, and the way her small round ears splayed and flicked as she spoke—noticing similarities between her and himself, wondering if they were more than just species similarities.

But a town skipping through time like a stone across the surface of a pond simply made no sense, and there was no such thing as a phoenix.

On the other paw, mermaids did exist. Mama Angelica was proof enough of that. Could a phoenix simply be an albatross who had learned some clever trick of showmanship for using fire to scare a village of squirrels into believing they'd been cursed? Even if that were the case though... skipping across time? No, Elijah couldn't believe that.

When Shaun finally came back, the flitting of his tail had slowed, and he seemed nervous. "I have good new and bad news," he said.

"Did you find an expert?" Elijah asked. He really didn't know what to expect from a squirrel who generally believed that he lived in a cursed village and could never leave. It was both sad that Shaun allowed himself to be boxed in by such a clearly ridiculous superstition and kind of charming that he was able to still wholeheartedly believe in the kind of magical story that's generally aimed at children.

"Not really," Shaun admitted, his delicate paws clasped together in front of him. "It's been generations since the albatross came to Treegadoon, and so all of us are going on the stories that our parents were told by their parents who were in told turn told by their own parents."

Elijah's muzzle quirked into a tight smile as he held back as much of his amusement as he could. He didn't want to laugh at Shaun. He genuinely liked the red squirrel, even if he was clearly a bit naive. But apparently, he had a whole village backing up his naiveté, so it wasn't exactly or entirely his own fault. Elijah really would have to bring Mama Arlene here. She'd be fascinated by meeting an entire city of squirrels who were ruled by a superstition that kept them from traveling out into the wider world and discovering its wonders. As a consummate traveler himself, Elijah hoped he could persuade Shaun to see reason. Perhaps not right now—Rosalee's family still needed to be found, and Elijah's boatful of tasty jellyfish needed to be brought home. But he would return. He was increasingly sure of that.

Shaun continued, unaware of Elijah's storm of thoughts, and said, "The bad news is that no one has heard of another otter washing into our town during the storm last night. However, some of my friends claim that the crescent dune island to the north of Treegadoon is actually within our borders and counts for the curse. Apparently, a couple of them snuck out and camped there overnight when they were younger. So, if he washed up there, then he would have skipped forward through time with us."

"A dune island?" Rosalee asked hopefully. She turned her gaze back to Elijah and asked, "Can we go check it out?"

"Of course," Elijah answered. He had promised to help her, and if they found her actual family, then she could forget this nonsense about skipping through time and him being her lost baby. Everything could get back on track.

* * *

As Shaun led the two otters back through the maze-like bridges and spiral stairs that crisscrossed between all the trees of Treegadoon, Rosalee turned the tables on Elijah and asked him to talk about his life. He seemed amused that she wanted to know about his parents, his playmates growing up, the way he'd celebrated his birthdays, and really every tiny detail of the life she'd missed while he'd grown up, but he wasn't averse to talking about it.

Rosalee could have listened to him talk about his childhood forever. There was something wistful but also restful about hearing of her child's life as if it were simply a story to be told rather than a hurdle to be cleared. Something to listen to rather than live through. All the travails had been overcome, the obstacles avoided, and every growing pain healed. It was over for him, but it was all fresh to her. As he talked, images of a young Liam playing among a band of sea lion children danced before her eyes. She pictured it all so clearly. Even the hard times—like when he'd almost drowned and become afraid of swimming—were simply amusing tales now, for better and worse.

Rosalee wondered what it would have been like to live through those times, and she did find herself a little envious of the Mama Arlene and Mama Angelica that Elijah spoke of so fondly. But mostly, Rosalee wanted to meet them. She wanted to go with her son, who was now called Elijah, when he went back to his home, and because she believed in the curse of Treegadoon, she feared deeply that she wouldn't be able to.

Shaun parted ways with the otters when they arrived back at the tree where Elijah's boat was docked, leaving the otters to descend to sea level on their own. However, he did press a paper sack of nut-butter sandwiches and joiberries on each of them before he left, and he wished them luck. The sparkle in his eye as the squirrel said goodbye to Elijah was quite charming. The sparkle dimmed as he wished the same to Rosalee.

The cloud in the squirrel's eyes summoned a storm in Rosalee's stomach. It looked like to her like Shaun knew he would see her again—like he knew the curse of Treegadoon would bring her back to here—and she didn't want to believe he was right. So, she shoved the feeling away as best as she could and followed Elijah down to his little boat.

Elijah uncovered the boat and made space between the piles of jumbled jellyfish for Rosalee to sit down and join him. Then he unmoored the vessel, shoved off, and began rowing northward between the many wide tree trunks toward the alleged crescent dune island.

The more Rosalee urged Elijah to tell her about his past, the more complicated her feelings became—like she was hearing about an alternate timeline, where she'd been there, but since she was only hearing about it, years and years after the fact, so many details were lost. Precious little details about the quirk of his smile, the happy dances and wiggles of an overexcited child, tiny moments too small to preserve in story had already washed away for ever on the tides of time, and Rosalee couldn't call them back by listening to a grown man tell her about his memories.

And yet... There was such a freedom to jumping forward like this. She already had a grown child. If she wanted another, she was young enough to have another. But she didn't think she would. She and Martin had loved Liam. Another baby wouldn't be the same, and it had all been so much work. This trick of time had traded her first-person experience of raising Liam for the freedom to be young and carefree herself again. It was so much to process, and she'd had so little time to process it. Seasons had passed for Elijah in a blink of an eye for her, and she thought, she'd like spend many seasons sorting out the way she felt about it. Right now, it was almost like the feelings were piling up inside her, too deep for her to feel them, saved way in a place deep, deep inside being buffered so they wouldn't overflow, flooding her, washing her away in their overwhelming power.

For now, while the complicated feelings piled up inside her, on the surface, all she could feel was entranced by every little thing that Elijah said, every movement he made as he rowed the boat. He was the most fascinating, mesmerizing being she could possibly imagine—just like he had been as a newborn infant, first settled in her arms. It was like meeting him for the first time all over again.

Elijah kept rowing as the trees thinned around them. There had to be hundreds of trees in Treegadoon, and near the middle, they grew densely close together. But around the edges of the city, they grew more sparse, and the bridges between them high above looked like threads in the sky.

When they finally cleared the last of the trees, Rosalee saw the glittering golden edge of the dune island in the distance. It was close enough to be an easy swim for an otter between Treegadoon and the island, but far enough to be a difficult swim for a squirrel. A very difficult swim for a squirrel.

Elijah made quick time rowing to the island, but then he kept the boat a calculated distance from the shallows, where it wouldn't get grounded on the sand. He rowed around the island toward the east, letting Rosalee look at the shore, searching for signs of her lost husband.

"I think I see paw prints on the sand," Elijah said as the reached the narrow end of the island. He steered the boat out around the sharply curved peninsula, bringing them to the other side of the sand bar that served as an island. "This place isn't much bigger than the island I'm from," Elijah observed.

"The one with the sea lions?" Rosalee asked, biting back her desire to tell Elijah that he was from further inland. He'd been born in a coastal town but most definitely on the mainland. Regardless, she knew Elijah still didn't believe she was his mother, and she didn't want to fight with him. If he never believed her, maybe she could live with that, as long as she still got to be near him. Rosalee could be friends with her son. She could live with that.

Elijah's boat followed the coastline, and Rosalee saw more and more paw prints on the sand, until a campfire came into view. Small, puffing smoke, and cheerily red even under the direct sunlight of midmorning. Martin was tending the fire, throwing driftwood on it and looking solemn. There's nothing more serious than a solemn river otter. Their whole beings—from tail tip to wide muzzle—are made for expressing joy. When Martin looked up and saw Rosalee and Elijah waving eagerly from the approaching boat, his round face brightened, and the expression completely transformed him

Martin ran right out into the water, unbothered by soaking his tattered clothes, and swam the last part of the way to the edge of Elijah's boat. He threw his front paws over the edge and clung on. Rosalee leaned over and wrapped her arms around him, leaning her own head against his. "Oh, Martin," she said, whispering right by his small round ear. "I didn't know if you'd made it."

Martin sobbed, unable to answer her, far too stricken by the profound, pressing weight of their shared loss and his fault in the matter. He had lost their baby, Tiny Liam, Little Lee-Lee, in the tossing waves of the prior night's storm, and he would have to tell her. But Rosalee knew what he had to be feeling. She knew he thought their child was lost, and she wasn't sure how to tell him otherwise. *Elijah didn't believe her. Would Martin?*

* * *

ELIJAH AND ROSALEE each grabbed one of Martin's paws and pulled him aboard the small boat. Immediately, he fell into Rosalee's arms, wrapping his arms around her as well, and he whispered to her, "I'm sorry, I'm so, so sorry," but she countered each apology with a whispered back, "It's okay, it's okay, dear, he's here," until Martin pulled away from her, just enough to look into her eyes. Confusion met reassurance, and a flicker of hope was born.

Rosalee pointed with a webbed paw at Elijah and said, "It won't make any sense, but we've fallen through time, Martin. This is... Elijah. *You know him.* Look at the notch on the webbing of his left paw."

Martin looked at Elijah, and suddenly, the otter rowing the boat felt very, very uncomfortable. He'd helped this woman find her husband, but now she was trying to comfort the distraught man by repeating absolute nonsense to him about skipping across time and curses cast by fiery mythical birds.

This was such a horrible tragedy, and Elijah wanted nothing more than to be away from it. He knew intellectually, abstractly that losing a child must be one of the worst possible pains—something he couldn't really even imagine—but to look at the face of this tragedy and see how it had broken Rosalee so thoroughly that she was living in a complete fantasy... It was too much, and Elijah wanted no more part in it.

"I'm sorry," Elijah said to Martin. "The squirrels in the nearby city—" The thick copse of trees that made up Treegadoon was still visible rising above the sea to their south. "—spun us a tall tale, and Rosalee seems to have fallen for it. I don't know what happened to your son, and I wish I could stay and help you search—" This was an outright lie, but sometimes, it's the sort of lie an otter simply has to tell. "—but I need to get home to my own village with my jellyfish-hunting haul."

Martin looked around himself in the small boat, taking in the piles of translucent tentacles for the first time. "How delicious," he remarked diffidently, clearly struggling to know how to react to the untenably bizarre situation he'd found himself in, faced with an otter his own age who looked uncannily like he could be brother to both himself and his wife insisting that they weren't caught in some kind of time distortion.

Under normal circumstances, Martin had to agree that time folding in half around him was very unlikely. These weren't normal circumstances, and he didn't know what to think. But he could see in Rosalee's eyes that she believed wholeheartedly that Elijah was their son. Their Little Lee-Lee. Baby Liam.

Martin shook his head and held a paw to his temple. "Your village," he asked, "do they have more boats? Might they be any help in mobilizing a search force—" He was going to say, "for our lost child," but the words choked in his throat, unspoken, too hard to say. Either their child had just grown up in the blink of an eye, or he'd been lost in the storm alone all night, not yet old enough to know how to swim. The last Martin had seen of Baby Liam, the child had been clinging to a broken crate. It was possible the wooden crate had proven seaworthy enough that the infant had ridden it like a toddler-sized boat through the storm all night. But not likely.

Not impossible. Not likely.

Not the best mix of probabilities for all of Martin's hope to rest on. But not the worst, and he couldn't let go of hope. Not yet.

Reluctantly, Elijah admitted to himself that the sea lions would probably be very helpful in a search and rescue operation. They wouldn't even need boats. Sea lions swim nearly three times as fast as river otters and are adapted for swimming in the ocean. But then, Elijah realized, he could also get back to them faster with less weight in the boat. And that served his purposes quite nicely. So, he said, "Yes, my village is mostly sea lions, and they would be happy to help you search for survivors lost in the storm. If I leave you both here, then I can get back to them quite quickly and get the search started."

Martin nodded, happy with the suggestion. "Yes, then we can stay here and begin searching directly. How far is this sea lion village?"

Rosalee looked much less happy, quite concerned in fact. "No, we should stay with Elijah." She believed to the deepest depth of her heart that if her son left Treegadoon without them, they wouldn't see him again until he was a very old man. Her heart was already wrestling with the complexity of her infant child aging instantly to be her own age. She didn't think she could handle missing his life entirely. "We have to stay together," she insisted. Fervently.

Martin looked confused, but he shrugged and put an arm around her shoulders. "If Rosie insists, then I'm with her. I'm sure a couple more otters in your boat won't slow us down too much. Besides, we can take turns rowing."

"Actually, for a longer trip," Elijah said, "I'll be using a motor my mother—she's an inventor—built for powering the boat automatically. And it'll take an hour for me to get back to the sea lion village alone. With the two of you? I don't know how much longer it will be."

Martin looked at Rosalee, brow raised in a questioning expression, but she shook her head firmly. She had no intention of leaving Elijah's side and allowing him to jump to old age before the sun rose on Treegadoon tomorrow.

"We stay together," Rosalee said, staring down at the

tentacles piled all around her in the boat. "I won't leave you again."

Martin thought for a moment that Rosalee meant she wouldn't leave him. He still didn't understand that she truly and completely believed Elijah to be their infant son, but he realized—sensing the tension in the boat between the other two otters—that there was something significant happening between them. There was a connection. He could feel it too. Elijah, although entirely new to him, felt familiar in a way he couldn't describe. And like Rosalee earlier that morning, he found his panic about his lost son inexplicably soothed by this stranger's presence.

Martin's logical mind told him that Elijah seemed like a very confident, competent otter—surely, all he had to do was see the successful haul of jellyfish in the boat around him to know that! Any otter who could catch so many jellyfish—including one larger than an otter!—all by himself clearly knew what he was doing, and if this otter was going to help them search for their child, well, then Baby Liam was all but found already.

Another part of Martin's mind—perhaps even more logical than the first—picked away at this explanation, telling him that a competent stranger's help would count for very little if Baby Liam had already drowned in the storm. But... That part of his mind held little sway, so long as Elijah was sitting right there. And Rosalee was right: Elijah did have the exact same notch in the webbing of his left paw as Baby Liam. Martin remembered when Rosalee had found it and worried that they'd injured their brand new perfect baby already, but he'd spotted the notch almost as soon as Liam had first been handed to him. It wasn't an injury, just a quirk, and it was such a particular thing for Elijah and Liam to have in common.

Tentatively, Martin reached out and grabbed Elijah's left paw. The other otter looked surprised but didn't object as Martin gently touched the notch in his webbed paw. "An old scar from when I was quite small," Elijah explained. "I can't remember how I got it."

"Actually," Rosalee whispered, wrapping her arms tightly around herself like she needed to be hugged or maybe to hug someone else but couldn't, "you've had it since you were born."

Martin let go of Elijah's paw, and the two otters stared at each other for a long moment.

"I think we can afford to lose a little time," Martin said, measuring the words out carefully. "Surely, the advantage of us being there to talk directly to the searchers and tell them everything we know about the storm and ship will be enough to outweigh a little time lost in getting there." Martin's mind was working overtime to try to make this situation make sense, trying to find logic in the face of the fantastical. Because like Rosalee, part of him knew: he was already reunited with his lost son.

Elijah sighed deeply. He no longer wanted to be mixed up in Rosalee and Martin's mess of a tragedy... But at least they were both sounding more reasonable and much calmer now. He didn't understand that it was his own presence that had calmed them down. He didn't believe in the curse of Treegadoon. He believed in the science and rationality that his inventor mother had taught him. Perhaps, if he brought Rosalee and Martin home with him, then his mothers could deal with them.

"Alright," Elijah said. "If that's what you think is best, then I'll get us on our way." He bustled about the boat, properly covering the piles of jellyfish so they were secure and setting everything straight. Then with everything in its place—including his two passengers—Elijah secured the oars he'd been using to the sides of the boat and turned on the motor his inventor mother had built.

The little motor roared to life, and the boat revved up, taking off like a strong wind had caught its non-existent sails. The little boat shot like an arrow through the water, and Elijah pivoted the angle of the motor to steer it, keeping clear of the hazardous trees as he began heading home.

"It's so fast," Rosalee said, breathlessly as the wind whipped past her. "So much faster than I'd imagined..." And maybe, maybe she meant more than the boat. Maybe she meant the whole day—meeting her son as an adult, oscillating between loss and wonderment, tragedy and joy, storm and eerie calm. It was too many feelings, simply too, too much.

The sea lion isle was south of Treegadoon, so the boat had to circle the copse of trees before it could continue on through clear, empty sea. And as they passed the towering trees, Rosalee and Martin felt a building sense of foreboding. The sensation was unattached to anything specific, just a feeling, but when someone feels something, they usually try to figure out why. Rosalee worried that the motor on the boat was unsafe, but also, she could clearly see that Elijah was familiar with it and had probably used it safely many time before.

Martin worried that he was wrong to abandon the site of where he'd lost hold of his infant son, terrified that he was making the wrong choice in staying with this strange otter named Elijah, no matter how comforting his presence had seemed only moments ago.

As the small boat finally rounded past the last of the trees, facing a clear stretch of blue, the discordant dissonance warring inside both Rosalee and Martin rose to a fever pitch, and every nerve in each of their bodies screamed with utter conviction and no regard in the slightest for rationality that they simply couldn't leave Treegadoon. There was no room left for laying a carefully constructed framework of logic over the top of the feelings urging them to stay. There was only room left to act, and Martin jumped over the side of the boat right away. He'd had less time to acclimate to the idea that Elijah was his son, and it was easier for him to let go.

Rosalee, on the other paw, felt torn in two, and the power of the curse was barely able to overcome her motherly attachment to the otter trying to drag her away from a mystical place that had laid claim to her, deep beneath her pelt, deep inside her heart. Rosalee belonged to Treegadoon now, and even Elijah couldn't draw her away. With a broken-hearted sob of inarticulate confusion at her own actions, Rosalee also jumped over the side of the boat, and Elijah found himself zooming away from the otter couple he'd sworn to help.

* * *

Alone in his boat on a clear sea in the glow of early afternoon, Elijah found he could almost believe the whole morning had been a daydream, perhaps caused by nibbling on a psychotropic jellyfish tentacle. *Were there jellyfish whose flesh could cause such hallucinations?* Elijah wasn't sure, but perhaps one of his mothers would know. As he sailed onward toward home though, he realized: there were still two sacks of nut-butter sandwiches and joiberries in the boat with him, and that was hard, physical evidence that he had met with someone out here on the sea this morning.

Though, Elijah began to wonder if the specifics of his memories could be at all accurate, because it was simply too, too strange that he'd met a village of squirrels who believed their entire city skipped across time like a stone across a lake and a nice, young otter couple who seemed utterly, irrationally convinced that in spite of the lack of an age difference between them, Elijah was their son.

Well, he supposed he would have an entertaining tall tale to tell the young sea lions around the cooking fires at home while they prepared his lion's mane jellyfish for the feast tonight. A feast provided by him.

By the time Elijah had pulled his little boat up on the

shore of the sea lion isle, his confusion about Treegadoon had melted away like morning mist under the beating sun of midday. He laughed and joked with the sea lions who helped him drag the heavy lion's mane jellyfish across the isle to the cooking fires. The giant jellyfish had to be handled very carefully due to its poisonous stinging tentacles which Elijah had become half-convinced he must have been grazed by when he'd first hauled it over the side of the boat earlier that morning. It would explain a lot.

The sea lions danced their funny dances—involving a lot of swaying in place—around the fires as the spoils of jellyfish baked into flat breads and simmered into soups. The lion's mane jellyfish was wrapped in a woven cover of seaweed and then roasted over one of the fires on a spit, slowly turning and sizzling as it dripped grease onto the fire below. It all smelled wonderful. Even though jellyfish itself is generally a bland meat, desired more for its fun, chewy texture than its flavor, the sea lions had salted and spiced everything, throwing in peppers, tubers, and fancy mushrooms, so the fires radiated sensuous, sumptuous smells along with cheerful flickering light and deep, compelling warmth—the kind of warmth that sinks right into the sand and slips under an otter's thick fur until it feels like it's warming you from the inside as much as the outside.

Elijah decided he wouldn't tell anyone about Treegadoon after all. He didn't want to think about Rosalee and Martin, still looking for their lost baby, so eager to avoid tragedy that they'd almost followed him home like ducklings imprinting on the first being they saw after hatching. It was all too weird and sad. Elijah preferred to stay rooted in reality, anchored to the home he'd known for as long as he could remember. And yet...

Elijah kept touching the notch in the webbing on his left paw. He'd never thought about it much. The notch had been there for as long as he could remember, and he'd always assumed it came from some injury when he'd been a careless, carefree toddler, unaware of the dangers of sharp rocks and cooking knives. But now, Elijah couldn't stop thinking about the way Martin had grabbed his paw and what Rosalee had whispered about it being a mark that had been with him since birth.

The notch did seem more like a birth mark than a healed wound. There was no scar. Just a notch in the webbing. And even more telling, he didn't remember how he'd gotten it. So, it really could be something that had been with him since birth.

The more Elijah thought about it, the more he couldn't deny that there was a sliver of his life unaccounted for, before Mama Arlene and Mama Angelica had taken him in. If there weren't, then Rosalee wouldn't have been able to slide into it, worming her way into claiming a part of his past for herself. She wouldn't have been able to claim to know him.

Perhaps other adopted children worry about their birth parents and wonder if they're still out there. Elijah never had. Maybe it was because he was already a fish out of water by being a river otter surrounded by sea lions, or maybe it was just the way his personality worked. He didn't know. But now, for the first time, he couldn't stop wondering: who were the otters who'd been his parents before Mama Arlene and Mama Angelica? What had happened to them? Were they lost at sea?

They couldn't be Rosalee and Martin. That didn't make sense. But they could have been a lot like Rosalee and Martin.

With a sigh, Elijah realized that he had to know. He had to close the door on this fantasy and slide shut the narrow gap where Rosalee had inserted herself. She was not his mom. Both of his moms were here, enjoying the feast with him, sharing in the life they'd built for him and welcomed him into as a lost, wayward child.

But why had he been lost? The question echoed and echoed in his mind, until his whiskers turned downward and his shoulders slumped. It wasn't hard for his two mothers to read the despondency in his demeanor which clashed considerably with the festive atmosphere around the cookfires that evening.

Mama Arlene sat down beside Elijah on the driftwood log where he'd settled to watch the dancing and feasting. Mama Angelica came up on his other side and stretched out comfortably on the sand. Most of the sea lions preferred laying on the sand to sitting on logs, but Mama Arlene and Elijah had pulled a nice driftwood log up close enough to the cooking fires for them to share with each other long ago, and it didn't get in the sea lions' way enough to be a problem.

"I expected you to regale us all with some tall tale about how you caught the lion's mane jelly," Mama Arlene said. She had a twisted, gnarled driftwood stick with her, and as she spoke, she idly drew curlicued patterns in the soft, dry sand.

"You're a very good storyteller," Mama Angelica added. "But it's also okay if you don't have a story to tell." The sea lion looked at her river otter wife, quietly communicating that they shouldn't push their son to talk if he didn't want to.

"I have a very tall tale, actually," Elijah mused. "Almost too tall. As tall as a redwood tree towering up to the sky." If the curse were true, then Treegadoon would be gone soon. Gone for years and years. But it couldn't be true, because that simply didn't make sense.

Elijah told Mama Arlene and Mama Angelica his toweringly tall tale, and when he was done, he held up his left paw, pointed to the notch in the webbing and asked, "How did I get this? Did I cut it on a rock or a knife when I was small? I can't remember." The past is a place that grows dim over time, and the light of his memory simply didn't shine that far back.

But Mama Arlene shook her head, and Mama Angelica said, "We don't know. Your paw has been like that for as long as we've had you. It never looked like a cut to me. It looked more like a good luck mark."

"A good luck mark?" Elijah asked.

Mama Angelica explained that sea lions thought minor deformations like his notched paw were a sign of good luck when they were found on newborn infants. "It's like fate has put a mark on you, promising a piece of good fortune in your future, already paid for by an inconsequential price exacted while you're still in the womb. Very lucky."

Mama Arlene smiled with the kind of forbearance she always showed for her sea lion wife's more mystical beliefs. Then since the conversation had lulled, the river otter inventor launched into a pensive monologue musing on how a whole forest could have come to be growing straight up out of the ocean—whether they might be a special kind of tree that thrived in sea water or perhaps whether the coastline had moved to engulf the forest after it had already grown. It was a fascinating subject, and she found she had a lot to say about it before winding down into quiet thought.

"You don't believe in a city jumping across time or a curse cast by a phoenix though," Elijah stated, knowing it to be true. He knew his mothers well.

"No," Mama Arlene agreed. "But I'm always up for an adventure, and I do love a good mystery. So, we should go find out what you actually saw and see what more we can learn."

While the two river otters had continued talking, Mama Angelica picked up one of the sack lunches her son had carried home from the alleged mythical isle of squirrels who had fallen out of time. The sea lion opened the sack up, examined the nut-butter sandwiches inside and then exclaimed with surprise at the sight of the purple heart-shaped berries. "Are these... *joiberries?*" Mama Angelica asked in utter surprise and bewilderment.

"Yes," Elijah answered. "That's what Shaun called them. Why?"

"I've never seen joiberries before," Mama Angelica said in wonder. "Only heard about them and seen drawings in history books. They went extinct hundreds of years ago..." Her dark brown eyes got a misty, faraway look, but then her attention snapped back, locked on the pretty little berry held with the tip of her flipper. She asked, "May I try one?"

Elijah nodded, and as Mama Angelica popped the purple berry in her muzzle, he pulled another one out of the lunch sack to offer to Mama Arlene.

"They're lovely," the river otter inventor said after eating the joiberry. Her sea lion wife had her eyes closed, savoring the flavor, but when she opened them, she looked very serious.

Mama Angelica said, "I'll come with you. I want to see this place as well."

Elijah felt like a young pup, well cared for by his parents. The mysteries of the squirrel city had been daunting when he faced them alone, but he wasn't afraid to go back there with his mothers. If Rosalee and Martin were still mourning their lost babe, still trying to drag him into their tragedy, then surely Mama Arlene and Mama Angelica would know how to handle them.

The family agreed they would voyage back to Treegadoon the next morning.

* * *

THE WATER SPARKLED in the early morning sunlight the next day. Both river otters—Elijah and Arlene—rode in the little boat with its motor running. Angelica swam alongside. As a sea lion, she was too large to fit comfortably inside the small boat, but Arlene had rigged the boat with a net that could be thrown out behind it and trail along attached to the back. Angelica could rest in the net like a hammock if she grew tired of swimming before the trip home.

The sky was clear, and they could see for leagues in every direction. And there was no sight of any trees growing out of the ocean. Elijah shouldn't have been surprised. He wasn't the first resident of the sea lion village to go exploring, and he'd never heard of Treegadoon before. And if it had been real, how could he not have heard of it? Surely, there would have been word passed around.

Elijah was beginning to feel like an absolute fool and to suspect that his mothers had only come along on this voyage to humor him. Well, that, and also to see if they could figure out why their son had spent the previous morning hallucinating—had he hit his head? Gotten dangerously dehydrated? Eaten something poisonous?

And yet, there were the joiberries. All three of them had eaten the joiberries, and Mama Angelica insisted she'd only ever seen sketches of them in historical scrolls before. So, they must be growing somewhere, even if it wasn't in a city of trees rising straight up out of the ocean.

* * *

Elijah and Arlene sat in the boat together, eating day old nut-butter sandwiches, and silently staring out at the empty sea. Sparkling, green, beautiful. Totally empty. Angelica floated on her back beside them, and Arlene occasionally tossed purple joiberries at her sea lion wife who snapped them straight out of the air with her muzzle like it was some kind of game. The sack lunches that Shaun had packed made a lovely breakfast. But when breakfast was done, Elijah had to admit—there was no Treegadoon. Somehow, in spite of the sack lunches, he must have imagined it.

"We should go home," Elijah said, despondently. He'd looked forward to seeing Shaun again. He'd wanted to prove the superstitious squirrel wrong and open his eyes to the wonders of a rational worldview. The marvels of science that could be discovered when superstitions were put aside. And in spite of himself, Elijah had hoped to hear good news of Rosalee and Martin—that they'd found their lost baby and gone on their merry way.

Instead, Elijah was left with the broken fragments of an unfinished story, as if he'd woken up in the middle of a dream.

"If we can't find where the joiberries came from,"

Mama Angelica suggested, "perhaps we can use the remaining ones to grow some joiberry plants of our own."

Mama Arlene looked in each of the two paper sacks, shaking them a little to rearrange the contents and get a better count of how many berries were left. "Yes, I think there are enough left for that, but this does mean you should stop eating them."

Mama Angelica's whiskers spread widely as her pointed snout twisted into a grin. "Then you should stop throwing them at me!" she countered.

Mama Arlene laughed and folded over the open tops of each sack. Then she set them aside, saving the remaining berries for later.

Elijah was just about to start the motor up on the little boat when, suddenly, a thick fog rolled in all around them. For a moment, he thought he'd gotten something in his eyes, but then he heard each of his mothers exclaim in surprise.

"I've never seen a fog come on so quickly!" Mama Angelica said.

"The air got warmer," Mama Arlene observed, ever the acutely focused scientist, looking for telling details and useful explanations. "I wonder why..."

And that's when Elijah looked up and saw the trees towering above them. The shade from the trees mixed with the haze of the fog, making everything darker, which would almost explain how Elijah didn't notice the trees immediately, but it didn't explain how they'd sprung up around their boat when they hadn't been moving at all.

"Remarkable," Mama Angelica breathed.

"I guess the trees explain the warmer air," Mama Arlene said. "Their branches hold the warmth in, but that doesn't explain..." She trailed off. There was no way her science could explain a whole forest appearing around them like a mirage. Unless it was a mirage... But she grabbed one of the oars from where it was attached to the side of the boat and used it to reach out and tap the closest tree trunk, gnarled, dark brown, and very real looking.

Wood hit wood with a satisfying clonk. Mirages don't act like that. They don't have substance when you touch them. They don't push back against the exploring tip of an oar and cause your boat to wobble in the calm water.

Mama Arlene made a begrudging sound of acknowledgment. The trees were real, not a trick of the light.

Mama Angelica barrel rolled onto her belly, splashed her tail, and swam circles around a few of the tree trunks before returning to the side of the boat. "This is amazing," she said. "You say there's a dune island to the north?"

"Yes, that's right," Elijah said slowly. He felt disconnected from his body, from reality, like he'd fallen backward into a dream. But then a familiar, chittering voice shouted from above, and Elijah looked up to see a red squirrel's face looking back down at him from a bridge way up in the forest canopy. *It was Shaun!* The red squirrel was real, and he was smiling in a beguiling way, like he was a mythical creature himself. But then, young people in love always think the object of their affection seems at least halfway mythical, and Elijah definitely had a crush on Shaun.

Elijah waved and called up to the squirrel: "Hallo! Shaun! I came back!"

The squirrel's grin widened, but then his face disappeared as he went scurrying the rest of the way across the bridge he was on. He made it to a tree and began spiraling down the stairs around its trunk far faster than a river otter could ever hope to. All in all, it took barely a few breaths before Shaun was down at sea level, grinning like a child on their birthday, facing a pile of colorfully wrapped presents, fully convinced the wish they'd made on the candles gracing their birthday cake was about to come true.

"Elijah?" Shaun asked, unbelieving yet believing at the same time. "Is it truly you? *Actually you?* And still young like me? *Like yesterday?*"

Elijah wanted to scoff at Shaun's ridiculousness. *Of course they were both the same age!* But the trees... they had appeared as if out of nowhere. They had appeared in a sudden fog. And all Elijah could manage to say was, "Yes, it's me," before his words dissolved in happy laughter, overwhelmed by the power of a boy he liked smiling so beatifically at him. He took the oars up in his paws and rowed his small boat over the platform at the bottom of the tree Shaun had come spiraling down.

Angelica kept apace with the boat, swimming alongside, and as she did, the sea lion caught the eye of her river otter wife. Angelica and Arlene looked at each other, each recognizing that the other had seen the simple truth of their son's crush bare on his face. Together, they shared the kind of silent amusement that parents share when they see their child take another step toward becoming more grown up. It's a kind of communion that can't be voiced, because it would wreck the moment if the child saw it happening.

Arlene and Angelica had both heard about Shaun the night before. They'd known he was squirrel tour guide who'd told ridiculous stories about curses and pressed sacks of nut-butter sandwiches and joiberries on their son, but neither of them had managed to fully interpret the wrought tone in Elijah's voice as he'd talked about the squirrel. They hadn't realized Shaun was so young and so pretty. Some of their son's urgency and confusion about Treegadoon made more sense now. Young people have a way of getting carried away by their hearts. Arlene and Angelica should know. They'd both been young and in love at least once before.

"Wait," Shaun said, the joy on his face dissolving like cotton candy in a sudden summer rain as Elijah stepped out of the boat to join him on the dock. "Did you camp on the dune island last night? You must have. You can't have really left. That must be why—"

Shaun's words came in a rush, but Elijah just laughed even more as he stood beside the squirrel who only came up to his shoulder, even counting the bright red tufts on the top of his pointed ears.

"No," Elijah said gently, getting his laughter under

control. "I went home—all the way home—and brought my mothers back with me to see your city." The river otter gestured at both his otter and sea lion mothers. "Mama Arlene wants to see how your buildings are constructed, and Mama Angelica would really, really like to take some cuttings home from your joiberry plants."

"It's unbelievable," Shaun said, wonder returning to his voice. The pretty young squirrel looked up at the river otter, and their smiles reflected between each other like they were mirrors, and with each reflection their smiles just grew brighter.

While Elijah was completely focused on Shaun, his mothers both kept looking around, marveling at the signs of the city high above them, and as they watched, more and more squirrel faces had began staring down from the bridges and platforms above. It looked as if the whole city were rushing out to see them, even more so than when Elijah had been greeted by a crowd yesterday.

In spite of the pretty squirrel boy staring up at him, Elijah collected himself enough to ask, "Did Rosalee and Martin find..." He faltered over referring to the idea of a missing baby and settled for saying, "...anyone else from the shipwreck?"

Now Shaun began laughing, a bright, musical sound. "How could they?" the red squirrel managed after his peals of laughter quieted down. "That shipwreck happened many years ago, when you were a baby." The squirrel sobered and looked from one face to the next of the three visitors to his town, finally acknowledging the mothers that Elijah had brought along with him.

"You still don't believe," Shaun said with surprise. "You've finally broken the curse we've lived under for countless eons, and you still don't even believe in it." He shook his head and drew a deep breath through his buck teeth, trying to steady himself. Shaun had lived under the curse of Treegadoon for his whole life. The idea of disbelieving it had never truly occurred to him until yesterday, and it still seemed strange to him. A denial of everything he'd known his whole life long.

"I suppose it would be a disbeliever who could break the curse..." Shaun pondered out loud. "If you'd believed, you would never have bothered to come back, no matter who you'd left behind here. You would have known better than to expect to find us again before you were an old man."

Neither Elijah nor his two mothers knew what to say to that. It's one thing to know intellectually that another person wholeheartedly believes in something you find ridiculous, but it's quite something else to look them in the eye while they state their ridiculous beliefs as plainly and matter-of-factly as you might tell someone that the ocean has a way of getting things wet. And more than that, the two river otters and one sea lion could now see the squirrels of Treegadoon swarming all around them, crowding onto the closest bridges and platforms. The whole city—its entire population—must have turned out to see their arrival. So, whatever they said or did next, from this point on, Elijah and his mothers would have quite the audience.

* * *

Far above the lapping ocean waves, among the crowd of squirrels, two river otters followed the movement of the smaller creatures around them, confused by the commotion and still heartbroken from their loss the night before. Neither Rosalee nor Martin had wanted to leap out of Elijah's boat the previous morning, and they'd spent the rest of the day together trying to find their way past the ineffable borders around Treegadoon, trying to follow in the path of their wayward son. But no matter how hard they'd tried to swim away from the trees, they always ended up right back among them.

Long after sundown, Martin had given up in despair and cried all night long. Rosalee had worn herself out, alternating between swimming and taking short breaks to rest her body, unable to give up so long as her limbs could still move. By sunrise, she finally joined her husband in absolute despair, facing the certainty that they'd never see their son again as either an infant or a grown otter.

The squirrels of Treegadoon had been kind to the tearful otters and found a spare room with a comfortable cot where they had crashed, wrapped in each others' arms, each trying not to sob, trying not to be the one that dragged the other down by wallowing in their shared despair, both dreading that they would eventually have to share words with each other, face the topic of what had happened to them head on... and if they couldn't find a way to face this unimaginable loss together, then they might have to face losing even more before the ordeal was done.

The two of them had risen from their dreary half-sleep to the sound of squirrels chittering and chattering, paws scuffling and claws skittering, as every resident of Treegadoon hurried to see the impossible: a visitor who'd left and returned the same age the next day.

For even though Elijah and Arlene were convinced they knew what was and was not possible, over the millennia, the squirrels of Treegadoon had seen visitors come and go, reappearing the very next day for them, impossibly aged over the course of a single night, telling wild stories of waiting and waiting for the trees that rose out of the ocean to reappear. Waiting for years and years. Waiting a lifetime to spend one single day more in Treegadoon.

And, sure, most of the squirrels of Treegadoon had not personally met such a visitor, but they had heard the stories from parents and grandparents they trusted. And furthermore, many of the squirrels of Treegadoon had shared an experience similar to Rosalee and Martin's thwarted attempts to leave—finding it impossible to escape the gravity of their small town, no matter how much their young, rebellious hearts cried for adventure on the high seas or exploration of further shores.

What Elijah had accomplished with his simple visit

home and return the next day should have been impossible, based on everything the squirrels knew of the rules that governed the small corner of the universe that comprised the entirety of their available world. They had lived under the curse of a long gone, long remembered phoenix every day of their lives.

Until today.

Today as the throng of squirrels and two teary-eyed otters stared down at the ocean below, a rosy mist began to rise off the water around Elijah's boat. The tendrils of mist twisted and twined, shining more and more brightly with the colors of sunset, like melted gold coalescing. The bright fog gleamed and came together, creating the hazy form of a giant bird with its wings outstretched. With a flash too bright to look at, the formless shape solidified, and the phoenix from the legend returned to the city that had turned her away so long ago.

Should the city welcome her now? When the albatross had visited Treegadoon in the distant past, she had brought ruination on the squirrels' city. But these were not the same squirrels who had turned the albatross away. These squirrels were the great, great, great, great grandchildren of those original squirrels, and they had grown up in a very different world. They had grown up in a world that had been closed off, shut away from the natural passage of time, and locked up like a pretty gem—too beautiful and valuable to be looked at every day, collecting dust and wasting away on its pedestal.

These squirrels were eager for something new, for

some connection to the world outside their small, unchanging home. These squirrels cheered at the sight of the phoenix returning to them, immediately ready to open their homes and hearts to the powerful visitor.

The phoenix's curse had changed them.

The phoenix spread her wings—as wide as the bridges spanning the distance between trees in the village—and her long pinion feathers dripped with fire. The sparks falling from her wings sizzled as they hit the cold ocean water below.

Elijah's muzzle fell open, and Mama Arlene's eyes narrowed. Mama Angelica swam up closer to the side of their boat, avoiding the bits of fire falling from the giant bird's wings.

Shaun fell to his knees and averted his gaze from the phoenix's glory, and all the other squirrels in the city—like a pattern made from dominoes—saw his reaction and followed suit, falling to their own knees and lowering their own eyes, until only the four river otters—two in the boat and two on a platform high above—were left standing tall, uncowed by the sight of a flaming bird four times their size.

The fiery albatross let herself sink down to the level of the water, landing with her webbed feet and sizzling feathers on the lapping waves. She floated on the water like a pile of sea foam, and steam rose all around her. But slowly, her flaming hot feathers cooled, and the fiery flickers of flame died down, leaving her wings a tarnished, ashy shade of gray and her body as snowy white as that of any normal albatross. Her dark eyes stared judgmentally at the smaller animals gathered all around her in the trees.

The albatross looked at the squirrels like a parent might when their child has disappointed them, but also, in dealing with the natural consequences of their actions already been punished more than enough. Like the bird wanted to say something snarky, something cutting and incisive, but she held her long, hooked beak shut.

Silence echoed between the trees. The only sound came from the lapping wavelets of the sea. Not a one of the squirrels dared speak first, and none of the visiting otters nor sea lion felt it was their place.

Finally, after many long moments, the albatross flapped her wings once, causing a stirring among the nervous squirrels watching, and then said simply with a voice that echoed like a fog horn cutting through a storm, "The curse is broken, as you've clearly surmised. As of this morning, Treegadoon has rejoined the normal stream of time."

Sometimes the most effective thing to say is nothing at all. Even so, after a few moments, brave or perhaps foolish squirrels here and there among the crowd began chittering, *"Thank you!"* and other empty niceties or expressions of gratitude. The chirruping rose in volume as one squirrel took heart from another until the entire crowd was cheering and whooping and celebrating.

The albatross flapped her wings again, bits of fire fanning into existence as the air whooshed under them, and a gasp of fear fell across the crowd of squirrels, quieting them again.

"Off with you all!" the albatross squawked. "You've learned your lesson, paid the price, and our story together is done. Unless you wish to have another lesson taught to you? Hmm?"

More gasps came from the crowd of squirrels, but this time, they were accompanied by the skittering sounds of scurrying paws as almost all of them rushed back to their individual houses or other nearer rooms where they could shelter away from the malevolent gaze of the malicious bird who'd cursed their entire town for many generations. The few brave squirrels who didn't immediately turn tail and run to hide were pulled and pushed by their fellow citizens, until the only squirrel left in sight was Shaun, standing beside Elijah at the level of the sea.

* * *

THE ALBATROSS FOLDED her wings behind her and sat floating on the ocean for all the world like nothing more than a massively large sea bird. She looked at each of the remaining fuzzy mammals in turn—the tearful pair of river otters still on a bridge above, the river otter in the boat beside the floating sea lion, and the river otter standing on the dock beside the one squirrel who hadn't scurried away to hide. They were all watching her with varying degrees of curiosity, wonderment, confusion, and fear.

"I see there are a few loose ends left from my spell to untangle," the albatross sighed. "A few innocent casualties, as it were. "

"*Innocent casualties?*" Rosalee hissed between teeth sharp enough to tear the feathers from the throat of a bird four times her size. Even though she spoke quietly, her words echoed in the relative stillness of the city, now devoid of any trace of its main inhabitants. The squirrels were all too afraid of the albatross to cross her. Not so with Rosalee. She might be a river otter, but right now, she was a classic mamma bear. "Is *that* what you call this?" Her voice twisted with pain and loss.

Elijah felt strange listening to her. He was beginning to believe that he really was the child she'd lost. And yet, he was right here. He was perfectly happy with this life. His heart broke for the mother who had lost him so many years ago... But he'd only been an infant then. The wound had healed for him long ago during dark nights when Mama Angelica had rocked him in her flippers and Mama Arlene had sung to him.

Elijah barely knew Rosalee now. He certainly didn't think of a river otter his own age who he'd met yesterday as a mother.

"Come down here and tell me what happened," the albatross squawked. "I have great powers, but I'm not all-knowing."

Rosalee and Martin looked at each other, and then they began the trek the rest of the way across they bridge they were on, followed by two more bridges and then spiraling down the stairs on the trunk of the tree where Elijah's boat was docked. When they made it to ground level, Rosalee looked like she was ready to roast the albatross with scathing words... until her eyes caught Elijah's, and then all the fire died inside her, and all that escaped her muzzle was a strangled sound of inarticulate grief and sadness.

Martin put a paw on her shoulder, trying to comfort her while also steadying himself. He looked at Elijah, tilted his head as if he were trying to measure or somehow understand the distance that had stretched out between him and the infant child he'd held in his arms only yesterday. A distance that had sprung up literally overnight. It was unfathomable. So, he turned to the albatross and spoke, stating simply what had happened: "The trick you played on this town robbed my wife and me of raising our child. Of knowing him. Of being there for his life. You kept us in stasis while he lived an entire life without us."

Martin gestured with a paw to the grown otter standing on the dock beside him and Rosalee.

The albatross nodded, her long beak bobbing up and down with the expression. "The love that binds you has served its purpose in freeing Treegadoon from their curse. You've played your parts here. Would you like me to send him back to you? You would always be remembered here in Treegadoon for the parts you've played. I won't change how you've affected the squirrels here, but I could send the three of you back so that as soon as you leave Treegadoon, you'd find yourselves in the past, and you'd find your son, still an infant, still waiting to be found."

Elijah wanted to object, but he found himself speechless at the idea of losing his entire life, starting over and becoming a different person who had never known Mama Arlene, Mama Angelica, or the sea lion island at all. Fortunately, he didn't have to say anything at all—both of his adopted mothers immediately, unhesitatingly cried out, "No!"

Angelica followed her declaration with a repositioning in the water, flipping from floating on her back to facing the albatross more directly, as if she were ready to fight to protect her son. A sea lion fighting an albatross would be quite the sight if it happened. Arlene, on the other paw, continued talking and said, "Even if I don't believe you can travel through time, I don't want you messing with my son."

The albatross's face creased around her beak, creating the avian version of an enigmatic smile. "I see the young man in question is claimed by two sets of parents. And what does the young man want for himself?"

Everyone turned to look at Elijah. He felt like the fulcrum in the middle of a lever, and his slightest move might cause the lever to become unbalanced, letting the hopes and dreams of half the people here fall off the edge of it forever. But he couldn't hold still forever. "I love my life," Elijah said, steadfastly refusing to look at any of his parents—adoptive, alleged, or otherwise—as he spoke. Instead, he looked at Shaun who he hoped would show up a lot in his future. "I don't want to start over. I don't want a different one."

Even Rosalee and Martin couldn't be unhappy with that answer. What does a parent want more than for their child to live a good life? A life they're happy with, a life they're enjoying enough that they wouldn't trade it.

Even so, the phoenix had robbed them. Perhaps Rosalee could make peace with having missed Elijah's past, but she couldn't stand being a stranger to him now. "I don't want you to take Elijah's life away from him," Rosalee said, voice shaking as she dared to look at him again. It was frightening—even just looking in her estranged son's eyes. Yesterday, it had felt like they could be something to each other, like they could find a way to be connected, even if it wasn't the connection she'd expected to have with her child. But then he'd sailed away through a barrier that wouldn't let her through, and he hadn't looked back.

Something had died inside Rosalee when she'd seen exactly how little she had become to the child she'd carried in her heart, her body, and her arms until a storm and a whimsical phoenix had ripped him away from her. How easy it was for him to leave her behind forever.

"I just wish..." Rosalee's voice broke, but she wouldn't leave these words unspoken. She needed Elijah to understand how much it had meant to her when he'd been telling her stories of his childhood on the sea lion island. She needed him to let her be a part of his life going forward. "I wish I could share in the memories of everything I missed. I wish through sharing them, we could find a way back to each other."

It was such a small thing to ask coming from a mother who had been separated from her child.

"Is that all?" the albatross asked archly. "Well, that's done easily enough."

In spite of the seriousness of the moment—or perhaps because of it—Arlene broke out laughing. No one else did. When the river otter inventor got herself under control again, she said, "What do you plan to do, oh magical one, fuse our minds together, transferring the memories of raising Elijah straight from my mind and Angelica's to theirs?" Arlene waved a paw dismissively at Rosalee and Martin, less to dismiss them and more to dismiss the ridiculousness of her suggestion. Certainly, the albatross had pulled off a number of impressive tricks so far with the fire that fell from her feathers and the way she had cowed an entire city of squirrels, but Arlene knew how magic tricks worked. They were tricks. Not magic.

"If you consent," the albatross squawked primly, "then yes, that's exactly what I plan to do."

Arlene snapped her muzzle shut a little too quickly, revealing that she'd had more ridicule ready to bound off the tip of her tongue.

"Wait..." Angelica said from her place in the water. The sea lion looked very concerned—there was a lot to be concerned about. "You wouldn't take our memories away from us, would you? We'd still have them too?"

"Of course," the albatross answered. "My intention in

none of this has been cruelty. Only justice. And now, only kindness."

As the albatross said the word 'justice,' Shaun's tufted red ears splayed, and he stepped a little closer to Elijah. The young red squirrel was witnessing events that would become the new legends of his people, and he was the only squirrel here to see them. It was a heavy burden for a young person, and right now, all he really wanted to do was get to know the handsome river otter who'd come to town, full of stories of the wide world, and freed his people from a curse that had hung over their pointed ears since long before either one of them had been born.

Elijah offered a paw to Shaun, and the squirrel eagerly grabbed it. They were both in over their heads, but on the bright side, this experience would bond them together.

"I consent to sharing my memories," Angelica said. Elijah wasn't surprised. His sea lion mother had always been the parent he could count on to overflow with generosity and kindness. She was always a warm pair of flippers ready to hold him and a soothing voice ready to sing his cares away, even now that he was all grown.

Arlene looked more skeptical. The gears in her mind were turning as fast as they could, going over what she had seen today, what she had heard from Elijah last night, and how she could possibly make sense of this young couple—two river otters—who looked like they truly could be the parents of her adopted son, if they'd been displaced through time by many years. Except skipping across time like a stone skips across a lake was clearly impossible.

Or was it?

Could this albatross be a visitor from the future? A future where technology that allows minds to blend together, sharing memories, had become commonplace?

How much more was there to discover about the rigid rules that governed the workings of this magnificent world —a place already so magical that it had allowed such amazing creatures as otters, sea lions, and squirrels to even exist in the first place?

Arlene didn't know. And she didn't know how much she didn't know.

But she knew that Rosalee and Martin were looking at her with hopeful, pleading eyes that looked so, so very much like the eyes of her son.

What harm could come from consenting?

Arlene bowed her head and said, "I agree to sharing my memories as well."

* * *

THE ALBATROSS HELD out her wings and said, "Each of you come forward and put your paws against my feathers. I will be the conduit for you."

Angelica was the first to move, swimming up close to the tip of the albatross's left wing. The albatross lowered her wing until the tips of the longest pinion feathers brushed the surface of the water, making it easy for

Angelica to roll onto her back and touch the ashy-gray tip of the wing with her flippers.

Rosalee, Martin, and Arlene a moment later all followed suit, stepping right up to the edge of the dock where the albatross's right wing was in reach. Each of them laid a webbed paw against the ashy feathers.

As soon as all four of Elijah's parents were touching the albatross, sparks began crawling over her wings like embers glowing in the dregs of a fire when a breeze hits it, blowing new life into the heat.

Elijah felt strange watching this process, knowing that memories of his life and his childhood were being shared with people who were relative strangers to him. It felt a little like a violation, but also, they weren't his memories to control. They were Mama Arlene and Mama Angelica's memories. Adjacent to his, but not his. And if they were willing to share their minds in this way, risk this kind of vulnerability, then he fundamentally had no say in the matter.

Perhaps if Elijah had objected, his adopted mothers would have honored his request to hoard their memories for themselves, but it wasn't his place. It would have been a controlling and miserly action, and he was better than that. If his mothers could be so vulnerable for the sake of broken-hearted strangers, then he could certainly withstand the lesser vulnerability of allowing it to happen without interference.

Shaun sensed Elijah's vulnerability in this moment,

and the squirrel squeezed the river otter's larger webbed paw with his own smaller, more delicate paw.

Elijah noticed that all four of his parents had closed their eyes. When the sparks died down and stopped crawling across the albatross's feathers, all four parents opened their eyes and for a flash of a moment, their eyes were filled with the ember glow of fire. The moment passed, and Elijah found himself wondering if anything had actually changed. Unlike his inventor mother, he hadn't imagined a possible story to explain how the albatross could be empowered by science from the future, and he still doubted.

But then Mama Arlene turned to him and said, "I remember finding the notch on your paw when you were a brand new baby." There was wonder and surprise in her voice. Elijah's cool and collected scientist-mother was overflowing with emotion. "*I remember it.* You were so tiny."

"So tiny," Mama Angelica echoed from her place floating in the water.

"I've never seen you that tiny before," Mama Arlene continued, her voice filled with simple, straightforward wonder. She had no doubts any more. "The notch was never an injury. You've had it since you were born, and I *remember* finding it on you."

However the albatross had accomplished it, the giant fiery bird truly had helped Elijah's four parents to share their memories of him with each other.

Rosalee stepped toward her son shyly, nervously,

spreading her arms in an inviting way. She was full of joy, knowing how good his life had been so far and being allowed to know the details of his past—the past she had missed—so well. But she still deeply craved a connection with who he was *now*.

Elijah looked uncertainly at first Mama Arlene, who nodded, and then Shaun at his side who smiled encouragingly. He didn't look to Mama Angelica, because he knew what she would say, and in fact, the warm-hearted sea lion went ahead and said it anyway: "Go on, Elijah, give your poor birth mother the hug she needs! You wouldn't keep me waiting like that."

Elijah laughed. He'd kept Mama Angelica waiting for hugs many, many times over the years, and she knew it. He supposed Rosalee knew it too now. But still, Elijah took his sea lion mother's point to heart and opened his arms to the mother who'd lost many seasons of his life. She fell into his arms and squeezed him as tightly as she could, as if she could secure him to her with her arms and stop time from ever driving them apart again.

After a few moments, Martin came in and joined the hug, and then so did Mama Arlene. Even Mama Angelica pulled herself out of the water, up onto the dock beside the four river otters, and they made room for her blubbery bulk in their now five-way embrace. They had become a complicated sort of family with one pair of parents closer in age to littermates to the shared child, but even so, they were definitely a family.

* * *

THE PHOENIX LEFT while Elijah's family wasn't watching. Only Shaun saw the feathered magician spread her wide ash-gray wings, flap them once, and then with a mischievous wink, disappear in a flash of shimmering fire that continued to dance in the air like a mirage for long moments after she was gone. Her presence had left ripples in so many lives.

Treegadoon was a beautiful but exquisitely delicate gemstone of a city, founded long before a time that could properly protect it.

If it hadn't been for the phoenix's interference, Treegadoon would have been washed away by ocean storms long before the island of the sea lions was populated, drawing the attention of a quirky river otter inventor who brought steam power and electricity to cities all along the coast when she settled there to be with her sea lion love.

However, since Treegadoon had skimmed across the surface of time, disappearing when the worst of the storms occurred, the lovely city in the canopy of the trees escaped its natural fate and was still around for Arlene to examine it.

The river otter inventor taught the squirrels to light their nights in the forest canopy with twinkling lights, but she also figured out clever ways to protect the city from storms. The squirrels added lightning rods throughout the city to direct any harmful bolts away from the trees themselves; they constructed wind sails that could be tilted and tuned to the angles of the wind, protecting the whole forest in a slipstream that directed the worst gusts and gales around them; and they reinforced the trees with metal cables, anchoring them more firmly to the sandy ocean floor far below.

Finally, and perhaps most importantly, the sea lion island—which had been growing crowded from its swelling population for some time—set up a satellite colony on the crescent-shaped dune island to the north where Angelica could grow a garden of joiberries, and the sea lions helped build stone wave breakers at intervals all around the small forest, so the largest waves would break apart before hitting the trees at all.

Although the squirrels never knew it, the phoenix had protected them, saving their city until Elijah—bound to Treegadoon by Rosalee and Martin's love for him—could bring them a savior scientist and an ally city. The squirrels even set up platforms with pulley systems that allowed the much larger sea lions who now lived nearby to occasionally come visit their neighboring city in the sky.

And sometimes, when Elijah went out hunting jellyfish—because he still loved chasing down the delectable, tentacular treats—he brought Shaun with him. Even though the squirrel didn't share the river otter's love of chewy jellyfish flesh, he loved escaping the confines of the city where he'd grown up for a day of adventures on the rolling seas.

19

THE MUDDY UNICORN

THE SKY WAS a the kind of empty blue that foretells a sunny, uneventful day, as untouched by actual weather as a day can be. Alivia couldn't stand it. She wanted to frolic in mud puddles, dancing under the droplets of a gusting storm. She wanted to prance and twirl on her cloven hooves, shake raindrops from her snowy mane like a waterfall, and spear the thorn-sharp tip of her horn into as many individual drops of water as she could. She wanted to play rainy day games.

Alivia was a unicorn who loved the rain.

But she lived among a herd of other unicorns, and most of the others loved sunshine. They liked bright, clear days when the sun glistened on the pearlescent curves of their twisting horns, gleamed on the downy fuzz of their milk-white flanks, and glittered in the curling locks of their ice-white manes. They liked to sleep in green

The Muddy Unicorn

meadows where the long grasses rippled from gentle breezes. They did not like it when Alivia caused trouble.

And Alivia's favorite form of trouble was dark, grumpy, gray rainclouds that fairly bristled with their overburdened atmosphere, chock full of too much moisture, ready to come pouring down at the slightest provocation. If the rainclouds sizzled with a little electricity, threatening to crack with thunder and flash with lightning, then that was even better in Alivia's estimation.

For years, through her entire colt-hood, Alivia had fought with the other unicorns in her herd, casting spells to call rainclouds down on their meadow. The clouds rarely lasted long. Before the clouds could do more than scatter a few raindrops—barely more wetness on the grass than from dewdrops on a foggy morning—some other unicorn would cast a counter-spell, causing an extra beam of sunlight to burn the rest of the raincloud away, melting into a harmless fog that wouldn't get a unicorn's pretty pelt all covered in mud.

Alivia had even tried sneaking into the nearby forest and casting her rainclouds there, but one unicorn or another from the herd always spotted them anyway. Even obscured by trees, raining on a forest adjacent to their meadow, the other unicorns took offense at Alivia's rainclouds. They didn't like it when she came back to the meadow all covered and caked in mud, her shining pelt dulled and brown. Too ordinary for a unicorn. Covered in mud, she looked like a common deer with an unusual, singular antler on her brow. The other unicorns wouldn't stand for it.

So, Alivia let herself be boxed in by their expectations. She learned to settle for prancing along the rocky edges of the nearest stream, a narrow trickle of water which bordered the far side of the unicorn herd's meadow and then cut its way through the forest, winding and wending a twisty path.

Alivia liked the feel of water running over her cloven hooves, wetting the tufts of downy white fur at her ankles. She liked to dip her horn into the water and stir up silt from the creek bed with its pointed tip. She watched tadpoles and tiny fishes dart about in the little mudstorms her horn whipped up. She imagined being one of them. A tiny creature, barely more than a wiggling tail, darting back and forth under the water, growing up to one day develop big, jumping legs and a tongue long enough to dart out and pull down dragonflies from the sky.

Alivia thought she would have liked being a frog. They spent a lot more time in the water than she did. The creek that ran beside her meadow wasn't deep enough for her to swim. She could lay down in the creek, but even then, the babbling water only wetted her folded legs, chest, and belly. She could never be fully immersed in such a shallow body of water. She had tried using magic to shrink herself down, small as a frog, but she'd only succeeded in losing a few inches of height while staying basically unicorn-sized.

And so, one day, Alivia decided to follow the babbling

brook as far as she could and see where it would take her. There must be lakes or, at least, deeper rivers ahead if she followed the water downstream. And if there weren't, well, perhaps she could get enough distance between herself and her herd that no one with magic would notice her casting raincloud spells and stop her.

Alivia walked all day, gamboling her way downstream. Her delicate hooves danced over the wet rocks, only splashing through the crystalline water when she felt like it. She played games with herself, seeing how many rocks she could step upon between wetting her hooves, and then seeing how far she could splash before too many rocks blocked her way and she had to hop over them. It was a pleasant if somewhat lonely way to spend a day. Alivia was used to the company of other unicorns, and she both loved the freedom of being away from the others and also missed their familiar if somewhat judgmental presence.

Who was Alivia, she wondered, if she wasn't the difficult, iconoclastic unicorn hassling all the others with her inexplicable, profoundly unnecessary rainclouds?

"I am sea foam, melting in sunlight. I am white water rapids, coursing across a rocky river bed. I am the stream," Alivia said aloud to herself, testing the sound of her voice in the air, even when there was no one to talk to but the stream itself.

One of the rocks in the stream answered her back.

"Your hooves tread more heavily than stream water. Please step carefully. I wouldn't want such a dangerous cloven thing to land heavily on my back."

The rock who had spoken to Alivia was round and green. On closer examination, she found a small head, four feet, and a tiny pointed tail poking out around the edges of the rock. It was an especially pretty rock, decorated with hexagons laid out in a geometric pattern.

"I've never met a turtle before," Alivia said. She'd heard about them. But they were rare enough in the unicorn's meadow that she had never seen one. Though, she knew what it must be. The funny creature seemed kind of magical to her. "I'm Alivia. What's your name?" She stared levelly at the little creature, which involved lowering her head and making sure not to accidentally poke it with her horn. Though, she wanted to. She wanted to tap the tip of her horn against its convex back and see if it sounded hollow or maybe chimed like a bell. But she didn't. She knew it wouldn't be polite. She wouldn't have liked it if any other animal—especially one much larger than her—came traipsing up and poked her without permission.

After a long pause, as if the turtle were trying to remember something he hadn't needed to know for a long time, he said, "Geode. It's a kind of pretty rock. My mother named all my hatch mates after different kinds of rocks."

This seemed perfectly sensible to Alivia. She half-suspected turtles were simply enchanted rocks anyway.

"Would you like to travel with me?" Alivia asked. "I'm following the stream downriver, looking for a place with deeper water where it might rain more often than here." She didn't bring up *why* it never rained up here. If this turtle, Geode, was unfamiliar with local unicorn politics, she didn't want to be the one to inform him.

"More rain?" Geode asked, ponderously. "That does sound lovely. But I don't think I can keep up with a creature that has legs as long as yours. My people are notorious for traveling slowly."

"If you'd like," Alivia offered, "I'd be happy to let you ride on my back." She had been finding the silence around her from the lack of other unicorns oppressive. "I would enjoy the company."

The turtle assented, and Alivia used a little levitation magic to make him float up from the bottom of the creek bed, through the air, to just above the middle of her back where she dropped the spell, allowing him to settle gently on her white fur. Alivia could have simply picked Geode up with her mouth—he was small enough, and her flat teeth were gentle enough—but she felt like showing off for her new friend.

The unicorn and the turtle traveled together for three days and two nights as the stream widened. They traded stories of frogs, salamanders, and birds each of them had known. Geode told a story about how he'd recently, against all odds, beaten a jackrabbit at a race. Alivia continued to avoid talking about the other unicorns, but Geode didn't seem to find that odd. Apparently, turtles like him were usually solitary creatures, not living in herds, so he wasn't fazed at all by the idea of Alivia being the only unicorn around.

For her part, Alivia was amazed that Geode had lived

so close to a unicorn herd his whole life—only half a day's travel away—and never known about them. The world was a bigger place than she had known, large enough for creatures who lived in one part of it to know next to nothing about the streams, forests, and meadows only a short voyage away.

It made Alivia wonder: what creatures were out there who she knew nothing about? What might she find at the river's end? She knew the babbling brook began at a spring in the mountain peaks on the far side of the forest beside the meadow where she had lived and grown—some unicorns traveled there, a pilgrimage to visit the ice-capped peaks and play in the ever present snow. Alivia had been invited on several such pilgrimages, but she had never gone. She'd heard enough about snow to know it didn't interest her. She liked her water wet, not crystalline and powdery. She wanted mud, not more sparkling whiteness. But for all that she'd heard about the stream's origin, she didn't know where its water wended to, what she would find at the river's end.

On the third day of her travels, the water of the stream deepened. Alivia found herself sloshing along through water as deep as her knees. By sunset, she could nearly swim, and Geode alternated riding on her back with swimming along beside her. She had trouble keeping from laughing at the way he floated along the water's surface. Rocks don't float, but this turtle did. He looked like a floating rock, and again, she was struck by how magical he seemed. A rock come to life, behaving in ways that a normal rock never would.

Of course, if you asked the other unicorns, Alivia behaved in ways a normal unicorn never should, muddying her hooves and dirtying her pristine horn. So, she was not one to judge.

Before settling down for their third night together, Alivia frolicked through a meadow beside the river which had grown so wide, she could no longer hop across it in a single jump. She had to swim from one side to the other. She grazed the clover and sweet grasses of the meadow as the sky turned gold, then pinkish red, and finally a deep, satisfying purple. When she made it back to the gurgling rocks beside the river to find her friend, Alivia was surprised to discover Geode had invited another animal to join them on their journey—a snow-white swan named Orange Beak.

Orange Beak had been raised by ducks. A tale as old as... well, mermaids who want to walk on land. The adopted swan had long been embarrassed by her glaringly white feathers, wishing she blended in better with the brown- and green-feathered members of her duck family, and she was clearly immediately smitten with Alivia's shining white fur. They matched each other in a way Orange Beak had never matched anyone before.

So, Alivia slept beside the babbling river that night, listening to the water gurgle and burble, as her head rested on a turtle's back, as if his green shell were a pillow, and a swan roosted on her back, as if their matching colors meant they could blend together, becoming a creature of hooves and wings, like the mythical Pegasus from ancient Greek stories of the gorgons.

Alivia had heard the stories of her distant winged cousins, but she'd never met one of Pegasus's descendants herself. The unicorns in her herd had been somewhat snide and judgmental about how equine bodies weren't suited to flying in the sky. But then, they were equally snide and judgmental about Alivia's love of rain and mud. So, she didn't really trust their judgements.

The next few days passed in a blur of bonding as Alivia, Geode, and Orange Beak swam down the ever widening river, sharing stories, playing games, and generally having the best time any of them had ever had. Occasionally, Alivia would cast a spell pulling a small raincloud down to shower them with beads of water, which her new friends enjoyed, but mostly, she saved her energy for traveling. All three of the companions wanted to see where the river would take them.

Alivia didn't think she'd ever go back to the meadow where she'd grown up, regardless of what they found at the river's end. She was happier with her new friends than she'd ever been with a bunch of unicorns who scolded her for getting her hooves wet. They'd have been horrified to see her swimming through neck-deep water now.

In spite of being the shortest, Geode was the first to spot the change on the horizon. The blueness of the sky ahead deepened, thickening into a much richer shade that spread across the very bottom of the horizon. It was a puzzle to look at it. None of them had ever seen the sky behave like that before. However, Orange Beak had heard stories from migratory birds who had passed by the part of the river where she'd lived, and so she was the first to figure out what it was they were seeing:

The ocean.

The river, which had been continually widening as they'd traveled, spread so wide that it opened into the mouth of a bay, and beyond the bay, the great blue ocean spread all the way across the horizon. As Alivia stood at the edge of the bay, looking out, the ocean filled one half of her world. She had never imagined so much water, more than she needed, but not more than she wanted. It filled her heart until it floated upward on a rising tide of joy.

The three friends—traveling companions who were already becoming much more than that: a strange little found-family—made their way to a beach at the edge of the bay where towering waves, crested in white foam, crashed onto the golden sand like thunder cracking, over and over again, creating a rhythm that resonated deep into their water-loving hearts.

Alivia felt her cloven hooves sink into the sand, leaving hoof prints behind her that spelled out the path she walked. Geode toddled over the sand on his short legs, dragging his belly, and Orange Beak flapped her wings, causing the glittering golden grains of sand to fly up and sparkle in the air. The three of them pranced, frolicked, splashed, and swam in the surf. Alivia's silvery white fur became marred with smears of sand; her shining mane hung in bedraggled tangles. She couldn't have been happier.

When the stars came out that night and shone down on Alivia, Geode, and Orange Beak, their celestial faces saw a trio of friends exhausted from dancing and playing, sleeping in a pile among the reedy grasses on a dune beside the shore.

The sky was clear, completely free of clouds, but Alivia didn't mind the lack of rain clouds anymore. Not when she had an ocean to play in, and friends to play with her, helping her to muddy her hooves. Instead of slicing the tip of her horn through raindrops as they fell, she could spear her horn into the waves as they broke around her. She could feel the power of the water rattle all the way through her body, sharp and cold, all the way down to her bones.

Alivia had never been meant to be a unicorn in a peaceful meadow; she was a creature designed for the raw wildness of an ocean shore.

ABOUT THE AUTHOR

Mary E. Lowd is a prolific science-fiction and furry writer in Oregon. She's had more than 200 short stories and a dozen novels published, always with more on the way. Her work has won four Ursa Major Awards, ten Leo Literary Awards, and four Cóyotl Awards. She edited FurPlanet's ROAR anthology series for five years, and she is now the editor and founder of the furry e-zine *Zooscape*. She lives in a crashed spaceship, disguised as a house and hidden behind a rose garden, with an extensive menagerie of animals, some real and some imaginary.

For more information:
marylowd.com

To read Mary's short stories:
deepskyanchor.com

For news, updates, discounts, and deals:
marylowd.com/newsletter

ALSO BY MARY E. LOWD

Otters In Space

Otters In Space

Otters In Space 2: Jupiter, Deadly

Otters In Space 3: Octopus Ascending

Otters In Space 4: First Moustronaut

Otters In Space Spinoffs

In a Dog's World

When A Cat Loves A Dog

Jove Deadly's Lunar Detective Agency (with Garrett Marco)

The Entangled Universe

Entanglement Bound

The Entropy Fountain

Starwhal in Flight

Entangled Universe Spinoffs

You're Cordially Invited to Crossroads Station

Welcome to Wespirtech

Beyond Wespirtech

Brunch at the All Alien Cafe

Xeno-Spectre
Hell Moon
The Ancient Egg

The Celestial Fragments (A Labyrinth of Souls Trilogy)
The Snake's Song
The Bee's Waltz
The Otter's Wings

Tri-Galactic Trek
Tri-Galactic Trek
Nexus Nine: A Tri-Galactic Trek Novel
Voyage of the Wanderlust: A Tri-Galactic Trek Novel

Commander Annie and Other Adventures
The Necromouser and Other Magical Cats
The Opposite of Memory
Queen Hazel and Beloved Beverly

Some Words Burn Brightly: An Illuminated Collection of Poetry

Furry Fiction Is Everywhere (with Ian Madison Keller)